ASH

ASH

JAMES RAYBURN

Copyright © 2019 by James Rayburn
Published in 2019 by Blackstone Publishing
Cover design by Sean M. Thomas
Book design by Kathryn Galloway English

Printed in the United States of America

First edition: 2019
ISBN 978-1-5385-0751-3
Fiction / Thrillers / Suspense

1 3 5 7 9 10 8 6 4 2

CIP data for this book is available
from the Library of Congress

Blackstone Publishing
31 Mistletoe Rd.
Ashland, OR 97520

www.BlackstonePublishing.com

"There are mistakes too monstrous for remorse ..."
—EDWIN ARLINGTON ROBINSON

ONE

Jane Ash fought herself out of a heavy, smothering sleep. She sat up—hot, disoriented, blinking at the fierce Asian sun hanging low in the bleached sky, fine sand falling from her dark hair onto her bare breasts. When she saw Victor Fabian standing naked with his hands on his hips, legs apart, staring out at the ocean, his hard paunch thrust before him, her internal GPS rebooted. She was on the beach of a spit of an island in the Chinese county of Changdao, part of a cluster flung like jewels between Bohai and the Yellow Sea.

Fabian was puffing on one of his ostentatious Cubans, leaking smoke as he turned to her and grinned, white teeth clenched on the black shaft of the cigar.

Jane heard the distant sound of an outboard engine and the whump of a hull on the water. She shaded her eyes and stared out at the ocean glittering like broken glass, spotting the speedboat cleaving the low waves as it came toward them. The same boat, helmed by a silent Chinese man dressed in a tunic, that had dropped them on this deserted fleck of land that morning. Wooden loungers, wide blue umbrellas, a stack of thick white towels fluffy as baby polar bears, and a gas-powered camping fridge stuffed with Krug, oysters, caviar, and foie gras had awaited them.

Victor, wearing slacks and espadrilles, had handed her down from the boat, ever the gallant.

"Charming, no?" he'd said in that unplaceable mid-Atlantic accent, his voice deep and self-satisfied, marinated in long-leaf tobacco and Michelin-starred food.

"It's beautiful," she'd said.

And it was. A small beach—cupped in the curve of a towering limestone cliff, fissured rock rising in a narrow column to the blue sky—empty but for them.

"Whose island is this?" she'd asked.

He'd flapped a matchstick dead after lighting his cigar, exhaling. "Just some chinky-chink who owes your Uncle Victor a favor."

His little running gag, the Uncle Victor thing. His way of lampooning the difference in their ages. She had no idea how old he was, but given how many years he'd hovered, Zelig-like, in the shadows of dictators and strongmen and martinets on five continents, she knew he must be at least seventy.

But age had not blunted his appetite for food, drink, money, and power. And for her. Invading her, smothering her.

Possessing her. The night before, lying with Victor on the massive bed in his Shanghai penthouse, high enough for helicopters to clatter beneath them, her groin aching, her cheeks blushing with beard burn, she had found herself suddenly longing to escape him. Longing to be home with her husband and son, far away in a small town near Seattle.

Victor, propping himself on an elbow, narrowed his dark, yellow-flecked eyes and stared down at her. "Something wrong, Janey?"

"Up here in heaven?" she said. "How could there be?"

He laughed, and so did she, but through the fog of booze and cocaine, she'd felt a keen sense of just how much of herself she had betrayed.

Victor's phone chirped, and he walked out onto the balcony to take the call. He spoke briefly, set the phone down on a table, and stood gripping the railing, staring out at the night, thick gray hair damp with sweat.

Then he turned and came back into the room, smiling, saying, "Janey, how about a little jaunt tomorrow?"

"A jaunt where?" she asked, desperate to be bounced free of her sagging mood.

"A desert island in Changdao. Wheels up at dawn, just a hop to Penglai, and then a quick boat ride out to paradise. We'll spend the day cavorting and be back here in time for beddy-byes. Yes?"

"Yes," she'd said. "*Yes!*"

And cavort they had. Even by his satyr-like standards he'd been insatiable, and the sun, sex, and champagne had sent her to sleep, naked on a cloth on the sand in the shade of an umbrella.

Jane covered herself with the cloth, eyes on the boat, the whump of its hull growing louder.

"Is it time?" she said.

"Yes, Janey, it's time."

Fabian was stepping into his pants, cinching them under his belly. Not looking at her. Something in his manner, some subtle withdrawal, taking the fizz out of the day.

As Jane stood and dressed, a flash of light on the boat caught her attention, and she leaned across and snagged Victor's Zeiss binoculars that hung from a chair. They were old and battered, sporting a dent in the left barrel that he swore was from an AK-47 round fired by a Cuban in the Angolan civil war thirty years ago when, the heady whiff of Luanda's oil pipeline in his nostrils, he'd palled up with the anti-communist rebel, Jonas Savimbi. The glasses had saved his life, he said, and he carried them with him like a lucky amulet. The only sign of superstition she'd ever seen him display.

She lifted the binoculars to her eyes and adjusted the focus ring. A man stood beside the boatman. A very short man wearing sunglasses, the wind flapping his loose clothes.

She recognized him.

A few months ago in the Shanghai penthouse, she'd woken in the middle of the night to the low drone of voices and, wearing one of Fabian's Savile Row shirts, had wandered down a carpeted corridor and seen Victor standing in the lobby talking to the short man, who'd been dressed in a sharkskin suit that had gleamed like gasoline on dark water. The man must have sensed Jane, for his eyes had slid across to her, and she'd felt the kind of fear that came from being in the presence of pure evil.

Victor had followed the man's gaze and had quickly shooed Jane off to bed.

When he returned to the bedroom, she said, "Who was that?"

"Johnny Yen. He's from Hong Kong."

"What does he do?"

"Oh, he hypnotizes chickens." She looked at Victor and he laughed. "He does odd jobs for me, my sweet."

And he'd kissed her and she'd responded hungrily, not even ashamed that her instinctual fear of the man in the lobby had left her aroused.

Now, on the beach, all she felt was terror. She lowered the glasses and stared at Fabian.

"Jesus, Victor."

He shrugged one hairy shoulder and exhaled twin plumes of smoke through his beak of a nose.

"It's not personal, my sweet."

Panicking, she looked around. The beach was encircled by the cliff. If she tried to swim, the boat would get her. Jane stared at the cliff, honey-colored in the afternoon light, gauging it for hand and footholds.

She'd rock climbed, back in the States, but always with a rope attached to her harness, reassuringly clipped to metal loops bolted to the stone. This was something else.

Jane looked at the boat. It was close enough now for her to see the passenger without the glasses. Johnny Yen stood staring at her.

She ran for the cliff, not looking back. She reached the stone and started to climb, finding purchase, her feet tearing on the rock. Longing for shoes. Longing for powder to stop her fingers from slipping.

But she climbed, losing a few seconds when she got to a vertical surface too sheer to scale. She edged to her right and found a crack and moved up, hearing her breath, trying to calm herself.

Summoning the face of her son, holding it in her mind.

She looked down and saw the boat scrape onto the sand, Johnny Yen flinging himself from it even before it had beached, running at the cliff in a compact, choppy stride. She saw Victor Fabian standing, watching.

Jane looked up. A long way to go to the summit. And if she got there? What then?

A chance to climb down the other side, perhaps. It was rocky, sharp rocks like fangs spiking up from the ocean. No beach. Impossible for a boat to pass. Rocks all the way to the next island. On the trip over she'd seen what looked like a small hotel built on the neighboring island's beach. Had seen people walking on the sand. Maybe she could swim to safety.

She climbed. Stopped, caught her breath. Looked down.

Johnny Yen was coming up toward her, moving at a terrifying speed. Swinging from purchase to purchase with the grace of a solo climber.

Jesus.

She saw her son again. Smiling.

Jane fought herself upward, slipped, hung on, lost a foot and a hand grip. Clung. Probed with her toes, finding a crack, her bleeding fingers somehow latching onto a hold.

She breathed.

Climbed on.

Jane looked down again. Saw the terrifying drop to the beach, Fabian a tiny figure on the yellow sand.

Johnny Yen was close enough now for her to see the spikes of his cropped black hair. He looked up at her and smiled. His teeth were small and sharp.

Jane sobbed and dragged herself higher, not far from the summit.

She felt his fingers on her leg and he tore her left foot from its hold. She lost her right foothold too, and held on by her fingertips, muscles and tendons like cords. Agony. She kicked out at him. Caught him on the side of the head and he slipped, but, like an insect, seemed to attach himself to the sheer rock.

She struggled on.

Bleeding. Wheezing. Short of breath.

He came again and this time, with a swipe of his arm, he took both of her feet out and then, with a superhuman surge, grabbed her right elbow and wrenched her hand from its hold. She was kicking at the rock, hanging by the fingertips of her left hand.

Impossible.

Johnny Yen was beside her and she could smell his sweat and

something else, something sour. He looked her in the eye and smiled and grabbed the hand that kept her on the cliff. He peeled her fingers free, and for a second she seemed to hang in space—then she was falling forever.

TWO

Danny Ash woke reaching for his wife, but his fingers found only emptiness. He sat up in bed, fighting the despair and grief that still threatened to overwhelm him a year after her death.

Ash left the bed, dressed in boxers and a washed-out Nirvana T-shirt. A slight, handsome man, he looked much younger than thirty-six.

He heard a woman's voice coming from the kitchen, so he stepped into the baggy khakis that hung over the chair by the vanity. Jane's vanity. He hadn't been able to get rid of it, or the makeup and lipsticks that clogged the drawer.

Ash stopped beside the door and composed himself, breathing away the lingering bad dreams. He stood straighter, ran a hand through his hair in a futile attempt to tame it, and found something that resembled a smile.

Ash opened the door and walked toward the kitchen where his neighbor, Holly Howells, washed dishes at the sink and his ten-year-old son, Scooter, sat at the table. Holly prattled on about anything that came into her magpie head. Scooter remained silent. He had not spoken a word since his mother's death, retreating into a muteness that, despite all of Ash's efforts, was impenetrable.

Ash, adopting a determinedly jaunty tone, leaned against the doorjamb.

"Hi, Holly. Hi, Scoot."

Scooter looked up from his bowl of Cheerios and nodded, his lank, dark hair—his mother's hair—falling over his eyes.

Holly smiled and lifted a hand in greeting, dripping eco-friendly dishwashing liquid.

She was somewhere north of fifty with wild corkscrews of graying hair, dressed in a cotton top and patchwork pants she'd sewn herself. She'd moved in next door a couple of months after Jane died. Ash called her his hippie angel. She earned a living making clay pots and new age paintings, and she'd adopted Ash and Scooter.

The boy loved her. That didn't mean he *spoke* to her, but he smiled and laughed at times, which was a real win in Ash's book.

It had been Scooter's birthday the day before, his first without his mother, and Holly had cooked and baked and decorated. Gone all out to cheer up the sad man and the silent boy. She'd almost succeeded.

Ash found a grin and said, "Hey, Scooter, I've got one for you." The boy carried on eating. "What did the green grape say to the purple grape?" Ash paused and waited until Scooter looked up at him. "Breathe, dammit! Breathe!"

Was that the hint of a smile?

Ash wasn't sure. But he did this every day, keeping up a long-standing dumb-joke tradition. Something they'd done for years, trying to outdo each other with the silliest gag. Now it was a one-sided enterprise. Looking out the kitchen window, down the slope toward the road, Ash saw a school bus clatter to a stop. The Anderson kids from across the way clambered aboard and the bus rattled off.

Scooter had caught that bus with the Andersons before he'd retreated behind the wall of silence.

Ash homeschooled him now. Or tried to. Scooter had undertaken his own education, via the internet. And he read books that were way too old for him. Ash had walked into his bedroom a few nights before and found him reading *The Catcher in the Rye.*

"Hey, you know that's my favorite book, Scoot?" he said. "When I was sixteen, I was sure it had been written about me."

Scooter looked up for a moment, then his eyes were back on the paperback.

Ash wished he could sit on the bed and yak to his son about those few wild days in the life of Holden Caulfield, but he just smiled and said, "Don't stay up too late, huh?"

He hesitated then leaned down and kissed the boy on the top of his head.

Scooter reached out and touched his hand for a moment. A fleeting touch, but it had filled Ash with hope and he'd left the room smiling.

Leaning in the kitchen doorway, the chirping of a cell phone had Ash reflexively patting the pocket of his khakis, even though he wasn't hearing the Moby ringtone Scooter had downloaded a few years before.

Astonished, he watched as Holly drew an iPhone from her floral pants. If she'd produced a handgun he wouldn't have been more surprised.

She said, "Yes. Okay. I'm ready."

Stowing the phone, she wiped her hands on a kitchen towel.

"Holly?" Ash said. "A cell phone?"

She looked at him without expression, offering no explanation.

This woman who didn't own a computer. Didn't have Wi-Fi. Didn't allow a cell phone into her home.

"The harm they do!" she'd said so many times.

Holly rooted in her brocade bag that hung from one of the kitchen chairs and lifted out something that resembled the insulin pen injector Ash's college roomie had used. She walked up behind Scooter who was still eating and jabbed the needle into his neck, pressing down on the plunger. The boy looked startled for an instant then slumped over the table.

Shocked out of his stupor Ash flew at her.

"Holly, Jesus!"

She punched him in the gut, hard, and, using some kind of martial arts move, tripped him up and left him lying on the floor. Holly unlocked the kitchen door, allowing a scrum of men in dark clothes into the room.

Two of the men swooped on Scooter, lifting his limp body from the chair.

When Ash dragged himself from the floor and tried to get to his son, another two men pushed him down, pinning him to the wood.

Holly looked down at Ash, her face a stranger's. When she spoke her voice was cold and flat with none of the hippie-dippie intonations he was used to.

"I'll go with the boy," she said. "If you do as you're told, he won't be harmed."

She followed the men as they carried his son out the back door.

The men holding Ash stepped back and allowed him to get to his feet. Through the kitchen window he could see a black van parked in the driveway. The men carried Scooter into the back of the van and Holly followed them in. The door slammed shut and the van drove away.

Ash made a run for the doorway. One of the men body-slammed him, and Ash hit the floor and felt blood on his lip.

He lay there, stunned. Then he got slowly to his feet and raised his hands.

"Okay," he said. "Okay."

The intruders looked at him with flat eyes.

He spun and ran full tilt at the far wall, hitting it with his shoulder. It held for a moment then the planks, which the builder, Ron Kebble, had wedged on the outside to keep the plasterboard in place when he'd abandoned Ash's house three weeks ago for a more lucrative job down the street, gave way, and the wall fell into space. Ash went after it, tumbling ten feet to the ground, the trees and the forest blurring past him.

He hit hard, landing in wet leaves and mud. He heard shouts from the house. Winded, he pulled himself upright and took off into the trees, sprinting in the direction the van had driven, fighting to free his phone from his pocket.

As he raced through the forest, his bare feet tearing on rocks and nettles, he didn't allow himself to feel any pain. He woke his phone. The face was cracked, but it flickered to life and he stopped, hidden behind a tree. He heard more shouts, voices getting closer. Ash dialed 911 then took off again, running for the road that ran parallel to his, phone held to his ear.

A voice said, "This is 911. What's your emergency?"

He slowed, ducking behind a tangle of weeds. "Men in a black van have taken my son. From 234 Maple Lane, Pearson."

The operator said, "I'm having difficulty hearing you. Please repeat your location."

Ash saw a black SUV driving along the road beneath him, heading in his direction.

He killed the call. Too late, he knew. They had already traced him.

Ash ran into the forest and emerged at a house under renovation. A carpenter was up a ladder hammering nails into stucco board. A chunky man stood beneath him. They laughed and the man on the ground turned and walked toward a shiny new Ford truck that was parked close to where Ash was hidden.

He saw that it was the builder, Kebble. The big man lowered his bulk into the Ford, its suspension moaning like a squeezebox. Ash, obeying some unknown impulse, edged forward and spun his phone into the flatbed of the truck as Kebble drove out toward the street.

Ash, in the tree line, followed at a jog, watching as Kebble accelerated away.

Nice, Danny. You've thrown away your best fucking means of getting help.

The black SUV swooped on Kebble's truck, blocking him. Men were out, weapons drawn, surrounding the Ford. A siren whooped and a patrol car sped up, the cops leaping out, guns pointed at Kebble. The men dragged the builder from his truck, and when he protested, one of them punched him. They spread him facedown on the road.

Ash retreated into the trees and ran deeper into the forest.

THREE

For a full minute, Victor Fabian didn't know who or where he was. It was as if all the signposts of his life had been erased.

He was alone in the back of a luxury car. The driver was Chinese—Fabian could see a slice of his face in the rearview mirror. A man sat in the passenger seat, talking on a cell phone. An American. Who he was Fabian could not recall.

Fabian looked out the window as the car halted at a towering gate. A gate to where? He didn't know. He glimpsed pagodas and lacquered wooden balustrades and a row of stone lions standing sentry.

A man in a black uniform and white gloves looked in through the car window. He had a rifle slung from his shoulder. Fabian felt a moment's fear.

The man waved the car on, and it rolled out into a busy road in a sprawling Chinese city. But which one?

"Sir? *Sir?*" The passenger had turned in his seat. "Mr. Fabian?"

Fabian. Yes. He was Victor Fabian. Yes.

And suddenly, as if with the snap of a carny hypnotist's fingers, Fabian remembered everything.

Remembered that he was in Beijing. That he was leaving the Zhongnanhai, the headquarters of the Chinese Politburo, adjacent to the Imperial Palace. That he had been stood up by an official of towering rank whose timid flunkies had fluttered around Fabian like moths, making apologetic whispers.

Fabian had no use for their groveling, he needed the signatures that would act like shock paddles on a huge project of his that was busy flatlining out in the Gobi Desert.

Fabian had aimed his beakish nose toward the door and strode through the endless corridors, blind to the lush floral carpets and the Ming vases and the scroll paintings. Angry, insulted, but knowing that the panjandrum, a fat little shar-pei called Sun Yongkang, had more than likely pulled a no-show so that he would have an excuse to visit Fabian's lair in Shanghai, where he would be plied with French champagne and Macanese cocaine and Jilin farm girls who still reeked of the paddy fields.

And then, as he'd been shown into the limousine, Fabian's mind had flown into a Bermuda triangle.

Gazing at the cherry blossom trees that grew against the vermilion walls of the compound, Fabian gave his head one violent shake as if his mind were some faulty appliance that needed only a jolt to restore it to order.

His longtime lackey, Ricky Pickford, was staring at him, blinking behind his glasses.

"Sir? Are you okay?"

"Yes, yes. Speak." Fabian sat taller.

"Our people moved on Ash."

"Good."

"But there's been a slight hitch."

"A hitch?" Fabian said, leaning forward.

"Yes. Ash escaped." Pickford blinked ever more urgently, semaphoring his anxiety.

Fabian stroked his long jaw, gathering his scattered thoughts like Scrabble tiles. Then he sat back and smiled.

"Unscripted, but I like it."

"You *like* it?"

"Yes. It only enhances the narrative."

"I thought you may want the Peaches alerted. To mop this up."

"No, no. The intention here is to discredit not to martyr."

"I understand."

"The boy is being held as insurance?"

"Yes."

"Fine. Then let it play out."

FOUR

Danny Ash stumbled deep into the forest that grew thick and wild on the hillside behind his house. His feet were bleeding, and shock and terror had left him disoriented and desperate.

A wave of panic took his knees and he sank down with his back to a tree. Forcing himself to breathe deeply though his nose, he tried to slow his hammering heart and tamp down the panic.

Fucking pull it together, Danny. Pull it together for Scooter.

He closed his eyes, breathed, and tried to find a still point.

He needed a plan.

Clearly the cops were no option. They were working with whoever had taken Scooter.

The media. He would go to the media. Speak out the way he had about his suspicions regarding Jane's death.

That must be what this was all about. He'd struck a nerve.

A little calmer, he stood and jogged to the top of the hill and looked out on the valley. The woods stretched down to a serpentine river and were busy reclaiming the abandoned sawmill far below. A new strip mall, an ugly concrete gash in the woodland, lay beyond the mill.

Ash started down the slope and came up behind a row of

mean houses. From his vantage point he could see into their
yards: junk, wrecked cars, unmowed lawns.

A big black dog, muscled and furrow-faced, was chained to a
withered tree in one yard. It had barked itself hoarse.

The house nearest to Ash had an American flag hanging limp
and sodden from a pole tied to its roof with baling wire. The
forest was kept at bay by a sagging wooden fence with missing
planks. A dirt bike with nubby mud-encrusted tires was parked
out back. Ash edged closer to a gap in the fence. He could see a
pair of work boots, thick with mud, left lying by the kitchen door.

The gap in the fence would allow his skinny frame to pass
through, and he was working up the courage to enter the yard
when the back door slammed open and a sway-bellied man in his
twenties with matted hair and beard tramped out.

He straddled the bike and kicked at it as if he bore it a grudge.
At last it caught and he worked the throttle, producing a rattling
roar and a belch of black smoke. He slalomed away and sped off to
the street, the noise of the bike pursuing him toward the strip mall.

Ash waited, looking for movement inside the house.

Nothing.

He turned sideways and fed himself through the gap in the
fence. He paused, waiting for a dog—inbred kin, maybe, of the
beast next door—to come at him with lolling tongue and yellow
teeth, but nothing happened. Crabbing over patchy grass strewn
with bike parts and rusted beer cans, Ash made for the boots.

As he neared the house, the self-important intro to a news
broadcast spilled into the yard and Ash caught the flicker of a tube
through a curtained window.

The image of a redneck with a shotgun flying out had him
grabbing the boots, ready to run. Then Ash heard a newsreader

speak his name and he edged closer to the window, a gust of wind lifting the filthy floral curtain and exposing the room within.

A massive TV rose like a shrine from a mess of beer cans, junk-food boxes, dirty dishes, and discarded clothes.

On Fox News a pinched-face anchor was calling Ash a fugitive terror suspect. And there he was on the screen. A mugshot from a DUI thing years before. A couple of glasses of wine with Jane over dinner had had him blowing .09 at a roadblock and the cops had booked him. He looked wild-eyed and sullen.

"Daniel Ash," the anchor was saying, "from Pearson, Washington, was born Mohammed Ashraf."

A lie.

That was his father, the medical student who'd fled Yemen for California in the late seventies, changed his name to Michael Ash and married Ash's Episcopalian mother.

The newsreader droned on: "Ash, with suspected ties to radical Islam, escaped capture earlier today and is on the run. His ten-year-old son has been taken into protective custody. An arms cache and explosives and chemicals used in the manufacture of suicide bombs were found during a search of Ash's house. Members of the public are warned that Ash is considered dangerous."

Ash became suddenly aware of the roar of the dirt bike and he clutched the boots, ready to bolt. Too late. The bike was already thundering into the yard. Ash dived through a peeling wooden door that stood half open and found himself in a cramped store room, stuffed with old furniture and piles of black trash bags, some leaking foul garbage.

Hiding behind the door, Ash could see a slit of the yard between the wood and hinges. The bike skidded to a halt and the bearded man dismounted, freeing a can of beer from a Walmart bag and chugging at it as he came toward the house.

The man stomped up the stairs, passing close enough for Ash to smell his sweat. He slammed inside, and the back door banged closed.

Ash waited a while before he crept out of the store room and sprinted across to the fence. There was a bad moment when the boot laces snagged on a nail in a wooden plank. Ash yanked the boot free and fled into the trees, breathing hard, listening for sounds of pursuit.

Nothing.

He sat and pulled the boots on.

They were way too big, even after he'd pulled the frayed yellow laces as tight as he could. But it was better than walking barefoot.

Walking to where, he wondered?

Where could he go where people didn't have TVs and smart-phones and computers and tablets?

FIVE

Victor Fabian was aboard his Gulfstream G650 en route to Shanghai, drinking Frapin Cuvée cognac and smoking a cigar.

His plane, his rules.

The memory lapse of earlier continued to plague him. It was not an isolated incident. It was merely the latest in a series of perturbing aberrations.

I am not myself, he thought.

Then who the hell am I? Or rather, who am I *becoming*?

Fabian pinched the bridge of his nose and tried to shake himself free of his gloom.

He looked across at Ricky Pickford who was "yessing" and "noing" into his cell phone. Fabian noticed that Pickford had a dusting of dandruff on the collar of his dark-blue suit and looked away in distaste.

Pickford ended his call and turned to Fabian. "Sir?"

"You have an update?"

"No, this is another matter."

"What?"

A lot of blinking and a bobbing of his Adam's apple before Pickford said, "It's about your daughter."

Fabian felt a distinct lurch in his chest, but kept his voice level as he said, "What about her?"

"Ms. Fabian continues to speak with your enemies."

"Yes?"

"Yes. She met with that investigative reporter from *The Guardian* in London yesterday."

"I see. And where is she now?"

"On the Eurostar to Paris."

"Any idea why?"

"Not yet."

"Mnnn." Fabian rubbed his eyes and squared his shoulders, keeping his voice light. "My enemies will trot out the same garbage they've been retailing for years. Let me know when Nicola starts speaking to my friends. Then I'll begin to worry."

SIX

In these days of rote terrorism, Eurostar's airline-style luggage and body scans meant you couldn't just waltz onto the Paris train at St. Pancras with an X-Acto knife—the one with the retractable blade that made a little snicker as it slid out—secreted on your person.

No, you had to be crafty. But, really, it wasn't so hard, now was it?

As Nicola Fabian, gangly and oddly beautiful with her tragic eyes and Modigliani face, locked the door of the train lavatory, she slipped the pin from her long brown hair. The hair a gift—like so many things—from her father. Her mother's had been mousy and thin, dishwater blonde.

The pin was Victorian, silver and coral, and sharp as a dagger. Avoiding her eyes in the mirror, she lifted the sleeve of her silk shirt and placed her arm, pulse up, on the cool metal of the sink, the skin of her forearm a palimpsest of scars.

She dented her flesh with the tip of the pin, feeling the bitter joy of the pain to come, conjuring the salt taste of her blood on her tongue.

But she stopped herself and said, "No, Nicky-Nicks. No. Not yet."

She returned the pin to her hair, washed her hands, and

went back to her window seat. Her overnight bag, a pretty little
Ted Baker spinner she'd bought on Daddy's account at Harrods,
rattled softly in the rack above her head.

She watched the Kent countryside blur by, the train a time
machine retracing the route she'd taken years ago to her boarding
school, an all-girls bullyfest near Maidstone. Her father had banished her there to keep her safe from the piece of human flotsam
that had been her mother, a fallen aristocrat, blue blood awash with
heroin, whom her father had married for her title—Nicola suffering
through a succession of hellish pubescent years while Victor Fabian
was in Africa or Asia or Latin America doing God knew what.

But she *did* know, didn't she?

Had known since she was ten, when she'd first googled his name
and been confronted with pictures of her father lurking behind
malignant-looking men wielding fly whisks or wearing absurd military regalia. She'd been confronted with the evils he had wrought:
snotty African babies with bloated bellies and skulls grinning from
the muddy soil of shallow graves in Mandalay, Kinshasa, or Pristina.

She'd deleted her Google search history and deleted her memory.

She lived for the sound of tires crunching on the gravel
beneath the gargoyles that guarded the entrance to the school.
Rushing to the window of her room and watching as her big,
handsome American father would emerge from a limo, smiling
his Cary Grant smile, ready to whisk her away to town for tea and
scones or, on rare occasions, an overnight in dismal Margate.

After her mother's funeral, her father had brought her to
America, to his house in Washington, DC. Nicola, gangly as a
stork, at twelve already her adult height, had sat slouched on
the sofa, knock-kneed, awestruck, watching him pace the room
drinking cognac and smoking cigars, holding forth in that

Wellesian baritone on matters of the day. She had convinced herself that she would live there with him forever.

But after a fortnight she'd been sent back to boarding school.
She'd spent her holidays with aged distant relatives of her mother's
in leaky manor houses overlooking tracts of grim countryside—
these ancients paid handsomely, she was sure, to suffer her.

It was on one of those holidays, in a filthy farmhouse in the
Scottish lowlands, that she'd learned the pleasure of self-mutilation.

He father would make sudden, unannounced arrivals,
smother her with kisses and fold her to his hot, scented flesh,
call her darling and baby and Nicky-Nicks. He'd spirit her away
for weekends in Antibes or the Cap or Sardinia, where he would
leave her alone while he huddled with dark men with nasty smiles
and then later try to make it all up to her with dinners and gifts
and frocks.

After school, she'd found herself at Oxford, where she'd tried
to study, of all things, economics. She'd lasted six months. After
dropping out, she'd dabbled in internet publishing, famine relief,
and gofering in the movie business. Her father's cash keeping her
insulated from the harsher realities of the world.

But she hadn't been able to hide, entirely, from her father's
actions. Not long after reading a report on how he had brokered
deals on behalf of Assad, she had seen the picture of the drowned
Syrian toddler on the Turkish beach. Three years old, in his red
T-shirt and blue shorts and little shoes, he'd looked like an American or English kid. And that had made it—obscenely—more
horrific and affecting.

Nicola had berated herself for this, knowing that her tears
were meaningless, that this was dead-child porn that elicited a
self-satisfied feeling of sadness among Western observers like her.

So she'd told herself that her father was who he was. She'd seen little of him and cashed his check every month.

Then a succession of anonymous emails had appeared in her inbox, filled with insinuations about Victor Fabian. Pointing her in the direction of her father's more recent misdeeds: Syria, the Ukraine, Indonesia, China.

Insistent enough to get her attention, they'd started suggesting she meet people.

People who could tell her the truth about her father.

So she'd met an alcoholic ex-MI6 man whose spoon had chimed like a beggar's bell against his cup as he'd stirred his tea in a Bethnal Green café. He'd told her a baroque tale about her father selling Romanian orphans, which may even have been true, but when he'd importuned her for a handout, she'd left in disgust.

Then came a little tête-à-tête at a coffee shop in Knightsbridge with a journalist from *The Guardian*, detestable in his puke-colored polo neck and smug liberal certitude. He'd gaily trotted out details of her father's association with the Ukrainian despot Viktor F. Yanukovych.

"Victor and Viktor," he'd said with a pursed smile. "It has a lovely ring, doesn't it?"

He'd sipped at his soy latte then carefully placed his cup in its saucer on the table, crossed his legs, looked at her blandly and said, "So, Nicola, how does it feel?"

"How does what feel?"

"To be the devil's daughter?"

She had lifted his cup and tipped it onto his head. The latte was hot, and he'd yelped, dabbing at his scalp with a napkin.

An overorchestrated version of "Yesterday" had played her out into the gloomy street, where an icy wind had slapped her as she'd hailed a cab. When she'd folded herself into its humid interior, she'd heard throaty, ribald laughter that, after a moment, she'd realized was her own.

These encounters had had the unwanted effect of making her feel more kindly disposed toward her father, who, with his bare-faced ignominy, seemed somehow more wholesome than these bottom-feeders.

More emails came. She ignored them for a few days then, the previous night, sitting in her Southwark flat, her computer had pinged and she'd opened her messenger app and read, *There's somebody else you should meet.*

She'd sat staring at the blinking cursor as she tried to compose a reply.

At last she'd written: *Who are you? I'll only play if you'll tell me your name.*

My name isn't important.

It is to me, she wrote.

There's somebody in France you need to talk to.

Don't be silly. I'm not going to France.

There's some urgency. She's dying.

Look, I know who and what my father is. I don't need to hear more about his dark deeds.

This is different.

Nicola had hesitated, then she'd typed, *How so?*

This is about your mother.

SEVEN

Ash, feet raw from where the too-large boots chafed at them, hobbled up the hairpinning mountain road, sweating, winded, searching for the overlook where the cop had questioned him and Scooter how long ago? Six months? Eight?

Seeing the lawman's gaunt face, eyes shadowed by his hat, leaning in toward him through the window of Ash's car, asking if he'd seen some hapless poacher.

Ash saying, "No, Officer, I haven't. Sorry."

The cop looking past him at Scooter who sat staring straight ahead through the windshield.

"And what about you, son? Seen anything?"

Scooter shaking his head.

"Only manners to reply to a question, boy."

Ash saying, "He doesn't speak."

The cop's shadowed eyes back on him. "He dumb?"

"I said he doesn't speak."

The cop swallowing, his Adam's apple bobbing in his skinny neck, then stepping back and waving a hand. "Okay, get going."

Ash had started the car and driven onto the road that carved through a carpet of forest.

He was the fugitive now.

He heard a vehicle, the engine straining as the driver shifted down, and he vaulted the silver guardrail and plunged into the bush. A cop car sped by, light bar flashing.

Ash started walking deeper into the forest, leaving the road behind. The undergrowth grew denser, the sky hidden by the tree canopy.

The smell of the peaty soil and crushed pine needles. The smell of his own sweat.

He needed water.

He thought of Scooter. Saw his limp body carried into the van. Saw the cold eyes of the woman he'd known as Holly Howells. The woman he'd liked and trusted.

Stopping a moment to get his breath, hand on the rough bark of a tree, Ash stared down at his stolen boots and wiped sweat from his face.

The silence was broken by the rasp of a rifle being cocked, and he felt the hard coldness of a gun barrel nudging the base of his skull.

EIGHT

Speeding through the lush fields of France, Nicola Fabian felt a surge of dread so profound that she leaned forward to order the driver to turn the Mercedes around and take her back to Paris.

But something stopped her. Some intuition that an opportunity awaited to close a chapter of her life. To shake herself free of the lassitude that had left her living in eternal monochrome.

So she sat back in her seat, hugging herself, her unseeing eyes on the bucolic pastures and cows at the cud, her mind on the internet exchange of last night.

Her anonymous chat pal had told her she needed to visit the detox facility north of Paris where her mother had died fifteen years ago.

When she'd asked why, the response had been an instruction: *Catch the 12:24 Eurostar from St. Pancras. I'll message you the reservation number shortly. A driver will be waiting for you on the platform at Gare du Nord.*

Almost immediately the number of her return ticket had popped onto her screen.

The exchange was over. She'd sat at her desk, staring out into the night, wondering who he was and why he was doing this.

Yes, she'd made up her mind that her correspondent was

male. Why, she couldn't say. Something about the bluntness of the messages, maybe? Although that wasn't any real indication of sex. Perhaps this gender attribution said more about her than the clipped prose did about its author? Said that she was more likely to respond to the whims of a man than those of a woman?

This insight had saddened her.

She'd fallen into a fitful sleep and awoken feeling wretched, resolved that she would be going nowhere.

But by ten she'd found herself getting ready, packing her spinner and taking herself to St. Pancras and boarding the train. Enduring the trip back into her childhood and the claustrophobic twenty minutes in the tunnel, before the train had emerged, mole-like, at Calais.

The driver, dressed in a dark suit, had been on the platform in Paris, holding a neatly hand-printed sign saying Mme. Nicola F., which had made her feel like a French soft-porn actress.

He'd taken her suitcase and escorted her to a black Mercedes, installed her in the rear, and driven her into the verdant French countryside.

The car, traveling along a narrow oak-lined lane, was filled with a muted ticking as the driver twitched the turn signal and swung off the road. He halted at a pair of high, rusted wrought iron gates that bore a faded coat of arms dominated by a winged dragon with a lolling tongue.

A very old, emaciated man wearing what looked to be the uniform of a long-forgotten war, dragged open one of the gates and stood to attention, his arm trembling as he saluted them.

The driver nosed the Mercedes through the gap and onto a rutted track that plunged into dense forest, the sky obscured by the trees, the interior of the car gloomy as dusk.

Through gaps in the foliage Nicola glimpsed snapshots of

decaying grandeur: A discolored marble statue of Adonis, toppled from his plinth, throttled by ropes of creeping ivy. A once-white 1930s Rolls Royce (hood ornament intact, the Flying Lady frozen forever as she was about to take flight) without wheels, doors or window glass, mired in mud, now the roost of a flock of diseased chickens. A Roman temple folly reduced to two columns and a jumble of masonry on which incongruously urban graffiti depicting a cock and balls had been sprayed in neon colors.

Finally the car broke free of the forest, approaching what must have been a perfectly symmetrical baroque château before its right elevation was consumed by fire, leaving blackened timbers pointing like lances at the low sky.

The Mercedes crunched to a halt beside a dry fountain, its wide basin filled past the brim with trash. As the driver opened her door she caught the landfill stench of putrefying waste.

"Mademoiselle Fabian?"

Nicola looked up as a young woman dressed in a starched white apron over a black dress and black leggings, her feet in clumpy, mannish shoes, scurried down the stairs.

She curtsied, her platinum blonde bob falling across her face, veiling her eyes.

"Dr. Rossignol awaits."

The nurse trotted up the stairs, pausing in the doorway of the ruined house. She led Nicola into a massive vestibule, paved with checkerboard tiles.

Plaster—reduced to powder as white as the wig of the long-dead nobleman who stared down from a stained portrait leaning against the doorjamb—flaked from the walls, revealing the time-worn brick beneath.

Two staircases, perfect mirror images of each other, swept up from the hallway. The stairs on the left reaching up to a landing; the staircase on the right, its ornate iron balustrade peeled back like the lid of a can of Spam, dangled over the void left by the fire.

The nurse ascended the undamaged staircase and, once she'd decided that it was sound, Nicola followed.

The beating of wings had her looking up and she saw that part of the domed roof had collapsed, leaving the room open to the heavens. Blackbirds, disturbed by their footfalls, pelleted skyward like buckshot.

The nurse led her along a dim corridor that tunneled into further devastation: torn carpets, peeling wallpaper, splintered doors opening onto rooms cluttered with debris.

The girl unlocked a door that was intact and pushed it open, revealing a bedroom shocking in its flawlessness. The pale walls were perfectly plastered and painted, decorative stuccowork and ceiling friezes unblemished, cavorting cherubs smiling down on a vast bed, its frame and headboard made of intricately carved pale wood.

A woman with white hair pulled back into a severe bun, wearing a black dress, sat on a chair near a pair of glass doors that overlooked the front of the château. She had a nasal cannula inserted in her nostrils, the thin tubes leading to an oxygen concentrator that sat beside her chair, the device clicking and sucking as it kept her alive.

Her face was emaciated, skull-like, but still made up, the lipstick and rouge foreshadowing the work of a mortician.

The woman extended a bony hand, roped with veins, the skin a tortoiseshell of liver spots.

"I am Dr. Marie Rossignol."

Nicola fought a wave of revulsion and touched her fingers to those of the old doctor. Her skin was dry as parchment.

"Please sit."

Nicola sat in the chair facing Rossignol, who coughed and fought for breath. The nurse hovered by the door.

The old woman dismissed her with a flick of her claw and the door closed. She stared at Nicola, the breathing apparatus providing an unsettling syncopation, like something out of a David Lynch film.

"You don't look at all like your mother," Dr. Rossignol said. "You favor your father."

"Why do you want to see me?" Nicola said.

"I am dying," the crone said. "I will live maybe one more month. I am, as they say, getting my affairs in order."

"And there's something you want to tell me about my mother?"

The old woman stared at her. "Do you believe in God?"

"How is that relevant?"

"She did not, your mother. Which is why she came here. All the so-called rehabilitation facilities in England follow the Minnesota Model. Do you know what that is?"

"No."

"That twelve-step nonsense. The surrendering to a higher power. To *God* in other words. *Tcha.*" A cough and a flick of the hand. "Your mother had no time for that, which is why this was her refuge of choice."

"Yes. It must have been. She came back ad nauseam."

"She struggled with her addiction, it is true."

"And you were always here to accommodate her."

The old woman regarded her with a steely eye and Nicola saw how formidable she must once have been.

"You are suggesting that we *fleeced* her?"

"Well, didn't you? Or, more accurately, fleeced my father?"

"Your *father*," the woman said and coughed. The spasm was

prolonged and Nicola was considering calling the nurse when the old doctor regained her composure and wiped her mouth on a tissue.

She fought for breath and said, "The last time was different. Your mother was healing. She was *clean*. Had been for three months. She spoke of you constantly, how she wanted to repair things with you. She wrote you letters."

"I never got any letters."

"Because I never mailed them. I burnt them." Dr. Rossignol looked out at the devastation. "Don't worry, I understand the irony. I wouldn't be so clichéd as to call it a punishment, but ..." A Gallic shrug. "Your father visited. He was not pleased."

"That she was in recovery?"

"Yes. He wanted, I suspect, a repeat of all the previous times. The previous failures. There was, I think, no room in his imagination for her to be healed." She sighed, pausing. "Before he departed, he asked me to do something."

Nicola felt a sick dread. She wanted to get up and leave, but she stayed in her seat.

"What?" she said.

A sigh. A cough. A shrug. "The overdose."

"You did that?"

"Yes. I did that. I gave your mother a sedative, and when she was asleep, I administered the lethal dose. She knew nothing." The old woman looked at her with watery eyes as blue as robin's eggs.

"Why?" Nicola said.

"You will have to ask your father."

"No. Why did you do it?"

The old woman laughed and coughed and when she had recovered she said, "For the money, of course. This place was failing. I was in debt. Your father offered me a great deal of money." Coughing again. "Of course it all came to dust. Less than a year later there was the fire and well …" Another shrug.

"How can I believe what you are telling me?"

Dr. Rossignol gazed at her. "Why would I lie? Anyway, I kept one of her letters. The last one she wrote to you. I don't know why. Maybe I knew that, one day, there would be this reckoning."

She extended a clawed hand and lifted a book on the table beside her chair. Proust's *À la recherche du temps perdu*. Underneath lay a letter in a sealed airmail envelope with a blue and red border. She held it out with a shaking hand. The envelope was yellowing and brittle.

Nicola stared at it for a long time before she took it. She recognized her mother's handwriting, an unruly cursive scrawl, but legible enough for Nicola to read her name and the address of her school.

She stood and walked out without saying another word to the dying woman. Clutching the letter, she hurried back to the car, the little nurse fluttering after her like one of the birds.

"Take me back to Paris, please," she said to the driver who stood to attention by the car.

When they were clear of the château, she opened the envelope carefully and drew out the sheet of lightweight paper.

My Darling Nicola,

I understand why you haven't answered my letters. I understand why you would be suspicious, but I will be leaving here next week and I really do want to see you. This time will be different, I promise.

She could read no more and slipped the letter back into the envelope and stowed it in her bag.

Nicola reached up into her hair and freed the pin and slipped her hand under the hem of her white shirt. She sat for a moment, then closed her eyes and jabbed the point into her belly below her navel, gasping at the sharp pain. The warm blood welled and soaked into the waistband of her jeans, and she exhaled long and deep as she felt the familiar release.

NINE

John Dapp, still half in the bag, burned his hand on the espresso machine in his Birdland kitchen. He'd been out too late the night before with a posse of kids he was grooming to embed within product teams at the Silicon Valley tech companies who laid heavy coin on him as a security consultant.

He said, "*Tamade*," as he sucked his index finger, after two years back in Northern California the Mandarin curse still coming to his tongue quicker than its English equivalent.

His beautiful Chinese wife, sitting at the kitchen table paging through *Vogue*, didn't look up. He knew deep in the marrow of his old spook bones that she was being unfaithful.

Dapp poured his coffee, holding his burned digit away from the cup, and looked at her. Remembering that day three years ago when, doing some off-the-books work for Apple at their Shanghai plant, he'd looked on as a female security guard had found the enclosure of an iPhone 5C in the underwire of Yingying's bra.

When he'd dismissed the guard and questioned Yingying alone in fluent Mandarin, she hadn't flinched, hadn't begged, hadn't offered him sexual favors like some of the women did when they were busted.

He hadn't needed to ask her why she was trying to smuggle

the part out of the factory. The math was simple. She earned $300 a month on the production line. Black marketers, who solicited factory workers by posting signs at bus stops and factory dormitories, offered six months' pay for Apple parts. Workers clenched these parts between their toes, threw them over fences, and flushed them down the john for retrieval in the sewer.

Dapp'd seen it all.

Including the underwire stunt.

The stolen parts mostly ended up in Huaqiangbei, in Shenzhen, Southern China. One of the biggest electronics markets in the world, employing about a half-million people and doing around $20 billion a year in revenue.

Yingying's composure had impressed him and he'd offered her a deal: she walked free if she informed on her coworkers.

She'd pursed her lovely lips in distaste, then shrugged and said, "Okay."

So she became his asset.

And after a few months, she became his lover and then, when Victor Fabian had done what he'd done, Dapp'd got her to the US and married her.

She'd acclimated to California with terrifying speed. An orphan, she had no family back in China and had no desire to return. Tall and athletic, she'd joined a gym and quickly become part of the workout culture that Dapp, a shambling, overweight bear of a man, despised.

When, after a lovemaking session, she'd pinched his roll of hairy gut-flab and suggested he join her at the gym, he'd lain back on the pillow, lit a Parliament, and said, "Baby, I'd rather be waterboarded than do those fucking circuits."

In the time Yingying had been in the States, she'd gone from having a few words of English to speaking near-perfect Californian, complete with redundant interrogatives at the end of her sentences. Just like the toned little gym bunnies in their Day-Glo athletic clothes who drove up outside the house and honked the horns of their SUVs for Yingying.

It was Dapp, earning good money—sure, not the obscene swag the twenty-year-old code-crunching geniuses pulled down, but enough to afford the bungalow in Palo Alto and the shiny new Lexus—who felt like an alien, missing the heady stink of gasoline and sewers and street food.

Missing the guttural slur of Mandarin in his ears.

And missing his wife who had morphed into somebody he no longer knew.

He poured his espresso and sipped it and watched her reading the glossy magazine with a terrifying avidity.

Was she screwing somebody? Some personal trainer with washboard abs and wandering hands? Some start-up billionaire looking for another notch on his belt?

A sick feeling deep in his gut told him she was.

So why didn't he prove it? He, who'd run the CIA's China desk for years. Who even now, out to pasture, could make a call and within a few hours know not only who his wife was boning but could have DNA samples of Yingying's lover harvested from their love nest's bed sheets—if he so wanted.

But he didn't want.

Didn't want to be right.

Didn't know just what on God's green earth he would do with that knowledge.

So he distracted himself. Drank more than he usually did. Worked longer hours than he needed to, but mostly channeled his fear and neurosis into exacting revenge on Victor Fabian. He could never forgive Fabian. Could never see that smug face looming over the shoulder of the president when he was doing grip-and-grins with rich Russians, Chinese, and Syrians without feeling a sick wash of rage.

Yingying stood and brushed by Dapp, laying a half-hearted air-kiss on him.

"Where are you going?" he said.

"Oh, nowhere. You know?"

"Have fun."

"You too."

She took her bag and went through to the garage, and he heard her Jeep start and reverse out and drive away.

Dapp sat down at the table and drank his coffee and tried to clear his mind of his suspicions.

He used the remote to ignite the wall-mounted TV and heard the blare of CNN. The coffee cup hovered halfway to his mouth when he saw the news of Danny Ash.

On the run. His child taken. A cache of explosives found in his house.

All Dapp's thoughts of his wife's infidelity were washed away by the sickening realization that this was his doing.

That his manipulation had destroyed Danny Ash's life.

TEN

"They came into your house and took your boy?" the bearded man asked, the light from the cabin's single high window showing a face as furrowed as a salt pan.

"Yes," Ash said, sitting with his back to the wooden wall, boots off, applying a foul-smelling yellow paste to his bleeding feet. He winced, his feet stinging.

The man looked at him. He had eyes pale as shards of glass.

"You don't tend those, you'll end up with the foot rot. Don't reckon a visit to the ER is an option for you."

"No."

"Then you best keep on rubbin."

Ash did as he was told, biting back the pain, looking around the hut.

A rough wooden table. Two hardcover books squared away with the edge. Ash couldn't read the spines.

A sleeping pallet against one wall, the blanket folded with military neatness.

A Dixie cast-iron potbelly stove, dented and beaten-up looking, like it had been salvaged.

An olive-green tin trunk. Padlocked.

A chair.

A hunting rifle, the one that an hour before had prodded the base of his skull, leaning against the wall, a pair of binoculars lying beside it.

When Ash was done applying the paste, the bearded man tossed him two lengths of yellowing bandage.

"Bind them good."

Ash started wrapping his feet and the man squatted, hands dangling between his knees. His hair and beard were long and matted, shot with gray. He wore clothes made from animal skins and his shoes were hand-hewn. He was a vision from the past, as if the fabric of time had been ripped and one of the Donner party had staggered out of a hundred and fifty years ago.

"You know who these people were who took the boy?" he said.

"No."

"They showed you no identification?"

"No."

"And now they're sayin you're some kind of a jihadist?"

"Yes."

"Are you?"

"Do I look like a fucking jihadist?"

The man scratched his cheek. His nails were long and dirty. "Just gettin the facts straight."

"I'm not a jihadist. They're framing me."

"Why?"

"Because I started asking difficult questions about my wife's death."

"What questions?"

"She died in China. Supposedly fell from a bridge that was under construction. But information came my way that she had been murdered."

"Murdered by who?"

"The Chinese." Ash paused. "And the government. Possibly."

"The American government?"

"Yes."

The man sniffed and tapped the baked mud floor.

"These questions, who'd you put 'em to?"

"I went to the media."

"The *media*," spitting the word out as if it were bitter to his tongue.

"Yes. And I was getting some traction."

"That right?"

"On blogs. And a mention in a piece in the *New York Times*."

"But what you were doin with this *traction* was drawing a target on your fool head." Those eyes staring at him, unblinking. "And the head of your boy. You made your son coffin bait." He cleared his throat and swallowed. "Think these people play by the *rules*?"

"No."

"No." Blinking, rubbing his eyes, sighing. "You have any plans? For findin your boy?"

"Maybe I'll reach out to the media again."

"Jesus, son, if a man cuts off your hand you don't offer him the other one. Not if you want to go on playin the piano, you don't."

"That's very colorful."

A flicker in the thicket of beard, like a woodland creature on the move. Then the eyes drilled him again. "Your stupidity put your boy in peril. You want him dead?"

"No."

"Then forget the media, okay? You purge the media from your goddamn mind. Understood?"

"Yes."

"Okay. This information you were puttin out, how'd you come by it?"

"I received anonymous emails."

"Anonymous?"

"Well, they were from Linda Lovelace."

"Like that cocksucker girl?"

"Yes. I think it was a play on Deep Throat. You know, the Watergate informant?"

"And you believed what they said?"

"They were persuasive."

"Persuasive? Emails from a stranger hiding behind some porno handle?"

Ash had no reply.

"I never heard the equal of this." The man shook his head. "And these emails had no tracks for you to follow?"

"No. They were untraceable. Believe me, I tried."

The man sighed. "I should have just left you there, up by the road. You woulda deserved it. But I owe your boy."

He stood, still lithe and limber. He lifted a couple of canteens off the floor and slung the rifle from his shoulder.

"I'm gettin water. Don't move."

He left, slamming the door.

Ash sat, feeling the throbbing in his feet, watching dust motes dancing in the light from the window—and then he was back at that mountain overlook with Scooter, the kid standing by the rail staring out, hands in pockets, silent.

Ash had brought him up there in the hope that time away from his iPad and his books would jolt some words from his lips.

Zip. Nada. Nothing.

Ash had floated a couple of comments his son's way,

low-key, banal stuff, but the boy had remained resolutely silent.

Silent as he'd been since his mother had died.

After a week of that silence, Ash had taken him to a therapist in Seattle, and the man had spent an hour with Scooter. Afterward, he'd left the boy watching YouTube on his tablet and had sat and spoken with Ash.

"He's grieving."

"I know that."

"And so are you."

"Yes."

"But you're an adult. You have more coping mechanisms in place."

"I sometimes wonder."

"He's a kid, albeit a very smart kid. And, from your description, a kid with a very developed interior life. We're not talking about a minijock who's going to leave his pain on the football field."

"No, that's not Scooter."

"Okay, so what if he's made some kind of pact with himself? Given himself some kind of structure, built a little life raft on the sea of grief?"

"And that pact is not to speak?"

"Without being too grandiose, what if it's a vow of silence?"

"Like a monk?"

"Yes. Maybe. That for Scooter this vow gives him a mechanism, a container. A feeling of some control. Some volition. I'm guessing, but my sense is that he has set a time limit for this silence. It's not permanent."

"One day he'll just wake up and speak again?"

"Yes."

"And meanwhile?"

"Meanwhile you do what you're doing. Love him. Support him. Wait."

"Wait?"

"Yes. It's not easy, I know."

Standing on that roadside looking out at the mountains. Waiting.

Hearing a noise in the bush.

A man appeared. A bearded man with long, shaggy hair and handmade clothes. A rifle was slung over his shoulder and some small creature—a squirrel?—dangled from his belt. He was limping and there was blood on his leg.

The man was breathless. Staring at them.

Ash stood rooted, as silent as his boy.

The silence was broken by the bone-saw shriek of a siren, getting closer. The man looked up the road.

It was Scooter who moved first, rushing to the trunk of the car, popping the lid, gesturing inside.

The man regarded the boy, the siren getting louder, then he looked across at Ash.

Ash saw something in his son's eyes, something more intense, more present, than he had seen in months. He nodded. The man clambered into the trunk, and Scooter slammed it shut and dashed for the car.

Ash followed, cranking the engine, wanting to escape the oncoming law.

Too late. The cops saw them and the cruiser braked with a little shimmy and backed up, blocking their path.

The deputy left his partner at the wheel, sunglasses flaring in the sun as he walked across to them.

When the cop leaned in and interrogated them about the

poacher, Ash's guts turned to water. But he found the courage to lie. Not for the wild stranger in the trunk, but for his boy.

The cop returned to the patrol car and it sped away, siren wailing.

Ash and Scooter sat there long enough for the sound of the siren to grow faint, then the man banged on the trunk.

Ash went around and freed him, and the wild man clambered out. He limped to Scooter's window and said, "You've got sand, boy. I thank you."

And with that he was gone, back into the forest, dragging his wounded leg.

Ash had started the car and driven down the hill.

"That was a brave thing you did, Scoot. Totally freaking nutso, but brave."

Scooter stayed silent but when Ash looked at the boy and saw that he was smiling, his heart had swelled and that had ended up being a good day.

The cabin door opened and Ash tensed. But the woodsman was alone, carrying canteens of water. He offered one to Ash.

When Ash was done drinking he wiped his mouth and said, "Who are you?"

"Nobody."

"You must have a name."

The man looked at him. "Bob will do."

"You some kind of a survivalist?"

"No. I'm just a fellow gettin through this vale of tears the only way he knows how."

Bob knelt at the trunk and unlocked it. He lifted out jeans, a plaid shirt, boots, and a John Deere cap. He laid the clothes on the pallet and set the boots on the floor.

He reached back into the trunk and removed an oilcloth that

he unfolded. Bob skimmed a driver's license at Ash, who stared at a youngish man with short black hair and a gaunt face. Carter Bew. Born the year before Ash.

The wild man stood. "We cut and darken your hair, I reckon you'll just about pass as him."

"Who is he?"

"Was. He was my boy. Dead now." Bob drank water. "Going on two years. I buried him myself, right out there." He jabbed a finger toward the forest. "I hadn't seen him for a long while then he come on out here from the city, skinny as you. Told me he had the AIDS. Nothin they could do for him. I nursed him till he died."

"I'm sorry," Ash said.

"You keep your sorries for yourself, son. Christ knows you gonna need 'em."

ELEVEN

"Scooter? *Scooter*!"

He saw his mom, laughing on the beach. Her dark hair blowing in her face. Running into the ocean shouting his name.

But it wasn't his mom shaking his arm. His mom was dead.

He kept his eyes closed, as if that would trap the terror inside him and keep him from crying out, from calling for his father.

Keep him from breaking his vow.

For that's what it was.

That doctor in Seattle had been right—Scooter pretending to watch YouTube, but standing with his ear against the man's office door, listening to him talk to his pop.

It was a vow of silence.

He'd taken it for a year, from the time he'd heard of his mom's death. The year would be up in thirty-seven days.

Or was it thirty-six?

He didn't know.

Didn't know what day it was.

Somebody shook his arm again, but he kept his eyes closed.

A man said, "He's still KO'd. Leave him be."

Scooter lay still and tried to figure out where he was. He could feel a vibration and hear the rumble of engines. Jet plane engines.

Like the time he'd flown with his pop to Disneyland back when he was a little kid.

He felt sick, and he prayed he wasn't going to spew. But he held it down. Swallowed back the sour crud that came up into his mouth.

His head was thick and sore and his thoughts spun like they were in a tumble dryer.

Kept on coming back to his mom.

Lying there, scared and wanting to barf, he felt she was real close, smelling the clean smell that was her and only her. Shampoo and soap, and something else, like maybe cinnamon on pancakes.

And then he was gone again, somewhere deep and dark.

When he surfaced later, he still kept his eyes shut. Listened. Moving, but bumpier. A car, not a plane. He opened one eye a crack. It was dark. He lay on the floor of a van. Somebody sat near him. A man.

Scooter closed his eye.

He tried to put it all together. What had happened.

Couldn't.

He remembered breakfast that morning and his father coming in and standing in the kitchen doorway saying "Hi," in that way he had that sounded all hopeful but just *so* desperate.

Scooter loved his father and felt bad for him. Knew he was suffering, too, after his mother died. Knew he'd suffer less if Scooter just opened his mouth and spoke.

But Scooter had this crazy notion that if he broke his vow— taken in the instant that his pop had told him the horrible news, that his mom had fallen from a bridge in China—he'd be broken too.

That his life would be over before it had even really got started.

He'd googled the suspension bridge that hung across a river in a province in southern China, near a city with lots of x's and z's.

One of the contractors was the company his mother had worked for. His mom was doing something called a site inspection and had fallen and died.

Looking at the picture, seeing how high the bridge was, how far she must've fallen, he understood why they'd never been allowed to see her body. How the coffin had stayed closed at her funeral.

And then, months later, his pop had sat him down at the kitchen table and said, "Scoot, listen, there may have been something bad that happened with Mom. She may have been working against China. And she made enemies. And those enemies killed her. I believe she was never on that bridge."

What his father had wanted him to believe was that his mother had been killed by some bad guys out there in China.

But he'd read some of the stuff online. Read interviews with his father on blogs, and his pop had said that their own people killed mom. That Americans had betrayed her. Did it for money.

For *financial gain*, his father had said.

For *greed*.

Is that why this was happening?

Why he was in this van?

Were these the people who killed his mom?

The van bumped and slowed and bumped some more. He opened his eyes and looked straight into those of Holly. For a moment, he felt real relief. He was safe. Holly had come to get him.

Then he remembered this morning. Remembered the moment when Holly, the woman he loved and had believed loved him, stuck something into his neck that had knocked him out.

As she looked down at him now, turned in her seat, one side of her face lit by the glow of the dashboard, he saw it was her, but not her.

"Scooter," she said. "You're awake?"

She was speaking in a voice that wasn't hers. Wasn't the voice his father, always with a smile, had called hippie-dippie.

His pop mimicking her, saying, "Wow, Scoot, isn't this just an awesomely *beeee*-utiful day?"

This voice was cold and flat. And she looked different too. That kinda wild, gray hair was pulled back from her face and tied up. She wore a pair of black-framed glasses he'd never seen before. And instead of those clown-like rainbow clothes she'd made for herself on her sewing machine, she wore some kind of dark pant-suit and a white shirt.

Looking all official.

She leaned in closer, and he saw nothing but coldness in the eyes behind the glasses.

"You'll be quite safe if you do as I say. Okay?"

He nodded, and she turned away, looking back at the road. She sat beside the driver. Out of the corner of his eye Scooter saw another man. Youngish with cropped hair, doing something to his phone that lit up his face.

The man pocketed the phone and said, "We're close."

He reached over and pulled a hood over Scooter's head.

Scooter fought, lashing out. He caught the man with his elbow and heard a muttered curse. The man grabbed him by the leg and squeezed hard.

"Leave him," Holly said. "I said, leave him!"

The man released Scooter. He felt Holly's hand on his chest as she knelt over him.

"Scooter, you need to calm down. You need to listen to me. It's about your father. Can you do that?"

Scooter stopped thrashing and lay still.

"The hood is just for a little while longer then we'll remove it. Okay?"

He nodded.

"I want you to listen carefully now. Are you listening?"

Another nod.

"Your father has done some very bad things. Things that undermine the security of our country. But we want to be fair to him. To give him a fair trial. Do you understand?"

Again he nodded.

"The better you behave, the more you show us that you are disciplined and obedient, the more lenient and fair we will be to your father. Is this understood?"

Nodding.

"Good then."

Holly patted his leg like she was patting a dog, and Scooter breathed through his panic and went deep, deep, deep inside himself, shutting his fear away in a tiny little box.

TWELVE

Like any house, a safe house needs cleaning. What with the 24-7 surveillance crews and the guests (that's what Uhuru Bakewell called them) obliged to stay in the house day and night, sometimes for weeks, or even months, on end.

So Uhuru had cleaned, swept, polished, scrubbed, and scoured the farmhouse, getting the place ready for the arrival of the new guest.

Two agents were already there. White men dressed in crisp leisure wear, who'd arrived in a black Suburban that afternoon, toting kit bags.

They were in the kitchen now, sitting at the wooden table he'd shone to a mirror with beeswax, drinking Nescafé and watching Fox News. There was a no-smoking rule in the house, so the younger, bigger, plug-ugly one went outside every hour or so and fired up a Marlboro.

Uhuru sat in the dark in his little crib by the garage, watching the cracker come and stand in the spill of piss-yellow light by the kitchen door, puffing, looking out over the oak trees. He finished his smoke and flicked the butt away onto the stones of the driveway, where a pile already lay like dead little worms, waiting for Uhuru to pick them up in the morning.

The agents were the kind of men who'd found it easy to ignore Uhuru's skinny black ass while he went about his business earlier. They'd made those small signs of irritation—tightening their mouths, clearing their throats like something was stuck in their craws—when he'd crossed their paths, but never once saying even one word to him.

Like he was invisible.

That was okay. That was just fine. Come morning, he still saw himself in the shaving mirror.

He was a vet. Marine. He'd taken a bullet to the right calf that'd left him a little gimpy and got him a Purple Heart.

He had a Silver Star too. But that was another fuckin story. What the hell, it had helped get him a security clearance, sure enough. Helped get him this gig.

Money paid into his bank account on the first of each month by Executive Protection Services. Who the fuck they were Uhuru didn't know, didn't care.

He asked no questions. Kept his head down, just doing the do these three years now. Dressed neat and clean in his pressed black sweats and Air Jordans, not making no eye contact with the agents or the guests.

Mostly the people kept here were men. Asian or Middle Eastern. Looking like the fuckers who'd shot at him in the sandbox.

Only one time had there been a woman guest. A Russian. Bird's nest of bottle-blonde hair piled up on her head and lots of gold in her grill when she smiled. Which she'd done a lot of when she'd first arrived. Spending hours on her face paint, coming out of her room dressed like she was going to a party. Tippy-tapping on her high heels, whale tail of her thong underwear peeking out of her too-tight pants. Giving the ofay agents the glad eye.

But over time, she'd got depressed and slovenly. Dumping used tampons and Kleenexes on the floor by her bed and leaving her unflushed toilet for him to attend to.

He hoped the new guest was some jihadist who prayed to Allah at dawn and dusk. Who made his own bed and cleaned his own crib, not wanting some *abed* like Uhuru to contaminate him with his black hands.

Sitting in his room Uhuru felt the little twitch and buzz of his meds. Seroquel to help him sleep and make the shadows stay on the walls. Zoloft for his tripwire nerves. Vicodin to relieve the pain in his leg where he took the bullet.

And a quaalude.

Well, man, the 'lude was just a little recreation, to ease him out a mite. To take his mind off of tomorrow.

For a while he'd been getting ever skinnier and had felt nagging pain in his gut, so he'd gone to the Baltimore VA hospital a few weeks back. A scan had showed something growing in his innards that had worried the doctor enough for him to order another appointment, coming up the next day, to "reassess."

Reassess.

Uhuru heard the crunch of tires on the gravel and headlights swung like searchlights across the rear of the house before a black van came to a halt.

The two men left the kitchen and spoke to the passenger who stepped down from the van. A woman. Small. Gray hair pulled back, wearing a dark pantsuit. She watched as the driver went and opened the rear door of the van and a guy climbed out. Young guy with that big dick way of walking that Uhuru knew so well.

He was followed by a kid maybe ten years old. Hooded.

When Big Dick took off the hood, the kid stood hunched,

checking the place out. Uhuru waited for another adult, a parent maybe, to appear, but none did. The driver slammed the van doors closed and got back behind the wheel. Big Dick went and sat up front, and the van drove away.

The gray-haired agent pointed at the door of the house and the kid walked slowly into the kitchen. She followed him.

Now, Uhuru had no time to ponder the circumstances of the guests. They came. He cleaned. They went away.

But a kid? Alone?

Man, that seemed whack to him.

Then he heard the voice of the man he admired most in the world, his one-time platoon sergeant, saying, "Now, Hoo, you just keep your shit tight and your eyes on the hills, hear?"

Church, Sarge.

Church.

THIRTEEN

Darkness fell and Bob lit a candle. The hut filled with the stink of tallow. Ash guessed the wild man had made it himself from the rendered fat of one of the animals he poached.

"You hungry?" Bob said.

"I don't know."

"When last you eat?"

"Yesterday."

Bob slung something at Ash. A strip of jerky, blackened and twisted as driftwood, landed in his lap.

"I don't eat meat," Ash said, standing and placing the jerky on the table.

The man glared at him then he growled and scratched out a small burlap sack from beside the bed. He skidded it across to Ash, who opened it and saw a pile of dried, shriveled black berries.

"Chokecherries," Bob said.

Ash tried one. It was bitter and astringent, but he realized he was ravenous and ate a handful.

The recluse sat with his back to him, chewing on jerky.

When they were done eating, Bob boiled water on the stove. He produced a straight razor, a fragment of mirror, and a gob of soap.

"Shave," he said.

Ash wet his face and lathered with the soap. He scraped away the pale stubble on his cheeks and jaw.

Bob propped his dead son's driver's license on the table and took a pair of scissors to Ash's blondish mop. He was surprisingly skillful.

"Were you a barber?"

"I was many things," Bob said.

The hair dying followed. Another of Bob's concoctions. The black dye burned Ash's scalp, but it transformed him into a close enough simulacrum of the man in the photograph to pass scrutiny.

Bob swept up the hair and took it outside and buried it by the light of a lantern. When he returned, he threw Ash a coarse blanket that smelled of smoke and something vaguely medicinal.

"Get some sleep."

"And tomorrow?"

"You got money?"

"No."

"You gonna need some. To get away from here."

"And go where?"

"One thing at a time."

"Where am I going to get money?"

"Jesus, where do you get cash, son? From a goddamn bank."

Bob snuffed the candle with his fingers and took to his pallet, and within seconds Ash heard the grate of his snores.

Ash sat against the wall, wrapped in the blanket, and thought about the day Scooter was born. In the delivery room, when the roiled infant had emerged bloody and bawling from inside Jane, Ash had hugged his sweating wife and taken his son into his arms and felt such pure joy that he'd been certain his heart was too small to contain it.

FOURTEEN

Leaving the taxi outside her apartment building, Nicola had no recollection of the journey from Paris. It was as if she'd been teleported—one second she was boarding the train at Gare du Nord, the next she was in the cab in the London night traffic, en route to her flat.

A plastic disc on her keychain allowed her access to the lobby of the graceless high-rise south of the river, the building almost postapocalyptically empty of noise or visible human presence.

She let the elevator haul her upward and, towing her spinner, she sleepwalked her way down a corridor paved in cold stone and let herself into her flat. After a moment's fumbling, she found a switch that ignited a bank of ceiling lights.

She stood in the doorway and saw the place as a stranger might. The open-plan apartment was as clean, neat, and anonymous as a recently serviced hotel room. She had a view through to the kitchen (just one wine glass upended in a drying rack) and the living room where characterless modern chairs and a couch bowed before a huge, wall-mounted TV.

She could afford better, her father's allowance was generous, but this was her hair shirt—this soulless box south of the river, with its low ceiling and faint whiff of on-the-cheap plumbing.

She closed the door, left her suitcase on the floor, and wandered aimlessly into the kitchen, staring at her distorted reflection in the chrome kettle, listening to the maddening thump of the clock. She turned to the knives in their block and fought down the urge to unsheathe one and use it on her flesh.

Though she wasn't much of a boozer, she distracted herself by crossing to the refrigerator and pouring a glass from a half-empty bottle of chardonnay. The wine had begun to sour but she took a long slug and carried it through to the living room, where she stood at the window gazing out at the city at night.

She only knew she was crying when a teardrop fell into the glass, rippling the surface of the wine.

Nicola crumpled down onto the sofa, surrendering to great whoops of sorrow. Feeling the folded letter against her heart, she remembered the last time she'd seen her mother.

It had been on the day of her twelfth birthday. A day that had begun miserably, waking up in her dorm room with her obese, farting roommate—the two disliked misfits exiled at the end of a far corridor. Waking to the tap of rain on the roof and water trickling down the tiny mullioned windows like tears.

The perfect soggy stage for her misery.

She'd washed and dressed, waiting to be summoned to the telephone, waiting to hear her father's booming voice singing "Happy Birthday" from somewhere remote and war torn. Promising her that he would see her soon, and even though she'd know he was lying, it would cheer her.

But the call never came, and she suffered through her classes. Her hated schoolmates were unaware of the occasion, which suited her just fine, and she drifted through the day alone in her world of gloom.

In the early afternoon, despite the drizzle, they were forced out onto the hockey field, where the strapping, jolly sadists used every opportunity to thrash her ankles and send her plunging facedown into the mud.

Filthy, bereft, Nicola was dragging her hockey stick across the quad, walking toward the showers, when a car came hurtling up the driveway, driven at such reckless speed that a couple of her tormentors were sent running for their lives.

The car, some kind of foreign sports thing with a soft leather top, skidded to a halt, and for a giddy moment she imagined that it was her father rushing in to smother her in cigar-scented kisses and bonhomie.

But when the door opened, she was horrified to see that it was her mother.

Jemima Fabian, tall, heroin-skinny, wearing designer jeans and high-heeled boots and, despite the chill, a man's wife beater that did little to hide her tits, used the door to pull herself from the low car. She folded herself across its leather roof as if she were about to be frisked, and rested her chin on her arms, staring at Nicola.

"Jesus, God, what the fuck are you wearing?" Which was rich coming from her.

Nicola looked down at her long, skinny pink legs emerging from her gym shorts and crossed her arms across her boy's chest. She knew she should run as far as she could from this banshee, but she didn't.

Her mother pushed herself back from the car, teetered a moment on her ridiculous heels, and threw her arms wide.

"Well, come and give me a bloody smooch, for Chrissakes."

Red-faced, intensely aware of the scrutiny of her fellow pupils and the teachers who had come out to stare, Nicola stepped forward and allowed her mother to embrace her.

Jemima stank. There was no other way to say it. She reeked of sweat and booze and stale sex and something burnt and chemical.

Nicola broke the embrace and stepped back. Jemima grimaced at her with a mouthful of rotten teeth.

"Why don't you go and shower and get dressed, and we'll toddle into Margate for some tea and cake?"

When Nicola just stared at her, Jemima made a shooing motion with her hands, setting her many bangles clinking like wind chimes.

So Nicola went and showered. When she approached her room and saw Miss Runcie, the housemistress, standing in the corridor, she was certain that the shrew was here to tell her that her mother had been evicted. That Nicola was safe to continue her miserable day alone, a prospect that now seemed quite pleasurable.

But instead the woman said, "Fabian, since it's your birthday, you've been granted two hours to spend with your mother. Back here in time for the supper bell, understood?"

Clearly the Findlay-Brown name still cowed middle-class toadies like Miss Runcie.

Nicola said, "Yes, Miss," and entered her room and crossed to the tiny window that offered a partial view of the quad. Her mother lounged at the wheel of the sports car, door open, smoking a pastel Sobranie.

Nicola, with as much pleasure as a condemned prisoner, dressed and went downstairs.

She was hardly in the car when Jemima gunned the engine and took off at speed, grinding those ruined teeth, eyes twitching above her Keith Richards cheekbones as she piloted the car through the country lanes.

A pub rose from the fields of gorse and Jemima skidded to a stop between a brace of muddy Land Rovers.

"Come," she said and hurried inside.

Nicola followed her into the funk of piss and beer.

A group of pink-cheeked farmer types wearing tweeds and wellies stood around a young man of debauched beauty. He was doing some kind of card trick on the bar counter and the men were cheering, shaking their heads and quaffing their pints.

And emptying their wallets.

The con man looked up and smiled. His teeth were white and even.

"Darling," he said. "Or should I say, *darlings?*"

He had the unplaceable accent of a newsreader, and his eyes, when they fixed on Nicola, burned with an intensity that caused her to look away, as if she'd stared at the sun without dark glasses.

He strolled over to them, his eyes never shifting from Nicola's. She felt as if she were being scanned, every inch of her measured and stored.

"This is Finn," her mother said. "My special friend." Lips curling away from those disgusting teeth in a carnal leer.

"How beautiful you are," Finn said to Nicola, putting a fingertip to her chin and lifting her face, forcing her to look up at him. "How *fresh.*"

Jemima leaned in and whispered something in his ear and he nodded and said, "In the fullness of time, my precious. In the fullness of time."

Then he turned his back on Jemima and put his hands on Nicola's hips and drew her to him, and she could feel his sinewy maleness.

"I believe birthday wishes are in order?" He moved her bangs aside and kissed her forehead. His lips were warm and dry and his breath smelled of nothing at all.

Finn took her hand and led her out to the car, Jemima staggering after them.

Despite her protestations, Jemima was forced to fold herself like a soiled flamingo into the tiny rear. Finn seated Nicola beside him, taking great pains to check that her belt was securely fastened. A hand brushed her chest, fingers patrolled near her groin.

Then he started the car, did a U-turn and headed away from Margate.

Soon they were on the M2 motorway.

"Where are we going?" Nicola asked.

"To London, of course," her mother said.

"But I only have two hours."

"Oh, fuck that," Jemima said. She leaned forward and put her lips close to Finn's ear and said, "Just a little. Just a teensy-weensy, itsy bitsy. *Puh*-leeze. As a reward."

"Okay, okay, okay," he said and nudged the turn signal and cruised into a Shell gas station.

He stopped near the restrooms and stood up from the car, tilting his seat forward so Jemima could unfurl herself, a knitted bag hanging from her shoulder.

Finn palmed her something and watched as she tottered off, then he leaned in and looked at Nicola.

"Not very close, you and your mum, are you now?"

"No."

"More of a daddy's girl then?"

She didn't answer.

"That's fine. That's not a criticism. I guess Jems was last in line when they were dishing out the old maternal instinct." He stared at her. "Precious little resemblance either. Well, maybe the height." She could almost feel the weight of his gaze upon her. "And the body type."

Her mother was back and she looked somehow younger and happier, glowing with whatever she'd injected into her bloodstream. Nicola found herself wondering where she did it—her bare arms were free of needle tracks.

"Come on, come on," Jemima said, clambering back into the car. "Let's get this bloody party started."

The drive to London was uneventful. Finn played some kind of art pop CD and Jemima, the drug rush like a revolving door that lit her up and then spat her back into gloom, fell asleep, a line of drool hanging from her lip.

"What are we going to do in London?" Nicola asked.

"Oh, we'll all have a lovely time," Finn said. "Just you wait and see."

They arrived at a warehouse in Shoreditch, and Finn rolled up a steel door and parked the car. He lowered the door and led them through what must have been a photographer's studio. Nicola saw a wheeled backdrop pushed off to the side—a strip of beach, blue sea, and palm trees.

Finn clattered up a metal staircase and unlocked the door to a flat.

The place was a mess—clothes strewn across the furniture, empty wine bottles filled with cigarette butts, junk food boxes and dirty plates thick with flies.

Finn lit a smoke and leaned against the back of the sofa. He looked at Jemima and said, "So? Is this happening?"

Jemima took Nicola's hand and walked her into the fetid

bedroom. Gray sunlight bled in around the edges of a red blind. The bed was unmade, with soiled, greasy sheets. More booze bottles and overflowing ashtrays.

Jemima patted the bed and, reluctantly, Nicola sat.

"Now listen to Mummy, Nicky. Finn is a very special friend. *Very, very* special. He is very kind to Mummy. In fact, he's the only person in this big cold world who looks after her, not like Daddy who used her up and cast her aside like a bloody toss cloth." Jemima sniffed and blinked and tried a ghastly smile. "So Mummy wants you to be nice to him too, okay?"

"Nice how?"

Nicola looked past the open door and saw Finn standing by the stereo, sipping a colorless drink from a tall glass, swaying to something she would later learn was middle-period Roxy Music.

"Come on, you see how beautiful he is. Beautiful and ever so skillful. God, just the thought of it makes Mummy go all swampy." Jemima closed her eyes. When she opened them they were terrifyingly blank.

Finn was in the room and the bed sank as he sat beside Nicola. His hands were on her and then his mouth and Bryan Ferry sang falsetto about inflatable dolls and disposable darlings, and it was nearly a week before three big, silent men who worked for her father kicked down the door and rescued her.

***

Nicola was dragged from the past by the buzzing of the messenger app on her phone.

She opened it. *Let's talk.*

No, she typed. *No more. You call me or I'm done.*

Shockingly, her cell phone rang almost immediately. Unknown number. She stared at the thing as if it were a serpent, knowing that if she answered, her life would change forever.

But she sniffed and wiped her nose on her sleeve and swiped the face of her iPhone and said, "Yes?"

"I've been messaging you."

An American voice, she was sure, but so flat and featureless it could have been produced by a machine, the call bounced, doubtless, through servers on four continents to remain traceless.

She sat up straighter. "Who are you?"

"My name is John Dapp. I was a CIA case officer. I knew your father."

"And who do you work for now?"

"Myself," he said.

"Why are you doing this? For money?"

She heard static, clicks, white noise, then he said, "No. Not for money."

"What then?" When he didn't reply she said, "Is it some sort of revenge?"

"Yes," he said. "Let's call it revenge."

FIFTEEN

Victor Fabian, naked but for his Patek Philippe wristwatch, stood on the balcony of his palatial penthouse on the 109th floor of the Shanghai Tower, which was by a mere 198 meters the second tallest building in the world. He smoked a Cuban, looking out at the lights of the Beaux-Arts buildings of the Bund reflecting in the snaking Huangpu River.

A helicopter churned by, taillights blinking, swooping like a firefly drawn to the pink-and-purple lollipop that was the Pearl TV Tower.

The fingers of Fabian's left hand found a scratch on his shoulder, a deep wheal caused by the debutante's long, lacquered fingernails. The scratch was weeping a little and he rubbed his fingertips together to dry them.

He turned his back to the city and stood splayed legged, smoking, staring into the honey-lit room. The girl lay on the bed. Unconscious. Not dead. No, things hadn't gone quite *that* far, but there was blood on the sheet beneath her and on the silk cord that bound her wrists behind her back.

Fabian cared nothing for this beautiful bumpkin from far Yunnan with teeth still stained by betel nut. She had been pro-cured by his manservant at a local beauty competition, and his man would spirit the girl away, pay her off, and restore the bedroom to its pristine state.

No, he cared about blacking out. About losing control.

Again.

He had no recollection of the last two hours. It was as if they had tumbled into a crack in time, lost forever.

And that scared the holy crap out of him.

There was a soft tap on the bedroom door, just loud enough to rise above the fusion jazz spilling from the hidden Harman Kardon speakers. Ricky Pickford, looking as uncreased and wholesome as the Mormon choirboy he had once been, entered the room. He set his bespectacled gaze on his naked master's forehead.

"My apologies, sir."

By way of reply Fabian wagged his cigar.

"I've just received a report from our man in London. He followed Ms. Fabian to Paris where she took a car from the Gare du Nord. He was able to speak with the driver later and establish her destination."

Pickford stopped, dangling this morsel. An irritating habit. He blinked and adjusted his glasses on the bridge of his nubby little nose.

"Go on," Fabian said.

"She went to what was once a drug rehabilitation facility north of the city. The Rossignol Institute."

He had Fabian's attention.

"She spent about forty minutes there and returned to Paris and boarded the train for London."

"I see."

Fabian found the self-control to blow a perfect halo of smoke that wafted toward Pickford as it dispersed.

"Someone is manipulating Nicola," Fabian said. "Mesmerizing her. Upsetting her equilibrium. I need to know who."

"I think I may have a lead."

"Oh, do you now?"

Pickford bounced on the balls of his feet and couldn't quite tamp down a little smirk.

"Well, tell me, Ricky. Tell me."

"I'd really rather *show* you, sir, if I may."

***

Fabian, showered and powdered, dressed in a mustard turtleneck and a pair of slacks, feet sheathed in oxblood cordovans, towered over Pickford as they fell toward the earth at over forty miles per hour, the express elevator rated the fastest in the world.

They came to a feathery stop, and the doors whispered open onto a vast underground parking lot, an empty expanse of strip lights and grid lines.

Not quite empty.

Fabian saw the head of his security detail, maybe five foot tall in her pumps, standing with a group of his close protectors around a black SUV. The bodyguards were all slight. This was the way here in Shanghai: small, fleet men and women who could kill with their hands and feet, and shoot too, if they absolutely had to.

Johnny Yen, hands in suit pockets, stood alone at the trunk of the silver Lexus parked beside the SUV. He was Cantonese, from Hong Kong. Spoke the Queen's English. Called these *Shen* Mandarin donkey fuckers.

Fabian followed Pickford. As they approached the vehicles, the bodyguards came to attention. He ignored them, looking at a man who sat in the rear of the SUV. A plump, balding Chinese of maybe forty, in a salaryman's suit. The man did not meet his eyes.

They stopped at the rear of the Lexus. Pickford nodded and Yen popped the trunk.

Fabian's nostrils twitched at the cocktail of shit and blood and fear.

A man lay in the trunk, hogtied and gagged.

He had been tortured, but he was conscious, staring up at Fabian with eyes that bulged like tubes of fried squid.

"What is this?" Fabian said.

"*This* is Wang Yuan," Pickford said. "One of our accountants. Apparently, he felt he wasn't adequately compensated so he did a little moonlighting."

"For whom?"

"After a little encouragement, he gave up a name."

That smirk, that pause.

Fabian restrained himself. "Going to share it with me? The name?"

"John Dapp, sir. He was in the employ of John Dapp."

Fabian exhaled slowly. "Interesting."

"I thought so."

"How did you root out this little mole?"

Pickford pointed to the man in the SUV. "That's his colleague. His friend. Apparently, this one's tongue got a little loose after a night of Johnny Walker and he spilled beans to his pal. Who, like a loyal soldier, brought it to me."

"And the nature of his intelligence?"

"Nothing significant. But I thought the fact that Dapp has eyes and ears on you *is* significant."

"Yes. Yes, it is," Fabian said.

"What shall I do with him?" Pickford said, indicating the man in the trunk.

And in that instant it was as if Fabian were standing outside of himself, watching as he held out a hand, palm up, toward Johnny Yen. "Your weapon please."

Without hesitation, Yen passed him a Glock.

Fabian took the pistol and cocked it. He adopted a two-handed grip and pointed it at the man in the trunk, who sobbed and implored.

Fabian shot him twice in the head.

He returned the weapon to Yen, who closed the trunk.

Pickford was staring at Fabian in astonishment.

Fabian looked across at the man in the SUV, who appeared to be weeping.

"Kill the informer too," he said to Yen. "If he sold out his friend, who knows what else he's capable of."

"I told him he'd be rewarded," Pickford said, his voice unsteady.

"And so he will be." Fabian pointed to the trunk. "Kill this man's family." Panning his finger to the man cowering in the SUV. "Spare his."

He turned and went back toward the elevator, Pickford skipping to fall in beside him.

The shakes hit Fabian as he walked and he stopped when his minions were out of sight. He put a hand to a column, feeling the cool cement, shocked to the core by what he had done.

It took tremendous control not to vomit on his shoes.

"Sir, are you okay?" Pickford said.

"Yes."

"It's just—"

"An extreme act, I know. But it doesn't hurt to show these people that I'm capable of doing whatever it takes."

Pickford stared at him, and then he nodded. "Of course, sir."

Fabian pushed away from the column and headed toward the elevator, Pickford half a step behind him.

"You did good work, Ricky," Fabian said, his voice calmer.

"Thank you, sir."

They stepped into the elevator and it rocketed upward.

"John Dapp has a wife, doesn't he?"

"Yes sir, she's Chinese. From Hangzhou."

"And where's Mrs. Dapp now?"

"In California. Palo Alto."

Fabian stood with hands in pockets, eyes closed, blue chin jutting. "I think this is a job for the Peaches."

"Yes."

"Let them make a house call on Mrs. Dapp."

"Yes, sir."

The elevator slowed and the doors opened.

Stepping into the corridor Fabian said, "Wives and daughters, Ricky ... Oh, how the women suffer for what we men do."

SIXTEEN

The jungle music woke Patty Peach, the glass of the hotel room window buzzing from the booming bass. A car door slapped shut and she heard the growl of a big engine as the vehicle sped off, taking the noise with it. She looked at the clock on the side table. Just gone 8:30 a.m.

Shocked, she sat up in bed, the sheet falling away from her white cotton shift. It was Patty's habit to rise at dawn each day, regular as clockwork. She scanned the room for Orlando, but he wasn't there.

"Orlando?"

No reply from the bathroom.

It wasn't like him to stray. She had no idea what could have drawn him from their budget hotel into the streets of downtown Phoenix.

Firearms were spread across the second bed. Three assault rifles. An Uzi. A sawed-off Remington. A selection of pistols. Cloths and gun oil. Cleaning their weapons soothed Orlando. And he was someone who needed plenty of soothing.

The door opened and he walked in, carrying a brown paper bag spotted with grease. He looked like teenager in his jeans and sneakers, a knit cap pulled over his cherubic blond curls. He was beautiful.

Patty observed him carefully. Who was he today? Her sweet, docile man-boy or one of his colder, angrier personas?

"Morning, Mama," he said, smiling.

She sighed her relief. He was all sweetness and light.

"Morning to you, my dear."

He stared at her with soft blue eyes. "Are you okay, Mama?"

"I'm okay, baby boy. I'm just fine."

He called her Mama, but he wasn't her son, though it was convenient to pretend sometimes that he was. She was barely a decade older than him. He was twenty-five and looked fifteen. She was thirty-nine and looked sixty.

She suffered from a mysterious premature aging syndrome. The quack doctors said it was some autoimmune thing, that her body was attacking itself. It made no sense at all. But she was weakening. There was no denying it. Forced to leave more of the work to Orlando.

He refused to speak of her inevitable death, but she knew it terrified him. In seventeen years they had not been apart for even a day.

Back when Patty was still with the ATF, she, with a small army of federal agents, had stormed the compound of a death cult in Utah. An angelic child had sat alone near the door of the community hall that was filled with the dead and dying, nodding his head, rocking, humming to himself.

She had lifted him and held him to her body armor and had never let him go.

When she had been unable to legally adopt him, she had taken him from the group home where he'd been placed by Child Protection Services, and they had gone dark.

Patty had found the transition from law enforcement to private contractor quite seamless. She'd had contacts, people who needed things done. Some with badges, others with attaché cases filled with money. A passably attractive young woman (as she'd been back then) with a small child in tow charted low on the threat matrix. Many was the time she'd left Orlando in the car with an ice cream and a comic book while she'd earned their keep.

And when, at the age of ten, Orlando had stabbed to death a hulking Latino teenager who had bullied him, she'd realized that he, too, had a talent worth nurturing.

And so they had become a team, doing the work that precious few were temperamentally suited to do. Rootless, moving randomly from city to city, living anonymously in a succession of cheap hotels.

Orlando clattered around her, making space on the bedside table for the bag he had brought with him.

"Why didn't you wake me?" Patty said.

"You looked so peaceful, Mama. And you need your rest." He lifted out two oily sandwiches. "BLT, Mama. Just the way you like it."

Patty's stomach heaved. She hurried from the bed to the bathroom and knelt by the toilet. The vomit came, scalding and acid, and she gripped the plastic seat with her veined hands.

Orlando was beside her, and he moved her gray hair and sponged her face, wiping away the yellow tendrils that dangled from her lips.

Patty gasped and spat into the bowl. She tried to stand but could not. He lifted her, and she leaned her forehead against the cool tiles and breathed.

She heard the splatter of the shower, and Orlando stripped the shift from her. He unclipped her bra and pulled off her panties. Ashamed of her wasted and sagging nakedness in the glaring florescent light, Patty tried to cover herself, but he gently pushed her arms away and put her into the shower and sponged her. Washed her face and her back and her skinny shanks.

He toweled her dry and led her from the room. Helped her into her modest underwear and thrift-store clothes.

Orlando sat her on the bed and used the hairdryer on her. He brushed her scant hair as he dried it, the heat from the nozzle burning her scalp. But she didn't complain.

Patty almost didn't hear the cell phone through the scream of the dryer.

Orlando cut the power and reached for the phone and held it out to her.

"Yes?" she said, clearing her throat. She listened, said, "Understood," and ended the call.

Orlando was already packing their arsenal.

SEVENTEEN

Ash woke with somebody kicking his leg and he opened his eyes to see a man in dark pants and a windbreaker standing over him, silhouetted against the light of the window.

"Relax, boy. It's only me." Teeth flashed in Bob's beard. "Don't I clean up nice?"

Ash stared at him. The woodsman had pulled his hair back into a ponytail and the unruly beard had been combed. He wore a white shirt under the windbreaker, buttoned at the neck. He sported a pair of sunglasses, looking like he belonged in a ZZ Top tribute band.

Bob dropped his dead son's clothes onto Ash's chest. "Get dressed. Time to move."

***

Scalp itching from the black dye Bob had rubbed into his hair, Ash followed the recluse down a winding track overhung with a canopy of giant spruce and western hemlock. The trees were draped with ferns and hanging moss. The dense forest was gloomy and preternaturally quiet, the moss absorbing sound like acoustic panels. This was bog land, and Ash swatted at mosquitoes.

He wore the dead man's clothes. They were a perfect fit. He didn't know whether to take that as an omen. Even the boots, well-used Timberlands, seemed shaped to his bandaged feet as if by a cobbler's last, and the pain from the chafing and torn skin had eased.

Bob, rifle slung from his shoulder, stopped, and through a gap in the trees, Ash could see down into the hamlet of Twin Forks. It was about ten miles west of his town. Smaller, hit even harder by the closure of pulp and saw mills.

Bob lifted his binoculars and glassed the town.

He lowered the glasses and walked on.

The forest ended at the potholed road that led into the Twin Forks. Bob unslung the rifle and leaned it against a tree. He hung the binoculars from a branch. The two men stood a while in the trees opposite a deserted Texaco station, watching. A truck with a shot muffler rattled by. A very big woman in a very small car sped past, shouting at a toddler who had his face pressed up against the window like a sucker toy.

When the road was quiet, Bob stepped out and Ash followed him, waiting for the whoop of sirens and a phalanx of black SUVs.

Nothing.

They crossed the road and walked past the boarded up Mr. Video, the outfitters, the feed store, the Burger King. Bob paused a moment outside a print shop and adjusted something under his windbreaker.

"Stay close," he said, on the move, Ash trailing in his wake.

The bank stood apart from the neighboring buildings, on a little patch of lawn. It looked like a small house, with a pitched slate roof and timber cladding. Only the Wells Fargo sign and a single Doric column betrayed its mercantile purpose.

Bob strode toward the doors saying, "Keep up, now."

He entered the bank and paused a moment, taking in the interior, Ash at his elbow. It was quiet inside, and Ash could hear the smack of a clock and the soft whip of the blades of a ceiling fan. He smelled jasmine floor wax. A happy smell that took him back to his childhood.

No customers. Just one teller, a young woman with blonde hair, dressed in a red shirt, smiling at them.

As Bob walked toward her, he lifted a pistol from under his jacket and rested his gun hand on the counter, barrel leveled at her.

"Don't make me use this, now."

Ash, shocked, stood rooted.

Bob took a burlap sack from his pocket and placed it on the counter.

"Kindly open the drawer and fill this. Only loose notes. No hundreds, no bundles."

The young woman stared at him in terror.

"Come on, missy, move now." Wagging the gun barrel slowly like a lazy dog's tail.

Ash felt a bead of sweat on his forehead and wiped it away, his finger coming back black. He stared at Bob and stared at the woman, who was filling the bag, her hands shaking.

Ash wanted to say something that would stop this. He said nothing.

The teller put the sack on the counter and raised her hands. Bob slung the bag at Ash who fumbled the catch and had to bend to retrieve it, holding it to his chest like a comforter.

Bob, pistol still leveled at the teller, walked backward from the counter.

"Move, son," he said.

Ash stayed frozen, as if his boots were glued to the linoleum.

"Move!"

As Ash unfroze and edged toward the doors, they swung open and a big redheaded man with a goatee, dressed in jeans and a Seahawks T-shirt, ambled in.

Bob panned the pistol toward the door, but for a moment Ash was between him and the big man, which allowed Goatee to draw a handgun from under his T-shirt. Ash jagged left and Goatee and Bob fired simultaneously.

A red stain bloomed on Goatee's shirt, and his second shot took out a window as he fell.

Bob fired again, and blood and brain sprayed from the big man's head.

Bob had a hand to his gut, holding himself, blood seeping between his fingers and dripping to the floor.

As Ash walked toward him Bob sank to his knees and dropped the gun. He looked up at Ash.

"Go," he said. "Go find your boy."

Then he keeled over onto his face, rivulets of blood reaching out for his dead son's boots.

A single plaintive siren was incoming and Ash turned and walked out the door, blinking at the brightness, still grasping the sack of money.

Then he realized he should run and sprinted for the forest as a cop car came barreling down the street.

Clutching the money, heart racing, breath sucking, he hurtled into the trees. Falling. Getting up again, palms bleeding onto the sack as he grasped it, Ash plunged deep into the muffled green woods.

EIGHTEEN

Nicola sat on her sofa in the pallid morning light and stared into space. She had succumbed to depression, its tentacles reaching out and drawing her into a morass of torpor and despair.

She roused herself and went to the window and stared out at the gray day.

She wanted to take a razor blade to the bathroom and slice into her flesh. To slice through the numbness. To feel something, even if it was only fucking pain.

But she dredged up some resolve from somewhere and, before she could change her mind, lifted her phone and speed-dialed.

The number rang for a long time and she hoped it would go to voicemail, but, eventually, she heard her father's booming voice: "Nicky-Nicks!"

"Daddy," she said, forcing away the ancient, corrupt face of the French quack who'd murdered her mother.

"How are you?" Fabian said.

"Oh, I'm fine." She tried to keep her tone light. Fun. The way Daddy liked it. "I want to see you."

"And I'd love to see *you*."

"No, I mean I really *do* have to see you."

A pause. "Anything wrong?"

"No, no. I just want to ask you something."

"Well, ask away, my sweet."

"I'd really rather do it face-to-face."

"Mnnn. Mysterious."

"Daddy! Don't you want to see me?" Revoltingly coquettish.

"Of course, I do. It's been far too long." She heard the flare of a match and then the little sipping sounds as he ignited a cigar. "As it happens, I'm leaving Shanghai later today. I have to take care of a little bit of business in DC, so why don't you hop across the pond? You can stay with me."

"Sounds lovely," she said. "I'll see you tomorrow."

"Perfect."

He was gone.

Nicola tossed the phone onto the sofa and reached for her tablet, reserving a hotel room in Washington.

NINETEEN

Ash reared up from the sleep that had poleaxed him, panicked, disoriented. He was in the forest, sprawled facedown on the muddy ground, still clutching the sack of stolen money.

The events of the last day slammed him awake.

Scooter.

Ash had run until he was exhausted and had fallen to the earth and allowed sleep to claim him.

He had a fucking history of this.

A history of escaping reality by shutting down and blacking out.

Ash saw himself asleep in a chair in a departure lounge, while a doomed plane rose into a hot blue sky.

Forcing this memory away he wiped mud from the face of the *shanzhai* Timex that Jane had picked up in Guangdong for his birthday a few years ago, its fakeness making the gift even cooler.

He'd slept for more than an hour.

Slept while his son was who-the-fuck-knew where.

He opened the bag and dumped the money between his boots and counted it. Over eight thousand dollars.

Ash closed his eyes, back in the bank with the dead men.

He blinked, clawed at his itching face.

He had no idea what to do.

Then he saw Holly Howells grab hold of Scooter and plunge that thing into his neck, his body sagging to the table, Holly's face hard and her eyes cold.

Who was she?

If he found her, maybe he would find his son.

Ash shoved the money back into the sack and hauled himself to his feet. He stared up at the sunlight lancing through the tree canopy. He was no woodsman, but he knew if he kept the sun at his back he would be moving in the direction of his house.

TWENTY

A barber came in each day to shave Victor Fabian. A small man in a white smock, with gray hair and a face as unlined as a baby's.

He huddled somewhere in the bowels of the staff quarters until summoned by the valet at a time determined by Fabian's whim. Then he was led through to the bedroom, carrying his warm white towels, bay leaf–scented shaving cream, and cutthroat razor.

The man never said a word—exquisite in his silence. The only sounds were the scrape of the blade against Fabian's bristled skin, and the little click of the scissors the barber used to trim the hairs that grew from Fabian's nose and ears.

It was Fabian's habit to sit and read the *Shanghai Daily* while he was shaved. It was a rag, but amusing in its toadyism. That morning he had laughed out loud when he'd read about yet another greedy American giant humiliated by the Chinese government. Laughed so hard that the barber had been obliged to lift the blade from his face and stand back, waiting until Fabian was composed again.

It was Marriott this time. Their websites blocked by the Politburo because they had listed Taiwan and Tibet as sovereign nations. The regime saying that the hotel chain "had seriously violated China's laws and regulations and hurt the feelings of the Chinese people."

Marriott had issued a groveling apology.

Hilarious.

Fabian stood now at the window of his bedroom, wearing a white robe, looking out at the smog, smoking a cigar. Thinking of the trip ahead and what awaited him.

He heard the door and turned to see his valet, Yi, with the barber.

"What's he doing back?" Fabian said.

Yi looked confused. "He has come to shave you, sir."

Fabian blew smoke. "Why? He was here an hour ago."

Yi shook his head. "No, sir."

"This is absurd. The man has attended me already."

"But, sir, your face."

Fabian raised a hand to his jaw and felt the rasp of bristles.

Dear God, what had his flawed mind conjured up?

A memory of yesterday? The day before?

"Of course," Fabian said, snuffing the cigar and taking his seat. "Of course."

Yi bowed and left the room and the barber approached Fabian, hunched, avoiding eye contact.

As his face was wet and lathered, Fabian recalled the chat with Nicola.

Nothing had been said about France, but the exchange had been thick with subtext.

It was that conversation that had done this. That had been the seismic depth charge that triggered this episode.

As the blade kissed his cheek, Fabian closed his eyes and saw his dead wife's face with hyperrealist clarity. Each enlarged pore and blemish. The crusted sores at the corners of her mouth. The pin-point pupils of her violet eyes.

Jemima leered at him, her ruined mouth revealed.

"Every dog, 'ey Vic?" she said in that louche Jaggeresque drawl she'd affected. "Every fucking dog has his fucking day. Isn't that right, my matey?"

TWENTY-ONE

For two hours Ash walked through the forest. He knew there was some risk keeping to the trail, but the alternative, hacking his way through the scrub and bush, would be impossible.

He was a good walker. In the year since his wife's death, he had taken to hiking. Stowing food and water in a backpack and heading off into the woods. He'd bought a book on birds and was able to identify some of the more common species. And he'd gained a passing knowledge of flowers and plants. After the anonymous emails had come, filling his head with information that had both enraged and terrified him, the hikes in the wilderness had been a way of ordering his thoughts.

As he'd walked, sweated, and breathed the clean, sweet air, he'd felt his mind stilling. Felt able to compose the statements he'd sent to the media. Statements in which he'd striven to strike the right balance between emotion and reason. Anyone reading them, he'd hoped, would see his pain, sure, but would think he was a sane, reasonable man.

That he was no crackpot.

But those carefully composed statements about the murk and contradictions surrounding Jane's death, that had taken him hours to draft, had, as the hermit had said, made him and his son targets.

And what had he achieved?

He knew nothing more about his wife's death than he had a year ago. Didn't know if there was any substance to what the anonymous emails had insinuated, that she had been killed elsewhere and then dropped from that bridge in Guangzhou.

Or who had done it.

What had Jane known that had made her so dangerous?

Who had so feared his own misguided attempts to find the truth that they had done this to him and Scooter?

As he hustled his way down the path, loose stones skidding beneath his boots, he saw his wife sitting at her desk in their house, typing on her laptop. Looking up at him with that slightly abstracted look as if he were a stranger, then smiling, letting him in.

When Scooter was a year old, Jane had taken a lowly job at a Seattle tech start-up that developed specialist bridge design and analysis software. She showed an aptitude that had surprised both her and Ash and rose meteorically. After two years, she started making enough money for Ash to ditch freelance manuscript editing for a couple of months and write a sitcom with his old buddy, Benno. A series about a twentysomething Seattle weed merchant who unexpectedly inherits a fortune when a distant relative dies, but he can't get his hands on the loot unless he spends a year working as a day trader on Wall Street.

Benno had a contact in LA, and there were emails and calls and suddenly they were invited to fly down to pitch the idea to a media-streaming outfit. The idea of a pitch scared the crap out of Ash, but Benno, who did open mic stand-up for fun, said, "No prob, dude. I've got this. You just say hi and smile and I'll smash the pitch right out of the fuckin park. I was born for this moment."

So they went to Los Angeles and found themselves in the streaming company's Santa Monica HQ. It was like an indoor summer camp for millennials, with beer on tap and an arcade area.

Ash and Benno were seated in a glass-enclosed conference room in front of a firing squad of überhip showbizzy types, all under thirty. When the head of development, a very thin fellow with a fearsome confection of gelled hair, indicated that they should begin, Benno froze.

Dried up.

Could. Not. Speak.

After a thirty-second eternity, all heads turned to Ash, and he fumbled and stumbled into the pitch. Hairdo Boy's eyes glazed over and he looked out into the open-plan space where some guys were shooting hoops. A freckled young woman actually started knitting.

Then something happened. A cocktail of terror and desperation hurled Ash into a weird kind of altered state. He heard himself finding a rhythm, tossing out one-liners, his delivery as punchy and zingy as a YouTube vlogger's. Suddenly Hairdo Boy was nodding like a dashboard dog. Knitting Girl's needles were stilled. There were laughs. There was even applause when Ash was done.

Knitting Girl walked them out and smiled at Ash and said, "We *will* call you."

Dazed, Ash followed Benno onto the sidewalk.

His friend scratched at his skully cap and said, "Fuck. Sorry, man. I choked."

"Yeah," Ash said, "you kinda did."

"But you ... Jesus, who was that back there?"

Ash, still stunned, shrugged, squinting up at the Ferris wheel on the Santa Monica pier.

"You killed, man," Benno said.

Ash laughed. "Well, maybe I *wounded*. Maybe I *maimed*."

"Dude, fuckin own it. You totally flat-out *killed*."

The flight back to Seattle was lost in a haze of celebratory drinks, and Ash and Benno spent the next few days waiting for the big call.

A week later, after hearing nothing, Ash found the balls to contact Santa Monica. The tidings were not good.

Haircut Boy had suffered a sudden plunge from grace after a tweet of his revealed an affiliation to an alt-right hate group. The broom that swept him into the street swept with him everything he'd contaminated with his touch.

Their sitcom included.

Benno announced he was taking off for an ashram in Goa, and Ash sank into a funk.

Jane gave Ash a couple of days to deal with his disappointment then took him out to dinner.

"I know you're crushed," she said.

"Just a little bent out of shape. But what the hell, there's always editing."

"Maybe not."

"What do you mean?"

"I've been offered a promotion. To VP of marketing."

"You? A *veep*?"

"Wild, huh?"

"No, it's great, Janey. Wow. I'm so proud of you."

"I'll be earning a lot more money."

"Yeah?"

"Yeah. Enough for you to stay home with Scooter and work on your writing."

"Janey, come on …"

"No. It'll be good for him. And you."

"And *you*?" Ash asked.

"I want this promotion." She sipped her wine. "But there's a teenie-weenie little downside."

"You've got to wear power suits? I think that'd be kinda hot."

She shook her head, suddenly serious. "Our software has found a huge market in China. They're building bridges like crazy. If I take the job, it'll mean spending a couple of months there every year."

"You okay with that?"

"It's not negotiable. What do you think, Dan?"

He held her hand. "If you want it, do it."

So she took the job and made a chunk of money. Bought their house, cash. And Ash stayed at home and felt less and less compelled to write.

Being with his son had been a rare treasure. Something that most fathers, slave to some deeply encoded hunter-gatherer imperative that drove them from the house each day and out into the workplace jungle, never knew.

It had been idyllic.

But Ash, sweating down the forest trail, knew that he was allowing his memory to be selective. Knew that he was glossing over why Jane had chosen to spend more and more time away from him, even though it had meant being apart from their son.

"You pushed her away," he said out loud. "You shut down and you pushed her away."

Guilt and terror took his breath, and he leaned against a whitebark pine, closing his eyes.

The yapping of a dog brought Ash out of his funk, and he realized his backyard was just beyond the tree line.

He looked across and saw old Mr. Carver from down the street, dressed in a straw hat and plaid shirt, out walking his Lab, Honey. Mr. Carver, a few yards away, didn't recognize Ash, but Honey did. She knew him and Scooter well, often coming into their yard for the treats the boy gave her.

Ash had encouraged the visits, the silent kid sitting with the dog, nuzzling her, laughing. Playing catch.

The dog bounded through the bush, wagging its tail, barking a greeting.

Ash froze.

Honey jumped up on him and licked his face. A young dog, barely more than a pup, a coiled spring of golden energy. He tried in vain to push her away, fending her off with the bag of money.

Fighting for breath, Mr. Carver hurried over, waving his stick.

"Honey! Honey!" He grabbed the dog, who was still yapping and wagging her tail. "I'm sorry, sir, but she likes you! Never does this with strangers."

Mr. Carver looked at him and Ash was sure the man must see past the cap and the hair dye and the redneck clothes. See *him*. But the old fellow apologized again and held the dog by her collar, allowing Ash to make his escape.

He walked a short distance then stopped and listened to the sounds of the man and dog receding, the Lab's barks growing softer. After a minute, he edged forward and crouched, looking through the trees at his house.

At first he saw no signs of life. The back door was closed. The wall that he'd shoved loose to escape had been replaced and shored up, supported by planks.

Then he saw the shape of a man in the kitchen, crossing the window. So they were still there.

Of course they were.

It had become the stage for the piece of theater they were enacting. They had brought all the essential props. The bomb-making materials. The weapons. The emails to and from Islamicist lunatics that they'd dumped onto his laptop.

All the necessary accoutrements of the jihadist that they had fashioned him into.

Ash edged back and walked through the trees until he was behind Holly's house.

No movement. The house quiet and empty.

He stashed the money in the bush and sat for five minutes. Ten. Nothing.

With the sweat of fear trickling down his forehead and ribs, he left the safety of the trees and inched toward the wooden fence, expecting a shout, the discharge of a weapon.

But all was still.

The fence was low and he scaled it easily. A bank of snowbrush hid him from his own house, shielding him from the men inside.

Crouching, Ash moved forward, toward the side of Holly's house, where there was a sash window that didn't lock.

He made it to the window, stopped. Listened.

He reached up for the window, feeling the flaking paint of the wooden frame beneath his fingers, and shoved. He couldn't move it. He tried again. Still, it wouldn't budge.

He stood a moment, breathed. Heard the sound of a car driving by and slowing before it accelerated away.

He grabbed the window and shoved again, and this time it flew upward with a loud clatter.

Cursing under his breath, he waited and listened. When he heard nothing alarming, he reached up and pulled himself through the window, landing on the pine floor of the dining room. He lowered the sash and stood, breathing hard.

The room had been stripped of all Holly's belongings. This was where she'd sat at the table and made her ridiculous clothes on an old Singer sewing machine, thumping away at the foot pedal. Squinting through her little granny glasses as she'd fed fabric under the stabbing needle.

No sewing machine. No clothes. No dire new age posters on the walls.

He walked into the living room.

Just a few chairs and a table, the furniture that had been here when Holly had rented the house. None of her clutter. No brocade cloths or bright lampshades. No art nouveau bric-a-brac. No piles of alternative healing books and crystals spilling out from everywhere.

Gone.

He edged toward the window and peered out of a crack in the lace curtain. He could see the front of his house. A couple of news vans with satellite dishes on their roofs parked in the street, people with cameras milling around.

Ash crossed the echoing room and went up the stairs.

The spare bedroom had been Holly's storeroom, a trove of junk, the door barely able to open. It opened now, swung wide onto barren emptiness and a shining floor.

Ash walked into Holly's bedroom. The mattress was stripped of the feather comforter, the gray ticking naked and obscene.

No pictures on the walls. No flokati rugs on the floor. No clothes in the walk-in closet, just two wooden hangers. He ran a hand on the upper shelf of the closet. Empty. Not even dust.

He conjured up the team of men and women who must have

come in yesterday. In his imagination they wore white coveralls and masks and surgical gloves. Carrying garbage bags, moving methodically from room to room, stripping them of their contents, wiping and dusting and Hoovering as they went.

Removing not just clothes and belongings, but fingerprints and DNA too.

The en suite bathroom was barren, nothing in the cabinet above the sink.

Holly Howells had been erased, as if she had never existed.

Which, he supposed, she had not.

There never had been a Holly.

Whoever had impersonated her had shed her like an unwanted skin and moved on.

Taking his son with her.

All that was left was the smell of patchouli and incense. The smell that Holly had carried on her clothes and wild hair like an aura.

Ash heard a sound. The front door opened and a heavy tread crossed the living room and started up the stairs.

He backed into the closet and closed the doors, feeling at once terrified and absurd, knowing this was no hiding place at all.

The footsteps got louder and came into the bedroom. Then a cell phone jangled and a man's voice said, "Yes?"

Ash could hear the man breathing. He said, "I'm in the next door house taking a last gander." A pause. "Okay, ten-four that. I'll be there directly."

The man turned and thumped back down the stairs, and Ash heard the front door slam.

Suddenly exhausted, he sank into a crouch. Resting his forehead on his knees, he closed his eyes.

The sweet smell was even more intense with his eyes shut, and he saw Holly reclining on her bed, feet tucked under her, drinking a cup of herbal tea, reading Louise Hay.

Ash opened his eyes, staring unseeing at the empty shelves of the closet. Slowly he focused and realized that he was looking at something wedged between one of the shelves and the wall. A tiny tongue of paper, small enough to have remained undetected, visible only from this low angle.

He reached forward, snagged the edge and pulled free a bar-coded rectangle. A torn stub of a Delta Airlines boarding pass.

A month before Holly'd told him she was splurging, flying to San Francisco for the weekend to attend a Reiki workshop.

But she hadn't gone to San Francisco.

She had flown to Washington, DC.

And her name wasn't Holly Howells.

It was Grace Zima.

TWENTY-TWO

Scooter sat at the table in the kitchen of the farmhouse staring out the window at the woman he knew as Holly Howells but had heard the men call Zima. This new, hard version stood talking on her phone, running a hand over her pulled-back white hair, nodding.

A glass of juice sat in front of Scooter untouched. A bowl of Cheerios stood beside the cup, also untouched. The black man—skinny like Scooter's father, but older and kind of used-up looking, like a wrung-out cloth—had given him the food and the juice.

He did the serving and the cleaning. The others ignored him. The men were eating the smelly, oily breakfast that the guy had cooked. They were yakking about football. To Scooter it was like they were talking Egyptian. He'd never followed sports.

The woman paced up and down outside on the gravel while she talked on her phone. It was cold and her breath came out in little puffs like she was smoking.

It was super weird thinking how close he had felt to her. That he had even lain on her big bed while she'd played old hippie music. Vinyl. The creased covers with guys with long hair and beards and girls wearing headbands. She'd hummed along and ruffled his hair, telling him about stuff in her life that he knew now was all lies.

All invented.

All *phony*, as Holden Caulfield would've said.

Phony like her supposed affection for him.

How could somebody do that?

Watching her through the window Scooter realized that this was what growing up was all about—coming to understand how the world lied to you. And getting smart and tough enough to deal with that.

Scooter stifled a yawn. He hadn't slept. Had lain awake in the narrow bed in the bare room, locked in. Scared.

After they'd shut him in he'd tried the window. It hadn't budged. Nailed shut.

He'd sat on the bed and cried.

He wasn't ashamed.

It was the first time he'd cried since his mother died.

He wondered where his father was.

Knew that was more lying, the stuff about him being a terrorist. No way his pop was into that kind of batshit craziness.

The woman finished her call and came back into the kitchen. She slipped the phone into the pocket of her jacket that hung on the back of the chair next to his and went to the kettle to make another cup of coffee.

The men were still jawing on about their football game. Keeping his eyes on her, Scooter reached across and dipped his fingers into the jacket pocket, feeling the cool, sleek body of the phone. She looked his way and he froze, staring at his food. When she went back to her task, stirring in sugar, he slipped the phone from the pocket and put it in the waist of his jeans, under his shirt.

Scooter stood and the men watched him as he headed for the bathroom. He went in and locked the door. The small room smelt of some kind of pine disinfectant.

He took the iPhone out of his jeans and sat on the john with the lid down.

Scooter knew that trying to call his father would be a really dumb move. Who then? All his grandparents were dead. Both his parents were, like him, only children.

"A family tradition," his pop had said.

There were some friends of his parents in Pearson and Seattle. Well, friends of his mom's, really, from work. His pop was kind of a loner, and he'd pretty much lost touch with them after Mom died. Scooter didn't know if he could trust any of them now. And anyway, he didn't have their numbers memorized.

He thought a moment, knowing he had to hurry. Then he opened Safari and went to Yahoo Mail.

Sending a message to his father's email address would be like sending one straight to these people. But he'd created a couple of Yahoo addresses for him and his pop years ago, back when he was maybe seven.

Scooter's address was Sonic and his father's was DrEggman. Kinda cringey now. Back then, he'd been addicted to playing an ancient Game Boy his pop had picked up for him in a thrift shop in Seattle. He'd found the 2D games kinda cool and retro. A nice change from the virtual reality of PlayStation.

Just him and his pop had known about the Yahoo addresses, which, like the Game Boy, were hilariously old-tech in the app-everything world.

They'd sent each other messages. Mainly dumb jokes and cartoons. *Really* lame stuff. After a year, maybe, Scooter had stopped sending emails.

Gotten too old for that silliness.

But when his mom died, after he'd gone silent, he'd gone into the Yahoo account and seen a whole lot of emails from his father, left over the years. Getting fewer and fewer and, for a long while nothing.

Then a new one, soon after his mom's death. His father saying that he loved him. That he knew he was in pain. Knew that he had chosen to be silent for a reason, and that he supported him. Was always there for him.

It had torn Scooter up, and he'd nearly replied. But he hadn't been able to find the words. Not even with his fingers.

Now, in the bathroom, he knew that this was the only way he could safely reach out to his pop. A long shot. But what else did he have?

He was about to compose a message, to try to tell his father that he was okay, when he heard a banging on the door and the knob jiggled loudly.

The woman shouted, "The little shit's got my phone!"

Scooter clicked out of Yahoo and went to the CNN homepage.

The door splintered, the lock flying, and the big blond man reached in, snatched the phone and threw it at the woman. "Check it."

He grabbed Scooter by the arm and flung him from the bathroom. His head hit the wall hard and he sank to the floor, dazed.

The big man picked him up and carried him back into the kitchen and dumped him on a chair by the table.

Scooter sat with his throbbing head in his hands, looking down at the floor, fighting back the tears.

He wouldn't let them see him crying.

He. Would. Not.

The woman messed with her phone a while and said, "It's okay. No calls. No texts. He was just trying to watch CNN."

"Be more fuckin careful, Zima," the big man said.

The woman gave Scooter a wicked-witch look, and he heard her climbing the stairs to the bedrooms, her footsteps loud and angry.

The blond douche went out the back door and lit a cigarette.

The other man, smaller, older, with dark hair and eyes set too close to his nose, sat opposite Scooter, drinking coffee. He put his mug down and tapped it with his fingernail, making it chime.

"Hey, kid," he said in a flat, even voice.

Scooter didn't respond.

"I think you should know that pulling dumb crap like that again will get you locked in your room indefinitely. You want that?"

Scooter stared at the table. The man reached out a foot and nudged Scooter's chair.

"Look at me, kid. You want that?"

Scooter looked up from under his bangs and shook his head.

"Your father's a traitor. He's going down." The man stood. "We're all you've got, kiddo, so get your head straight."

He went outside and joined the blond man, and they picked up again on their football talk.

The cleaner was at Scooter's side. He moved real quietly. Scooter felt something slipped into his pocket.

The cleaner left the room and Scooter took a wrapped stick of gum from his jeans, keeping it hidden in his lap. Wrigley's Doublemint. He didn't chew gum, but he slid it back into his pocket and watched as the skinny guy crossed the gravel and went into a room by the garage and closed the door.

TWENTY-THREE

A human pincushion of a girl sat behind the counter of the print shop, buds in her ears, eyes glued to her phone, moving her skinny shoulders in time to music. The phone's screen was reflected in bursts of color on the piercings in her nose and ears.

Ash had to wave a hand to get her attention and she looked up, blinking, and tugged the buds free of her ears.

"Um," she said.

Ash gestured toward an old mushroom-colored desktop computer and monitor that sat on a table near the self-service Xerox machine.

"Can I use that?" he said.

"Sure," she said. "It's mega slow, though."

"That's okay."

"Two bucks an hour. Pay when you're done."

She was already reattaching the ear buds, eyes on the screen. Ash went past the counter, emblazoned with Seahawks regalia, toward the computer. He'd ditched the sack in the woods and stashed the stolen money in the pockets of his jeans and jacket, and found himself patting at the cash, as if to make sure he wasn't leaving a trail of banknotes.

He was in a semideserted strip mall on the frayed edges

of town. He'd walked there from Holly's—or Grace's—house, through the forest, remembering the place from a few years ago, when he'd been out on a drive with Scooter and they'd needed water and he'd stopped at the 7-Eleven beside the print shop.

The surface of the computer table was ringed from coffee mugs and none too clean. The keyboard was grime-encrusted and the mouse was sticky. Ash grimaced and rubbed his fingers on his jeans.

First, he checked for anything on the bank robbery and found a report on the website of a regional news station. The man with the goatee was an unemployed mill worker. He had a wife and two kids aged six and three. Ash closed his eyes and tried to lay it all off on dead Bob. That didn't go too well.

He read on.

Bob hadn't been identified. The report said that the second robber had escaped with "an undisclosed sum of cash." There was a poorly rendered identikit of a man who looked like anybody and nobody.

Next, Ash did a Google search for Grace Zima. The computer, ancient hard drive wheezing asthmatically, was as slow as Pierced Girl had promised. The first hits were on Facebook and Twitter. A college student in Atlanta and a housewife in Indiana.

He did a deeper Google dive and saw the headline, "Homeland Security Agent Took $15M in Bribes." The machine chugged and clicked and an hourglass cursor appeared, blinking and rotating in the middle of the screen.

When last had Ash seen one of those? Surely not this century.

While he waited for the sands of digital time to trickle by, Ash looked at the door just as a uniformed cop walked in. A beefy guy with a sharp haircut. Ash tensed, checking for a back door and seeing none. The cop eyed him, then leaned on the counter and touched the girl's hair and she swatted his hand away.

"Fuck off, Lonnie," she said.

He smirked. "Baby."

"Whyn't you go *baby* your fuckin wife?" she said.

The cop leaned in closer and whispered something and the girl laughed, and he laughed too. Ash looked back at the monitor, the egg timer still blinking.

The cop said, "I'll see you later, okay?" and walked out, and the girl sat and watched him as he got into his cruiser and sped out of the parking lot.

The timer disappeared and an article from the *Seattle Times* stuttered onto the screen. It was from earlier in the year. Curtwood Coyne, a Homeland Security agent at Immigration and Customs Enforcement in Seattle, assigned to investigate the case of a Chinese businessman accused of sex trafficking, had been found guilty of taking hefty bribes from the man and his relatives in return for destroying evidence. All charges had been dropped against Coyne's ex-partner, Agent Grace Zima, who had alerted internal investigators to the bribery. Zima had resigned from Homeland Security eight months before.

Was this the person he'd known as Holly Howells?

He searched for images of the woman, but found only pics of an agile porn actress named Suzie Zima.

If it this was the same Grace Zima, who was she working for now?

He came up empty.

He googled Curtwood Coyne. More links to the corruption case. Then a link to a sex-workers advocacy group on Facebook that claimed to have played a major role in getting Coyne exposed. A lengthy post, high on emotion and low on facts, asserted that Coyne had been bringing Asian women into the country as prostitutes for years. That he was out of prison and working at the Dollhouse, a peep show in Seattle.

Ash googled the Dollhouse and got an address.

He knew he was wasting his time but he opened the old Yahoo account Scooter had created for him. Nothing new. He clicked out of there fast, ready to tear up when he saw the old emails from his sweet little seven-year-old.

Then, aware there was some risk that he was being tracked, he logged onto his cloud storage account, and searched the backups of his photographs. Ash found a picture of Scooter standing in their kitchen with the woman who'd called herself Holly, watching as she prepared him a meal.

She hadn't liked the camera. Had always contrived to turn away, but this picture caught her full-face, staring through her gray mop as she stirred a pot.

"Miss," Ash said, turning in his seat, waving at the teenager at the desk.

The girl was bopping, ignoring him.

He crossed to her and prodded her shoulder. She raised her pierced eyebrows.

"Can I print something?" Ash asked.

She nodded and walked with him to the computer and sat and clicked away and he heard chugging and expectorating. A color printout of Holly slipped from a printer's mouth.

Ash shut down his cloud account, cleared the Google search history, and paid the girl.

He folded the picture and put it into his pocket.

As he pushed his way out into the sunlight, he looked across the parking lot at a shop offering auto repair, detailing, and wind-shields.

And used-car rentals.

He hesitated for just a moment, then fished out Carter Bew's driver's license and walked into the shop's office like he was a solid citizen. Ten minutes later, after parting with seven hundred dollars in cash (two hundred for a day's rental and five hundred as a deposit because he didn't have a credit card), Ash drove away in a tawny red 2002 Honda Accord.

As he headed for the I-90 to Seattle, rain started to stipple the windshield.

TWENTY-FOUR

John Dapp parked his Lexus outside a small stucco house in East Palo Alto. Unmowed scrap of lawn. Sagging fence. Paintwork flaking like a skin peel.

It was a suburb of cramped bungalows and rent-controlled apartments, many rungs down the totem pole from Birdland.

Dapp unwrapped a Life Savers mint and sucked on it, preparing himself. These were not visits that he relished.

He left the car and walked up to the front door, aware of a lace curtain twitching in the living room window.

It wasn't necessary to knock, but he observed the courtesies, and smacked his knuckle twice on the door that needed a scrape and a paint.

It opened to reveal a tiny woman with a tight stew of graying curls, dressed in the kind of dress that hadn't been seen since *The Brady Bunch* was canceled.

"Hi, Mrs. Mung. Jimmy in?"

She fixed a pair of dead eyes on him and said, "Repetition don't make that no funnier, mister." Something slow and Southern in her voice.

"No," he said. "I apologize."

The woman admitted him into a cramped parlor, neat and

airless. Doily wonderland. She pointed a finger down a short passageway and folded her arms.

Dapp took a deep breath, and set off, sucking on his mint. He
stopped outside a closed door and could hear the soft drumming
of fingers on a computer keyboard.

He tapped at the door. The typing stopped.

A voice, high and reedy, said, "Mom?"

Putting his face close to the wood, Dapp said, "No, Jimmy,
it's me. Henry."

The man inside knew him as Henry Green.

"Hey, come in, dude."

Dapp opened the door and, even though he was prepared,
struggled not to gag on the stench.

The room was a geek cave lit by a bank of monitors, some tuned
to obscure sci-fi and horror movies, others filled with a torrent of
source code. The floor was crammed with stacks of vintage porno
magazines, graphic novels, and pulpy paperbacks. Every surface littered with the butchered innards of computers and gaming consoles.

A massive man, morbidly obese, squeezed into an egg yolk–
yellow sweat suit, was sprawled across a king-size bed, a laptop
almost invisible in the vast pudding that was his belly.

"Wassup, Henry?"

"Hi, Jimmy."

"Take a seat, dude."

Dapp moved a half-eaten plate of food and a stack of horror
comic books from a chair and sat.

"How are you doing, Jimmy?"

"Is that like a real question that requires a real answer?"

Dapp shook his head. "No."

"Glad to hear it."

Jimmy Mung was too huge to leave the room. Couldn't fit out the door. He did his ablutions in a bedpan that his mother emptied, and the stench of his leavings and his poorly washed flesh was something from the ninth circle of hell.

Dapp had found him during an investigation for a tech company that was being hacked. To save his own ass, another hacker had flushed Jimmy out. The fat man's unique circumstances had prompted Dapp to protect him in exchange for access to his skills. Rather than resent this extortion, Jimmy seemed to enjoy Dapp's visits.

Jimmy's stomach rumbled like a cement mixer and he slapped his rolls of fat.

"Gotta feed the beast soon."

"Then let's get to it," Dapp said, unwilling to see this man-mountain at the trough. "Got anything for me, Jimmy?"

The huge man sighed and coughed and shivered and shook like an ocean of Jell-O. "I looked at general activity in that area of Washington State. Somethin jumped out at me. A bank robbery this morning in a flyspeck called Twin Forks. About ten clicks from Pearson, where your boy lives. Old dude and young dude go into a Wells Fargo, and they hold it up. As they're leaving, a customer pulls a weapon and shoots the older dude. Gets shot himself. Both gunmen die. No surveillance cam, but there's a vague description of the younger dude who escaped. Not on the news yet, but the state cop's feed tells me the older robber has been ID'd as one Robson Bew. Some survivalist type, living off the grid. He has a son, Carter Bew."

"So the Bews robbed the bank?"

"You'd assume so. But, diggin a little deeper, I dug out some medical records for the younger Bew from a Seattle hospital two years ago. End-stage AIDS. Dude was skinny as a Brazilian supermodel, man. He refused treatment and discharged himself. Here's his driver's license." Jimmy tapped the keyboard of the laptop and the license appeared on a monitor. "Fits the description at the bank. Also, with a bit of finessing, isn't too far from your boy."

Danny Ash's face filled an adjacent monitor. Dapp got that little ping in his gut that, for a moment, made him forget the stink in the room.

"You thinkin what I'm thinkin, Henry?"

"Hope not, Jimmy. You've got a mind like a skid mark."

When the massive man laughed he sounded like a blimp that had sprung a leak. His flesh wobbled, the laptop lost in a yellow sea of blubber.

Jimmy coughed and gasped and said, "I'm *thinkin* what if Slim went home to his woodsman daddy to die? What if the old man dug a hole and buried his rancid ass and didn't tell nobody? What if your boy's Bonnie and Daddy Bew's Clyde?"

"It's a long shot."

"Yeah?"

"Yeah."

"Well, I did a little more sniffin," Jimmy said, "and found that Carter Bew hired a car in Pearson earlier today, from some rent-a-wreck outfit. A 2002 Honda Accord. They ran a regulation license check, and it got in the system." He burped into his fist. "So? Dead man drivin? Or your guy? I just started plate-trackin him. Looks like he's headin up to Seattle."

"That's good work, Jimmy."

"Hey, it's what I do, dude."

"Keep me looped in, okay?"

Jimmy grunted as he heaved himself toward the edge of the bed and lifted a chrome bedpan into view.

"Now I need a bathroom break. I'd advise you to vacate the premises. It's not gonna be pretty."

Dapp was already halfway out the door.

TWENTY-FIVE

Uhuru Bakewell sat in the diner drinking coffee so damn sweet that if he stood the spoon in the cup it would come to attention and salute him.

Well, what the hell, wasn't no sugar gonna kill him. Knew that sure enough.

The diner was catty-corner from the Baltimore VA Medical Center where he'd spent the morning being pushed, pinched, and prodded. Pissing, coughing, lying in a tube for what they'd called a PET scan.

Finally got to see a doctor, who'd looked at him with professionally sad eyes and told him that he had something called pancreatic adenocarcinoma. Cancer of the pancreas in plain English.

Stage T4. Meant it was going to kill him within six months.

The doctor had sighed and said, "Surgery is not an option, so we need to talk about making your last months comfortable."

That's when Uhuru'd clocked out and stopped listening. Nodded politely and got the hell outta there soon as he could.

He sipped his coffee and looked out the window and didn't see the traffic in Greene Street. No, he saw the black smoke rising from the burn pits in Helmand Province, Afghanistan, hovering thick over their camp. Sometimes the smoke was so dense he had lain on his bunk and breathed it in and out again, like he was smoking a damn stogie.

They'd burned all kindsa shit in them pits. Gasoline, oil, rubber, tires, plastic, Styrofoam, batteries, electrical equipment, pesticides, aerosol cans, explosives, casings, medical waste. Even animal and human carcasses. Used jet fuel to stoke the fires.

He'd heard it said that those pits were killing vets now.

Lung disease. Cancer.

Had the toxic smoke gotten to him too?

Didn't fuckin matter. His time was near done, sure enough.

He drank his coffee until the cup was dry. Set it down in the saucer.

He had no family to tell.

Daddy went to the store when Uhuru was three and never come back.

Mama's heart gave out when he was fifteen.

Kid brother gone ten years now. Shot by a drug dealer. Fuckin Tupac-lite.

Sister selling her crack-whore ass. Probably dead, but anyways dead to him.

For one weak moment he thought about tracking down Sergeant Dave Dolan and crybabyin on his shoulder.

Shut that down fast.

This was his shit. His and his alone.

What he did know is that he wasn't going to let this motherfucker take him down.

When things became too much—and by the sounds of it, that would be pretty damn soon—he would put an end to it all.

Dying didn't scare him. But becoming a useless sack of shit lyin in a hospital bed did.

Scared him a lot.

Scared his ass right out into the street. Him sucking car fumes, trying to chill.

He found himself standing by a newsstand and his eyes lit on a pile of superhero comic books.

Saw that big cracker throwing the kid against the wall this morning, then shoving him into the kitchen chair.

Felt hot shame for having just stood by and said nothing. Mr. Silver-fuckin-Star.

Uhuru flipped through the comic books. *X-Men. Captain America. Thor. Hulk.*

Who the hell knew if the kid even read these things? Maybe he read fuckin Shakespeare.

But Uhuru bought a *Spider-Man* comic, folded it into his coat, and walked off to get his bus back to the farm.

TWENTY-SIX

A man in a green hat. That's what the Chinese call a cuckold.

The Mandarin insult came to Dapp as he sat at a red light on the border of East Palo Alto and Menlo Park, drumming his fingers on the wheel of the Lexus in time to an old Bacharach tune, and spotted his wife's Jeep Renegade parked outside a cheap motel.

He couldn't read the license plate from where he sat and was ready to convince himself that the car was just a look-alike when Yingying appeared out of a room on the first floor, wearing her gym clothes and Jackie O sunglasses. She unlocked the little yellow Jeep and slid behind the wheel.

The truck behind Dapp honked and he pulled away, watching his wife's car recede in his rearview, patting his pockets for a pack of Parliaments. Until he remembered that he'd quit five months ago.

What should he do? Go back and confront her? Confront her and the guy with unnecessary muscles who'd been giving her the bone?

He didn't trust himself to handle a situation like that without resorting to the kind of extreme bloodletting that ruined lives.

No, better to do what any self-respecting green-hatter did: find a bar and get thoroughly shit-faced.

TWENTY-SEVEN

Slowing to a crawl in the traffic, on the trail of the yellow Jeep, Patty Peach couldn't help sneaking a look at Orlando sitting beside her in the rental van. When she saw his eyes were closed, his girlish lashes golden in the sun, she allowed her gaze to linger. Her constant fawning annoyed him, and he wasn't someone you wanted to annoy, so she had to be covert in her appreciation of his beauty.

The traffic started to move, and she took her eyes from Orlando. The sun angled into the van as she followed a curve, and she saw her reflection in the big windshield. Saw the deeply lined face, the turkey neck, and the gray, lifeless hair, cut mannishly short. Saw, for an instant, her face in death.

When she shook herself out of this indulgent reverie she realized she had lost the Jeep, and felt her hands trembling on the wheel. Then she saw the little yellow car darting up a side street like a ratter, and she swung the van to the left, nearly colliding with some boastful foreign coupe with a braying horn.

Patty settled in behind the Jeep and forced herself to calm down. To focus.

If she'd had her way, Patty would have killed the woman in the motel room. Killed the man, too. It was the kind of place where access was easy and people were inclined to mind their own business.

But Ricky Pickford had insisted that the work be done in the woman's home.

And done in such a manner that it sent a clear message.

The Jeep was winding through the leafy streets of privilege. Patty stayed a little way back, even though she knew that the van would go unnoticed in this neighborhood of milquetoast husbands who relied on blue-collar men to perform their household chores.

The Jeep's blinker flashed and the woman turned into the short driveway of a house painted pale meringue. The garage door lifted like a drawbridge and the Jeep was swallowed.

Patty parked the van outside the house, which, like its neighbors, was unfenced in the way of this smug, complacent suburb.

Orlando roused himself and sat, blinking, instantly alert. He wore beige overalls and took a matching peaked cap from the seat beside him and pulled it over his curls.

He leaned forward, opened a tool bag, and removed a length of cheese wire attached to two wooden toggles. Aware of Patty's scrutiny, he did a little playacting for her benefit.

He looped the cheese wire around the gear selector of the van, and, holding a toggle in each hand, pulled the wire taut. She saw it bite into the paintwork, and saw the pop of sinewy muscles beneath his sleeves.

Flashing her a beatific smile, Orlando loosened the wire and dropped it into the bag. He opened the door and steeped down.

"Are you sure you don't want me to come in with you?" Patty said.

He shook his head. "No, Mama. You rest. Anyway, it will be messy. Best spare your clothes."

Slinging the tool bag over his shoulder, he closed the van door and walked up the curved brick pathway to the porch.

TWENTY-EIGHT

No more flashbacks, Nicola Fabian said to herself as she sat in a taxi on her way to Heathrow, London a pewter-colored blur unspooling past her.

No more dips into the scummy pond of memory.

No more cutting, pricking, piercing, ripping, rending, or abrading.

No more.

From today, her life would be lived in a forward progression. Or, at the very least, in the moment.

Memory was her enemy. She needed to learn to forget. Of course, it was now contended, there was no such thing as forgetting. Forgetting implied that a recollection was forever lost. And that notion was considered unacceptable in this stridently online, wired, all-access culture. Memory loss was now said to be just a matter of retrieval failure.

Well, she would bloody well degauss her hard drive.

It was time to *live*.

And really, seriously, up to now her existence couldn't be called a life, so much as a lookbook for one—an assemblage of props and artifacts to lend some semblance of credibility to the idea that she was real.

Boo-fucking-hoo, so she'd had a messed-up childhood. Who hadn't? She couldn't click on her TV without finding yet another mucousy celeb oversharing the sordid details of their abusive upbringing.

It was a load of bollocks.

But for all her resolve, she couldn't quiet erase a nagging voice that said, Your father killed your mother.

Yes, the new Nicola replied, but who says the silly bitch wouldn't have just slid back into her rotten ways and carried on carving a swathe of narcissistic, heroin-fueled destruction?

Maybe, Old Nicola said. Maybe not. Your father never allowed you to find out.

When she discovered her fingers toying with the hairpin that she'd secreted in her jacket pocket, she folded her hands in her lap and sat up straighter.

It was time.

Time to claim her life.

And the way to do that, she'd decided, was to take down the man who resembled a many-armed Hindu deity as he plucked pleasures from the world's tallest trees.

It was time to fuck Daddy up.

TWENTY-NINE

John Dapp stood and looked at the body of his wife sprawled on the sodden throw rug in their living room.

Yingying, still in her gym clothes, had been garroted and the wire had bitten so deep into her throat as to almost sever her head. Her blood had geysered over the walls, the floor, and the furniture.

Somebody had been out to make a statement.

Dapp felt the puke rising in his gullet and turned to the door, a young patrolman putting out a steadying hand.

"You okay, sir?"

Dap nodded and walked out into the sunshine, squinting at the glare, drinking air.

The street was lined with police vehicles and ambulances. Cops were keeping the media back. Neighbors were rubbernecking with their camera phones trained on the house—no doubt this was already trending on Twitter.

Dapp, three sheets to the wind as his old dad had liked to say, had arrived home from the bar ready to face his wife. Ready to unleash upon her the full measure of his rage and hurt.

Instead he'd walked into the cops.

They'd briskly alibi'd him. The mixologist at the Menlo Park sports bar had confirmed that Dapp had been planted on a stool for the last two hours. Then they'd taken him in to see Yingying.

A detective in a suit a cut above his pay grade walked across the lawn toward Dapp.

"John," Artie Winslow said.

"Artie."

"Hell of a business."

"Yeah."

They'd had dealings in the past. Identity theft, hacking, cyberfraud. Winslow was smart and personable, the kind of cop who could move through the tech world without ruffling feathers, and Dapp had gone out of his way to cultivate him.

Winslow took his arm and walked him into the kitchen.

"What we know from your neighbors is that a van stopped outside your house, driven by an older woman. She stayed in the van and a teenage boy in overalls came inside."

Dapp felt like he'd been hit by a secondary quake, a little San Andreas opening in his gut.

He leaned against the refrigerator.

Winslow eyed him. "That mean anything to you?"

"No. Nothing."

Winslow looked at him and sucked his teeth. "Sure?"

"Yeah. Jesus."

Dapp closed his eyes. Saw Victor Fabian smirking, blowing a smoke ring that looked like a halo.

"John."

Dapp blinked himself back and looked at the cop.

"Yeah. Sorry."

"You going to be okay?"

"Sure."

"There are people we can call. Trauma professionals."

"No. I'm okay. Thanks, Artie." He pointed toward the living room. "You guys are still going to be a while here, right?"

The cop nodded. "Yeah. Techs still have to do their work. We won't be able to move, uh, Yingying, for a while."

"Okay if I get out of here?"

"Sure, man. You got some place to go? Some friends?"

"Yeah, yeah."

"We'll need to sit down a little later. Okay?"

"Sure."

"I'll call you with updates."

Dapp nodded and went outside and a couple of uniforms walked him to his car, keeping the media and their barrage of questions at bay.

Dapp got behind the wheel of the Lexus and sat a while, gathered himself, then he started the car and drove away.

Bye-bye, Birdland.

THIRTY

Ash sat in the Honda in the rain. He was parked outside a windowless bunker marooned beneath an overpass on the edge of downtown Seattle. The silhouette of a nude dancer twitched and spasmed on the roof above a pink neon sign that scribbled The Dollhouse onto the night.

Two dented cars were parked by the doorway, the neon reflected in their windshields.

Ash took the stolen money from his pockets and counted out a thousand dollars. He folded the banknotes and stuffed them into his right boot. The rest he wrapped in a road map he'd found in the glove box and shoved it under the seat. His fingers connected with a greasy junk food wrapper, and he wiped them on the upholstery.

An old truck rolled up and stopped beneath the sign. A middle-aged man in a windbreaker stood up into the drizzle and made for the stairs. He had the shipboard sway of a drunk.

Ash left the Honda and followed him, hanging back a little.

The drunk jabbed at a buzzer beside the door. The door opened and he went in and the door closed.

Ash waited a minute, standing in the rain, drops ramping off his cap, then he approached the door and hit the buzzer.

With a cluck like a scolding tongue the door unlocked and he pushed it open, stepping into a small lobby that stank of piss and stale sweat. It was lit by a lurid red lamp.

A hard-faced blonde stood watching him through a smeared window set into one wall.

The blonde left the window and appeared behind an iron gate. She was dressed in pink booty shorts and black vinyl thigh-high boots, with a white shirt tied at her midriff.

"Welcome to the Dollhouse," she said in a fifty-a-day voice. "You got any preferences?"

"I want to see Curtwood Coyne."

The blonde gave him a blank look. "Wrong answer."

Ash took a ten from his pocket and showed it to her. She shook her head. He added a twenty. She reached a hand through the bars and took the money before unlocking the gate and allowing him through.

The blonde locked the gate after him and slouched down a narrow corridor illuminated by a string of colored party lights. Rather than making the passageway look festive, the lights lent it a sordid and somehow menacing air.

They passed two red doors standing open onto identical rooms—dim, cramped spaces, each containing a black couch and a low table. A third red door was shut. The blonde walked past them all to a scuffed wooden door at the end of the corridor and pushed it open.

A big man with a bald head, a gut ballooning over his sweat-pants, sat squeezed into a closet-size space. He chewed gum like a hippo on a river bank as he watched a chunky TV monitor that rested on a steel table. The man had a black eye and a caterpillar of recently applied sutures crawling above his right ear.

He looked up at the woman. "Yeah?"

"Curt, this guy wants to see you." She stepped away leaving Ash in the doorway.

"Who the fuck are you?" the man said, chewing.

"I want to talk to you."

The man's eyes were back on the monitor. "'Bout what?"

"About Grace Zima."

The man looked at him and blinked. He picked at the scab on his head.

"Come in. Shut the door."

Ash stepped into the tiny room. It reeked of overheated armpits and groin overlaid with the ripe tang of recently ingested junk food. The monitor showed a garish color image from a camera mounted high on the wall of one of the rooms. A topless brown girl in a G-string gyrated her pelvis, dancing close to the drunk in the windbreaker who sat on a sofa.

The big man stood and moved with surprising speed. He shoved Ash against the wall and frisked him. He found a few banknotes, Carter Bew's driver's license, and the printout of the woman Ash had known as Holly Howells.

Breathing loudly through his nose, Coyne stared at the photograph, then he took Ash by the jaw and dragged his face into the light of the desk lamp.

The big man looked scared.

"Well, I'll be fucked. You're him. The fuckin jihadist."

"I'm no jihadist."

Coyne grabbed the money, the driver's license, and photograph and shoved them back into the pocket of Ash's jeans. Then he started pushing him toward the door.

"I want no part of this. Get the fuck out of here."

"I'll implicate you," Ash said. "I'll tell the media you helped me get explosives and weapons into the country."

The big man opened the door and propelled Ash into the passageway. He was breathing hard.

"We're closing, so get your ass the fuck out. I'll see you in the parking lot," he said. "Five minutes."

He slammed the door. The corridor was ablaze with light, every scuff mark and peel of paint revealed with forensic clarity. A thickset Filipina dressed in jeans and sneakers, her hair covered by a bandanna, was swabbing the floor with the vigor of a deckhand. The handle of the mop clattered against the wall, the fumes of industrial solvents bringing tears to Ash's eyes. The woman ignored him.

He walked down the corridor to the gate. After a little fumbling he found the release button and it opened. He went out the front door of the bunker and went out into the rain.

He stood a moment in the wash of the neon sign, then he walked over to the edge of the parking lot and sheltered under a tree.

After a few minutes a side door opened and he saw the bulky shape of Coyne. The man beckoned him.

Ash walked over.

"Who sent you?" Coyne said.

"Nobody."

"How'd you find me?"

"I saw on Facebook that you worked here."

"Fuckin Facebook." Coyne scratched at his head wound. "Anybody else know you're here?"

"No." Ash stepped in closer. "So that's Grace Zima? In the photograph?"

By way of reply Coyne punched him in the stomach and Ash folded and fell. The big man started to kick him, and Ash tried to protect his face. A kick to the head had him blinking away bright lights.

After a minute of sustained whaling, Coyne took a knee beside him, breathing heavily. "Now you go. You forget the fuck about me, hear? Come back and I'll kill you."

Coyne was gone and Ash lay blinking away rain drops, the dancing girl on the roof a palsied blur.

Drenched, Ash sat up and spat blood. He got to his knees and vomited. Standing, he walked unsteadily to the Honda.

Wincing, he lowered himself into the seat and started the car and drove away. He didn't know where he was going.

He just drove.

THIRTY-ONE

Dapp knew it was egregious fuckheadery, but he'd checked into the very motel room his dead wife had used for her daytime tryst, and now, in the wee small hours of the morning, he was sprawled on the bed, weeping. He'd stripped away the bedspread and lay with his face in the pillows, trying to catch a trace of Yingying's fragrance, a blend of lemon and sandalwood.

What remained of his rational mind told him that even in this dump, most likely the linen had been changed after she and her lover had checked out, but still he snorted and sniffed like a truffle hound, catching nothing more than the smell of bleach and mold.

All his righteous rage and hurt at her unfaithfulness had been replaced by overwhelming grief and guilt.

He had loved his wife. What she had done had wounded him grievously and, sitting in the sterile sports bar, he had entertained the usual cuckold's fantasies of bloody revenge.

But after a suitable time and suitable penance, he would have forgiven her. And, in the way of homely men who marry beauties, he would have convinced himself that her love for him was real and would endure.

He knew, of course, that she had seen this big *guizi* as a ticket out of Chinese purgatory. His bulk and physical unattractiveness had been rendered invisible by his usefulness.

But here in California, Yingying had blossomed, and her beauty had drawn her from his orbit.

He understood that she would have left him, ultimately.

That his purpose had been served.

But she'd not been given that chance.

He sat up and wiped his nose on his sleeve and reached for the bottle of Wild Turkey that stood on the burnt and stained side table.

The liquor was little more than symbolic. When he'd uncorked it after installing himself in the room, the first taste of the sweet alcohol had sent him to the bathroom for an extended bout of purging. He could do no more than swig at it and wash his mouth and dribble burning liquid down his throat.

He was sober. Grief and guilt ravaged.

But sober.

After he'd fled his house, he'd driven to the Palo Alto train station and parked the Lexus on a side street. He'd left it unlocked with the keys in the ignition. As he walked toward the brown-and-yellow building, he dumped his iPhone in a trash can, along with his driver's license and social security card. He kept the burner phone in his jacket pocket.

Dapp made for the digitally operated luggage lockers near the station coffee shop, punched in his code and retrieved the bag inside. He walked out and flagged down a cab and gave the address of the motel. He checked into the room using one of the array of driver's licenses he had inside the bag—along with a few bricks of hundred-dollar bills, more burner phones, a virgin iPad, and a Glock 17.

A sawbuck had encouraged the desk clerk to conjure up the dusty bottle of Wild Turkey.

Dapp knew that he was taking a dumb risk coming to this room. Odds were that the Peaches had been following Yingying and would have seen her here. But if Victor Fabian had wanted Dapp dead, the Peaches would have done his bidding.

No, Fabian had wanted to hurt Dapp.

Had wanted to leave him a message: mess with my daughter and I mess with your life.

The burner phone in his jacket rang. The only person who had the number was the massive hacker.

Dapp cleared his throat and answered. "Yeah?"

"Henry?"

"Uh-huh."

"Long story short: I've found our guy."

"Yeah?"

"Yep. Plate-tracked him. He's in a motel in Seattle."

"Okay."

"You online?"

Dapp powered up the iPad, hearing it trill, and watched it wink. "Getting there," he said.

"I've sent you a link. It'll patch you into a live security-cam feed."

"Obliged, Jimmy."

"De nada."

The big man was gone. Dapp scrolled for the link. A click and he was looking at a grainy monochrome image of the parking lot of a motel.

There were three cars in the floodlit lot. One of them was an aging Honda Accord.

Dapp sat on the bed, his hands hanging between his knees,

the iPad propped up on the table, gazing at the little slice of drizzly Seattle, thinking about himself and Danny Ash.

Thinking about how they were both on the run, holed up in cheap motels.

About how they had both worn green hats.

About how both of their wives had been murdered by Victor Fabian.

But there were a couple of telling differences.

Dapp didn't have a son who needed saving.

And he'd sure as shit never dipped out on catching an Airbus A350 that'd been blown out of the sky.

THIRTY-TWO

Ash lay on the hotel bed staring at CNN, seeing images of a broken fuselage and aircraft parts strewn across the ocean. Seeing bodies floating facedown in the water.

He had his cell phone in his hand. He hit redial and yet again heard an electronic voice saying something in Arabic and he ended the call.

On the screen, the clothes of two bodies were whipped by the blades of the hovering helicopter.

Ash hit redial once more.

It took him a moment to realize he was hearing Jane saying, "Hello! Hello!"

"Jane. It's me."

"Jesus, Danny! Jesus Christ!" She was sobbing.

"I'm okay. I missed the plane. I'm okay."

"God, Danny, it's all over the news. We thought—"

"I know—"

"We thought you were dead."

"I know. I've been trying to reach you. There's been no cell phone service and the landlines are down."

He heard a rattle and an echo as she went to speaker phone.

His son said, "Pop?"

"Hey, Scooter. I'm fine, buddy. I'm fine."

"Pop. I was so scared, Pop."

The pain in his ribs woke Ash from the dream. Confused, disoriented, he realized that he was lying on the bed of a Seattle motel room, looking at Scooter on the TV screen. His son held a handwritten note that said, *Dad, please give yourself up.*

Ash lunged for the remote, boosting the audio, but the news anchors were back, giving an update on a mass shooting in a midwestern shopping mall.

Ash surfed. CNN. Fox. The alphabet channels. No Scooter.

Had he dreamed it?

Then he landed on some regional news affiliate and there was his huge-eyed son, pale, blinking, holding up the note.

And gone again, replaced by a gnomish weatherman who looked like he was wearing somebody else's dentures.

Ash clicked off the tube.

THIRTY-THREE

"They had to hold a gun to my head," Scooter said in an imaginary conversation with his father. "No, seriously, Pop. They held. A motherfreakin gun. To. My. Head. Mic drop."

He sat in the upstairs room in the dark, at the table by the window, looking out at the distant rash of light pollution from some unknown city. He wasn't crying. He was beyond crying.

"But I put one over on them, Pop. I sold them a real bill of goods."

In his head, he used the same outdated slang that he and his father had bantered in back in the day. Scooter knowing it had been his father's way of saying, "Hey, aren't we all cool and ironic, me and my so-smart son?"

Even the nickname his pop had given him. Rockwellian, he'd said. Scooter had googled that.

Earlier, before the whole gun thing, he'd found the *Spider-Man* comic book the small man had put under his pillow. Who else could have left it there? Scooter hadn't read a comic in years, but the fact the man had done this had made him feel less alone, and he'd sat on the bed flicking through it, catching that old ink and paper whiff.

When he heard footsteps on the stairs he slid the comic book back under the pillow and went and sat at the table.

The woman came in carrying a cup of cocoa with a sprinkle of cinnamon on top, just the way he liked it.

She held the mug out to him, but he didn't touch it and she set it down on the table next to a yellow legal pad and a black marker.

"I need you to do something, Scooter. To help your father."

He stared at her.

"I want you to encourage him to surrender. That way he'll be safe."

Sure, he thought. I'll believe that when hell freezes over.

"The longer he's on the run, the more chance there is of something bad happening to him. There are people in this country who're a little too gun happy. You understand what I'm saying?"

Scooter looked out the window. He could see the blinking lights of a plane and wondered where it was going.

"Now," the woman said, "I know you won't talk. So ..." She opened the legal pad and held up the pen. "I want you to write something. A message. Telling him to give himself up."

He shook his head and turned his back on her.

"Scooter," she said, "I really need you to do this for me."

The door opened and the big man stood there. The ugly one. The bully.

"Maybe he needs some encouragement," he said.

"I've got this," she said.

But the bully came in and he had his gun out and he put it to Scooter's temple. "Write. Do it."

"Jesus, Coombes," the woman said.

"Do it." The guy cocked the gun, just like in the movies.

They wouldn't shoot him, Scooter knew. But he wanted this over. He wanted them gone.

So, he wrote the message. And he let them snap his picture holding it.

But he'd pulled one over on them.

Got them good.

And even the woman, who should've known better, hadn't picked up on what he'd done.

But his pop wouldn't miss it.

THIRTY-FOUR

Victor Fabian—dreaming of things done to him long ago, things so dark and so noxious that only his unconscious mind would dare poke a stick at them—heard the sound of a door opening and the low rumble of men's voices.

He sat up in his Washington bed, flinging back the covers, sweating, heart racing.

It took forever for his ailing mind to assemble a makeshift reality—the sixteen-hour flight from China on his private jet and the cocktail of cognac and Ambien to help him sleep had left him askew. He yanked open the bedside drawer and found the Ruger automatic pistol, wondering why the alarm had not been tripped.

He left the bed, dressed in his monogrammed pajamas, barefoot, thick gray hair falling across his eyes, and edged to the door, enough blue dawn light filtering through the curtains for him to find the handle and open it.

Outside on the landing, he stood listening to a squad of men entering the downstairs hallway. No attempt at silence. He heard heavy treads on the staircase, the wooden frame shaking like a gibbet, and a trio of men in zippered jackets and FBI caps appeared. His weapon was met with the muzzles of three others, amid yells to drop his pistol and get down.

For a moment, Fabian was seized by an almost ungovernable urge to fire, but he fought for control and won and opened his fist and allowed the Ruger to fall and lowered himself to the carpet. The men kicked the weapon away and frisked him. Lying there, Fabian was acutely aware, of all things, that his bare heels were cracked and calloused. That he needed to visit a salon on Ferguson Lane when he turned to Shanghai.

If he returned.

"Are you alone in the house?" asked a runt with morning breath as he knelt over Fabian.

"Yes," Fabian said. "What the hell is this?"

The men allowed him to get to his feet. Fabian smoothed his pajamas, running a hand through his hair, trying to tame his widow's peak.

He had to fight to stop his mind from skittering off like an eel in the deep.

"We have a warrant to search the premises," the skinny man said.

"Let me see it," Fabian said, extending a hand.

He held the document at arm's length, not wanting to have to ask for his reading glasses to be brought from the bedroom. He could see enough to verify its legality.

The little prick said, "Mr. Fabian, we ask that you sit downstairs while we execute the warrant."

"I want to call my attorney."

"You can do that downstairs."

More men, joined by a woman wearing blue gloves, were in his bedroom. They opened the closet, using their phones to photograph his suit collection, the flashes detonating like flak.

Fabian walked downstairs to where a bevy of feds was at work, unraveling his life. The front door stood open, but he saw no visible damage, so they'd chosen to pick the lock rather than use a battering ram. Small mercies.

He made for the phone on the chiffonier by the door.

A young man built like a defensive back tried to stop him, but the runt waved him away.

Fabian called Pickford and told him enough to light a fire under his backside.

This done, Fabian took to his favorite chair, a green leather wingback with chrome nail-head accents that had allegedly graced the office of J. Edgar Hoover himself. He opened a humidor of Havanas and removed one, sniffing at it.

Fabian inserted the cigar into a bullet punch cutter and clipped the tip. He struck a wooden match and waited for the sulfur to burn away before he held the cigar over the flame, rotating the Havana as he slowly toasted it. Satisfied, he brought the flame a little closer and lit the cigar, drawing on it gently.

The warm smoke calmed him, and he sat puffing, watching the to-ings and fro-ings.

Watched his laptop being walked out the door.

Watched piles of binders from his office upstairs carted away.

As he smoked, Fabian closed his eyes, tuning out the hubbub and stilling his mind, and started to compose his kill list.

THIRTY-FIVE

Scooter had written Dad. Not Pop.

Dad.

This came to Ash in the shower of the motel, standing under the tepid water in an attempt to soothe the aches in his body. His torso was as mottled as the hide of a piebald pony, the bruises red and blue and green-tinged. They would only get more garish and Technicolor in the coming days.

His ribs hurt and were a little spongy to the touch. Bruised not broken, he reckoned.

But the pain was forgotten when his memory flung back at him the image of his son holding the hand-lettered note.

He'd written, *Dad, please give yourself up*, when he'd only ever called him *Pop*.

A coded signal from behind enemy lines. Telling Ash that he'd been forced to write it.

Ash sobbed. And it had nothing to do with the pain in his body.

He sobbed for his son. His brokenhearted, self-muted son.

What had they done to him?

What were they doing to him now?

Ash flung open the mildewed shower curtain, tears and water

and snot dripping from his face, and dried himself on a towel as rough as a doormat.

He knew what to do.

He would find a pay phone and call the FBI.

Negotiate a surrender.

Give himself up in exchange for his son's freedom.

***

Dressed in Carter Bew's soiled and blood-stained clothes, Ash emerged from the second-floor room and stood on the landing, blinking at the feeble sunlight that prodded at the soggy clouds.

The Honda sat in the parking lot where he had left it, the windshield patterned with raindrops. Traffic hissed past the motel and a homeless man rooted in a trash can on the sidewalk.

Ash walked down the stairs, leaning on the railing, pain stabbing his ribs. He paused to recover his breath and crabbed toward the Honda.

As his fingertips touched the door handle a voice said, "Daniel Ash?"

He turned to see a big man with short, side-parted brown hair and the professionally blank face of a federal agent.

Ash raised his hands to shoulder height, searching for the SWAT team, the armored vehicles, the choppers, the snipers.

The man said, "Relax, Danny, I'm not law enforcement."

Ash, arms still raised, said, "Who are you then?"

"I'm Linda, man." When Ash stared at him blankly, the big guy said, "Linda fucking Lovelace."

THIRTY-SIX

In the rental car outside the motel, John Dapp looked Danny Ash in the eye and said: "The man who killed your wife and took your son murdered *my* wife yesterday."

Ash blinked. "Jesus."

"Yes."

"Who is he?"

"His name's Victor Fabian."

"Should that mean something to me?"

"No. He swims pretty deep in the cesspit."

Dapp started the car and drove.

"Where are we going?"

"To an airfield. We're flying to DC."

"Why?"

"Because that's where Victor Fabian is."

"And then?"

"We get him to tell us where your son is."

"Just like that."

"No. Not exactly."

"Who are you?" Ash asked. "And don't say Linda fucking Lovelace."

Dapp sped onto I-5. "My name's John Dapp. Until a few

hours ago, I was a security consultant for tech companies in Silicon Valley. For twenty years before that I was with the CIA. The last eight years as a case officer in China. Shanghai."

"You got ID?"

"I've got ID for John Dapp." He switched lanes, the wind from a semi buffeting them. "Jerome Lindsay. Peter Carter. Saul Abrahams. I could go on."

"So your identity is fluid?"

"'Be like water,' a *rōshi* once told me."

"You've never met a *rōshi*, have you?"

"No, I haven't."

"So, you're a liar?"

"Well, let's say a professional embellisher."

"Fuck." Ash looked at him. "How can I trust you?"

"What's your alternative?"

"Give myself up. Get them to release my son."

"My guess is you don't play much poker, do you?"

"Meaning?"

Dapp said, "*Meaning* that all your son has is you. You have value when you're out here. You have precisely zero value when you're in their hands. That clear enough for you?"

Ash nodded. "Yes. Yes, it's clear."

THIRTY-SEVEN

Uhuru Bakewell had to fight down a bout of dizziness as he scrambled eggs in the farmhouse kitchen. He took a step back from the stove and bumped into the big blond cracker who was standing at the fridge drinking milk straight from the carton.

"Whoa, easy, son," the fucker said, though Uhuru had ten years on him.

Uhuru bit back a reply and took a breath and finished cooking the eggs. He plated them along with crispy bacon and set the plates down on the kitchen table for the cracker and the gray-haired woman and the other guy.

The kid sat pushing Cheerios around in his bowl of milk, not looking at nobody.

The big asshole ruffled the kid's hair as he thumped down into a seat beside him. "No hard feelings, huh, little bro? About last night?"

The kid didn't acknowledge him, just carried on stirring the milk.

"What we got here is failure to communicate," the cracker said.

He was the only one who laughed at his joke.

Uhuru turned away, his rage making him even dizzier.

His rage and self-loathing.

He'd been sitting on the step of his room the night before, taking the air, when he'd looked up at the house and seen the gray-haired woman standing over the kid at the table in his room. He couldn't hear her voice, the window being nailed shut, but he could see the kid shaking his head. Then the big white man came in and gunpointed the kid, and it was fear that had kept Uhuru's ass glued to that step.

Fear that he was no match no more for that motherfucker. That if he'd started something he wouldn't've been able to finish it.

He heard Sarge, clear as a bell, say, "Goddam, Hoo, you shoulda gone up there, man. Shoulda planted that Glock deep in his redneck ass."

The boy stood up from the kitchen table and placed the uneaten cereal on the counter beside the sink. He did this every day. A well-mannered kid.

The boy didn't move away. Uhuru eyeballed him then glanced down at the bowl the kid was staring at. He saw the small piece of paper crunched up in the saucer the bowl rested in.

The boy gave him a look from under his bangs, and he turned and went toward the stairs. The woman followed him, ready to lock him in his room.

Uhuru took the paper and pocketed it.

THIRTY-EIGHT

"To get a no-knock warrant, the prosecutors had to show proba-ble cause that your home contained evidence of a crime, sir," Pick-ford said, piloting the black SUV through the streets of Capitol Hill. "They had to persuade a federal judge that you were likely to destroy evidence. It's a signal of intent."

The house hadn't yet been swept for listening devices, so Fabian had insisted on talking in the car.

"What's Schulz say?"

Bruce Schulz. Fabian's attorney. A pit bull in a Brooks Brothers suit.

"That they'll try to get you on violations of tax laws, money-laundering prohibitions and requirements to disclose foreign lob-bying."

"Is that all?" Fabian said, watching DC pass by through his sunglasses. How bland and white-bread it was after the East.

"It's enough."

"You reached out to the presidency?" Fabian asked.

"Yes. Very quietly."

"And?"

"They're distancing themselves, sir."

The SUV crossed Pennsylvania Avenue and Fabian looked

toward the White House. His intemperate side wanted to go down there and cause a ruckus. Remind that clown in the Oval Office who he was dealing with. The impulse was sound, but the venue was not.

He lit a cigar, ruminating. "Maybe it's time to break a little china?"

"Maybe."

"We can no longer sit and watch this Daniel Ash business play out. I want him found and shut down."

"It may take time."

"Then kill his son."

Pickford looked at him. "You're serious?"

"Yes. Get the Peaches in. Let them eliminate everybody in the safe house, Zima included. And tell them to butcher the child. I want it messy. Catnip for the twenty-four-hour news cycle. It'll make Ash raise his head. And when he does …"

Fabian made a scything motion with the flat of his hand.

THIRTY-NINE

John Dapp sat aboard the Learjet, busy on his iPad, reading a bulletin from the obese hacker about Grace Zima, a.k.a. Holly Howells.

After telling Dapp about Zima and handing over the creased and folded printout of her photograph, Danny Ash, his face gaunt with exhaustion, had fallen asleep.

There would be no sleep for Dapp. Not until this was over. Sleep would bring dreams. And dreams would bring back his slain wife.

The jet was flying to Baltimore, the nearest destination to DC that he'd been able to secure at such short notice. Back in Seattle he'd reached out to a guy based in Texas who was a partner in an executive jet charter company. For a decade, he'd flown for a private airline that had been used by the CIA to move weapons, matériel, personnel, and captives around the globe.

A few years ago, the pilot had been busted in Shanghai for transporting meth precursors from China to the Mexican Sinaloa cartel and was looking at a possible death sentence. Dapp used an asset close to the Politburo to secure his release. So the favor bank was overflowing with good tidings, and the pilot had organized for Dapp and Ash to hitch a ride on an empty leg flight back to Baltimore.

They'd flown out of a small private airfield near Seattle, and paperwork had been kept to a minimum.

Once the onboard Wi-Fi had gone live, Dapp had harnessed Jimmy Mung to get on the cybertrail of Grace Zima and find out what happened to her after she resigned from Homeland. Dapp was certain she was the key. Winston Ng, the Chinese businessman who'd bribed her ex-partner, had fingers in dubious pies in Beijing, Hong Kong, and the US.

And he was tight with Victor Fabian.

An hour into the flight, Dapp's burner warbled. Mung.

"Yes?" Dapp said.

"Zima is on the payroll of a company called Executive Protection Services. Registered in DC."

"Okay. What do they do?"

"Good fuckin question, dude. So far, I've found the names of twenty-seven people affiliated with EPS and traced all of them back to three Beltway-area PO boxes. Smells fuckin skanky, man."

"Yes, it does."

"I searched for some of those people in public databases and found that though most names were attached to dates of birth in the fifties, sixties, or seventies, all were given Social Security numbers between 1998 and 2003." The huge man belched and Dapp pictured him wallowing on his bed in that fetid room. "I'll shoot you an email with names and shit and keep on diggin. Maybe I'll come out in China."

"That's funny, Jimmy."

"Ho ho ho."

Dapp ended the call. Within minutes Mung sent him proof

that Zima was attached to Executive Protection, along with the names and addresses of people associated with the outfit.

Dapp had started enough front companies in his time to know when he was looking at one.

And it was like looking into a black hole.

FORTY

Rumpled and dyspeptic, Nicola Fabian was almost pleased to find her father's little toady waiting for her in arrivals at Dulles. Without complaint she allowed Ricky Pickford to drive her to the Capitol Hill house. No doubt she'd lost her hotel reservation.

The flight had been a bloody nightmare. Some idiot in coach had created a disturbance and had to be restrained by passengers and crew. The plane was diverted to Logan International in Boston. Word filtered through to business class, where Nicola was reading an early McEwan, that the man was carrying a screwdriver, Vaseline, matches, and some kind of communication from ISIS.

A pair of US fighter jets appeared over the Atlantic, took up positions on each wingtip of the Boeing, and escorted the plane to Logan. After landing and coming to a stop on a remote apron, a SWAT team swarmed the aircraft. Minutes later the man, burly and swarthy and probably drunk, was frog-marched past Nicola and out of the plane.

The skittish passengers were forced to stay on board for another hour before being allowed to disembark. Walking to the bus that ferried them to the terminal, Nicola saw their baggage spread out on the runway like a yard sale, sniffer dogs rooting through it.

Nicola waited in the terminal and watched conflicting reports on various networks. Fox declared that the man was a known Islamic extremist with "ISIS ties." CNN weighed in with a report that he was a drunken copier salesman from Istanbul whose demands for more alcohol in his mother tongue had spooked the crew.

Nicola was inclined to go with CNN.

At last the passengers were bussed off to some dreadful airport hotel, where (minus her baggage) she spent an uncomfortable night. Her sleep was fitful and dream-sodden, and she woke to find her strength and resolve of the day before diluted.

It took until nearly noon before a plane was found to fly the stranded passengers to Dulles. On landing, Nicola had discovered that her baggage had not accompanied her and despaired of ever seeing it again.

Pickford parked outside the house and escorted her in. He seated her in the living room, gave her a glass of spring water, muttered that her father would be down directly, and evaporated.

Sipping her water, Nicola closed her eyes for a moment and sensed a slight disturbance in the atmosphere. Without knowing how she knew, she was certain that something had happened here. It felt like a place after a natural disaster, where the order of things had been disrupted.

She opened her eyes and looked for any signs of disarray. When she saw none, she dismissed this tenuous intuition as the result of being tired and strung out. And understandably nervous about confronting her father.

"Nicky-Nicks!" That fulsome baritone coming from the stairs.

Victor Fabian made an entrance. He was sporting one of his absurdly expensive casual outfits: teal-colored slacks and a white silk shirt worn untucked, his sockless feet in a pair of black espadrilles.

He seemed his usual smug self, teeth impossibly white in his tan face.

But was that a tinge of yellow she saw beneath the suntan as he neared her? And did she detect just the slightest tremor in the meaty hand that he laid on her shoulder as he leaned forward and kissed her on each cheek?

Submitting to the brief embrace, she caught something acid under his persimmon cologne.

This diminishing of his usual sangfroid, albeit slight, somehow energized her, and she sat up straighter and blinked away fatigue.

"I gather your flight was an ordeal?" he said.

"A little."

"Word among those in the know is that it was all an overreaction. The product of this paranoid age. He was just a bellicose drunk."

"I thought as much. If he'd been blond and apple-cheeked, none of it would've happened. He could've lit a tiki torch and goose-stepped down the aisle and it would've been laughed off as overexuberance."

He snorted and reached for the carafe of cognac on the chiffonier, wagging it at her.

Nicola shook her head. "Too early for me."

"Not if you're still on London time."

When she shook her head again he poured a glass for himself and sat in his club chair. He crossed his legs and went about pruning and igniting a cigar the size of a bull's cock.

After he had puffed and sipped, he squinted at her through the scrim of smoke. "So, you said you have something to discuss?"

Being who he was, she assumed he knew that she had been to the French clinic.

"Yes," she said. "Something quite important."

Was the swinging of his foot just a little too mannered? Was there a clinch of tension in his shoulder muscles? Was he nervous? Was that even possible?

"Well," he said, smiling, porcelain veneers catching the light photogenically, "here I am."

"I want to ask you something."

"Ask away."

She paused and his leg swung like a metronome, moving from adagio to allegro.

"Will you give me a job?" she said, and his leg stopped swinging. He looked at her in surprise.

"A *job?*"

"Yes, Daddy, I want to work for you. I want to learn all about what you do." She smiled, just a nice English girl with too many teeth. "And who you do it to."

FORTY-ONE

Uhuru waited until he was back in his room, door locked, before he retrieved the scrap of paper from his sweatpants.

While he'd washed and stacked the breakfast dishes, he'd felt it like a hot coal in his pocket. But he'd let it be, just done his chores, nice and slow. Swept out the kitchen. Emptied the trash into a black bag and dumped it in the back of the Ford pickup. He'd dispose of it later on his run into town to stock up on supplies.

He sat down on his bunk—all tight with hospital corners, just like in the Corps—and looked at the note. It was on a strip of legal pad, neatly written:

> *Please tell my father where I am. Use this email. Only he and I know it.*

There was a Yahoo address. Name of some cartoon character, he figured.

Uhuru scrunched up the note and returned it to his pocket and went out and climbed into the pickup and drove for the gate.

The dark-haired guy was out walking the perimeter fence. He watched Uhuru drive by without acknowledging him.

Uhuru unlocked the gate and drove through, locking it after him.

He passed cornfields on his way into the small town. Passed a graveyard, a water tower, and a church. A small park with gnomes. Wide streets named Oak and Beech. Headed for the two-block downtown with a butcher, a general store, a diner named Wanda's, and a library.

As he parked the truck outside the store, Uhuru rubbed the kid's note between his fingers and looked across at the library.

He had been in there one time, seeking a Walter Mosley detective story. He kinda dug Easy Rawlins. The dog-faced librarian had shook her head, mouth as pinched as if he'd asked her for a big-booty magazine.

He'd seen the computers then. Three old desktops off to the side of the bookshelves. Two idle. One occupied by a fat ofay dude looking at porn, judging by his hypnotized eyes.

Uhuru left the truck and went into the store, returned the grunt of the guy behind the counter and bought what he needed. Food. Drink. Cleaning solvents.

He carried the bag outside and dumped it in the back of the truck. Stood and looked at the library. Rubbed the note between his fingertips.

No. Fuck this. This was not his shit. He had plenty of his own.

He shook a smoke out of a soft pack and lit it with a match, closing his eyes as he inhaled, feeling the burn. He struck another match and set fire to the kid's note, watching it twist and curl like a worm and fall to ash at his feet.

He got into the pickup and drove away.

Then he saw the kid's eyes, looking up at him through his hair and he saw the big cracker gunpointing the boy and he slowed the truck.

He'd burnt the note but the email address was still sharp in his memory. He just couldn't shake it.

"Dumb motherfucker," he said and threw a U-turn and parked outside the library.

Climbed out, slamming the door of the truck like it was to blame.

FORTY-TWO

When Ash awoke he had no recollection that his wife was dead. No recollection that his son was gone.

Then reality struck him in a Muhammad Ali–esque one-two: a blow to his jaw and a blow to the solar plexus.

He gripped the arms of his seat, lest the return of memory blast every atom in his body from the plane and into yawning space.

When he'd calmed himself, he saw that the big man sitting across from him had lowered his iPad.

"You back?" Dapp said.

Ash drank water and looked out the window at nothing and then turned to Dapp.

"Did you know her? My wife?"

"Yes."

"How?"

With a fingernail Dapp tapped out "Shave and a Haircut" on the case of his iPad and then said, "She was my asset."

Ash, who thought he was beyond surprise, gaped. "She worked for the fucking *CIA*?"

Dapp nodded. "Informally. It's common practice. She interfaced with a lot of Chinese businesspeople. It was useful to have insight into this."

"You *recruited* her?"

"I approached her, yes. She was reluctant at first. Then she became more amenable."

"So you coerced her?"

"No. Incentivized."

"Incentivized?"

"Yes. I was in a position to grease wheels. I helped her business."

"Come on, man. You *bought* her."

"It was a mutually beneficial arrangement."

Ash shook his head. "Jesus. And you think you know somebody."

Dapp scratched at his stubble. "China is a fucking tire fire. Chaotic and bewildering for a foreigner. I helped orient her. In return, she gave me some soft intel."

"You got her killed."

"No, she did that all on her own." Dapp held up a big hand. "I'm sorry. That was uncalled for. It's a matter of context."

"Then fucking *contextualize* it for me."

"Okay. Victor Fabian is a vulture capitalist of sorts. He targets trouble spots—Africa, Asia, Central America, Eastern Europe— and moves in on them. Where there's warfare and disaster and debt and deprivation, there are also serious business opportunities. And he's always had the backing, both tacit and active, of members of the Beltway elite. He's made a lot of greedy people very rich."

"Where does Jane fit into this?"

"A few years ago, Fabian shifted his gaze to China. Realized there was a mountain of cash to be made. He'd had some reversals of fortune. The Arab Spring had taken him by surprise. He'd backed the wrong horse in the Ukraine. China was virgin territory for him. He went in with the blessing of the presidency," Dapp scraped his unshaven jaw with a meaty hand, "and my cocksucker bureau chief was in his pocket."

"Okay. But did Jane know Fabian?" Dapp looked away. "Tell me."

"She was drawn into his orbit in Shanghai. He took her to the big table."

"And in exchange?"

Dapp shrugged. "There were rumors."

"Rumors?"

"Jesus, man, do I have to skywrite it?"

Ash stared at him. "Are you telling me my wife was screwing Victor Fabian?"

Dapp nodded. "Yes." He sighed. "I'm sorry."

"Christ."

"My advice is you write it off as an episode of aberrant behavior. Put it out of your mind."

"That's your advice?"

"For what it's worth."

"It's worth shit."

"Yeah." Dapp tapped his iPad again. "I know." He looked out the window.

Ash saw Jane's eyes as they made love to Mazzy Star's "Fade into You" the night he had proposed to her. Eyes that had never left his.

Ash purged the memory and turned to Dapp, who was reading his tablet again.

"I want to hear," Ash said. Dapp looked up. "I want to hear it all."

Dapp put the iPad on the seat beside him. "Fabian had a shot at a huge deal. Some massive construction project. A deal that would make him and his cronies tick-fat with money. Believe me, the White House had a major hard-on for this. But the Beijing Politburo had a quid pro quo."

"What?"

"They wanted the names of all the CIA's Chinese assets."

"Including yours?"

"Yes. Including mine."

"And Fabian gave them up?"

"Oh, yeah. He didn't fucking blink, man. My assets were arrested and executed. Some were public executions, to send a message. I lost twenty-seven people in two days."

"He gave up Jane, too?"

"Yes, he gave her up." Dapp looked at him. "Fabian took care of her himself. Well, he got his people to do it, but I'm pretty sure he was there. And they faked the bridge thing."

"How did she die?"

"This is speculation but from what I've been able to piece together he took her to an island in the Yellow Sea and she fell from a cliff."

"Fell?"

A one-shouldered shrug. "No."

Ash sat a while and took this in. "When you first contacted me, why were you so coy? Why weren't you explicit about Fabian and this CIA thing?"

"If I'd been too explicit, it would've been obvious that I was your source." He sucked his teeth. "I had a new wife. I didn't want her endangered."

"Yet you gave me more than enough to place me and my son in jeopardy?" Dapp said nothing. "Jesus. Did you ever consider the consequences of what you were doing?"

"Not enough. Clearly."

"You *knew* what these people are capable of. What the fuck were you thinking?"

Dapp raised his big hands, palms up. "Create enough chaos and the world will realign. Or it won't."

"That's it?"

"Yeah, that's it."

"Jesus."

Dapp looked haunted. "To be honest, I never expected you to get far enough to endanger yourself. I miscalculated."

"Miscalculated?"

"Yes."

"Fuck."

"I'm sorry." A shrug. "My stupidity also got my wife killed."

"Why did Fabian want her dead?"

"Fabian has a daughter. Late twenties. Lives in London. I was in touch with her. I made certain things known to her, about her father."

"So the killing of your wife was a reprisal?"

"Yes. And a warning."

"Why didn't he kill you too?"

"That would have been too easy on me."

"And Grace Zima? She works for him?"

"Not directly. I think she works for a private outfit funded by the administration. It's in their interests to keep what Fabian did under wraps."

"But he was involved?"

"Damn straight. He would have written the playbook."

"So your plan is to get him? Bring him down?"

"Yes."

"How?"

"Through his daughter. She's come to DC from London. I think I have motivated her."

Ash sat in silence for a minute, then he reached out an arm and said, "Let me check out something on your iPad."

Dapp hesitated then handed the tablet over. Ash googled Victor Fabian. Surprisingly skimpy information. A few blurred pictures taken with dictators and despots. Always the man in the background.

He tried to connect Jane to this creature. Couldn't. Sat thinking of the stranger his dead wife had become. Thinking of how his life had been dragged from its safe little moorings into a charnel house.

How much of what Dapp had told him was true?

He googled recent murders in Silicon Valley. It took a little searching but he read about the death of Yingying Dapp. That, at least, was the truth.

He looked down at the tablet and saw that, without being fully conscious of what he was doing, he'd opened that old Yahoo account and checked his email. A reflex. The rubbing of the frayed hem of a security blanket.

He blinked.

There was a new email.

Ash read the message four times and then he stood, looming over Dapp who was sitting with his eyes closed, massaging his temples.

"Dapp? Dapp!"

The big man looked up, squinting. "Yeah?"

"I've found him," Ash said. "I've found my son."

FORTY-THREE

The closer they got to the killing ground the calmer Orlando Peach became. His pulse rate slowed, his breathing deepened, his skin cooled. The voices in his head were nothing more than a whisper, like the distant wash of a freeway at night.

That morning when he'd woken, the voices had screamed at him. Howled and cursed. Mocked him. Spewed filth and obscenity, gloating in the knowledge that Mama would soon be leaving him forever. Leaving him alone.

The voices had driven him away from his weapons, out into the streets of Baltimore, where a cacophony of cars and horns had failed to drown them. He'd felt he was going to unravel and had rushed back to the hotel room.

Only when Mama had greeted him with the news that they had, again, been called to work, were the voices cowed, like wolves shrinking from a burning torch.

And as Orlando had packed the weapons into the trunk of the car, the grip of the voices was loosened entirely, and he felt the serenity that only the prospect of a day's honest work could give him.

But looking across at Mama as they cleaved through a cornfield made fiery red by the low sun, he felt again the certainty of her imminent departure, and his bubble of calm was pricked by a jolt of pure terror. Slowly, he breathed it away and regained his equilibrium.

"We're near," Mama said, nodding at the GPS suction-mounted to the windshield.

They were driving in an old green Chevrolet, soft on its springs. It was the kind of car that attracted no attention. The car of a retired school teacher. Or a Bible salesman.

Mama reached forward and unmuted the GPS. The electronic commands unsettled him, even though she had programmed it to speak in a female voice not dissimilar to her own.

The GPS told them to take a right onto an unpaved track.

Mama nudged the turn signal and the car was filled with a soft clucking. The Chevy swayed and bounced as the tires left the asphalt and found the dirt. When Mama stopped the car and turned to Orlando, a curtain of amber dust swirled around them.

She put her right hand in his, and it shocked him anew how bony and birdlike she had become.

She touched his face. "I love you, my baby boy," she said in her phlegmy, uncertain voice.

He felt a tightness in his throat. "I love you too, Mama."

She released his hand and clicked the car into gear. It rolled forward, gravel crunching under the tires.

Orlando reached beneath his seat and retrieved the sawed-off Remington and sat with it in his lap.

A chain-link fence appeared, the silver wire slicing the corn-fields into diamonds. When a high gate barred their way, Mama brought the Chevy to a halt and the car seethed and shook.

A thin, dark-haired man approached and looked at them through the gate.

Mama lowered her window and said, "Daltry?" The man nodded. "We are the Peaches."

Daltry unlocked the gate, and it swung open soundlessly.

Mama drove through and Daltry locked the gate after them. He came to Mama's window and leaned down.

"Everybody present?" Mama said.

"All but the cleaner. He's gone into town for provisions," Daltry said. "Coombes, Zima, and the boy are in the house. Should I ride with you?"

Orlando climbed out of the car, the sawed-off held at his side, hidden by the open door.

"Daltry?" he said.

"Yeah?"

"Whyn't you ride shotgun?"

Daltry nodded and came around to the passenger side. Orlando raised the Remington and shot him in the face with both barrels.

He placed the weapon on the hood of the car, grabbed Daltry by his ankles and dragged him into a thicket of scrub.

When he retrieved the shotgun and got back into the car, the suspension barely troubled by his bantam weight, Mama was laughing.

"Oh, Orlando, you are a tonic," she said. "Ride shotgun, indeed."

She put the car into gear and they bounced away, Mama still laughing fit to bust.

FORTY-FOUR

Dapp was on his feet and waiting at the hatchway while the plane was still taxiing. Terror had impaled Ash to his seat.

What if the email was a hoax?

Or worse, a trap?

When he'd voiced his fears to Dapp, the big man had looked at him and said, "It's all we've got."

"But is it enough?"

"It has to be," Dapp said. "Just believe your boy is there. Believe we're gonna get him."

"But what if he's not?"

"Ash, what I don't need right now is doubt. Doubt is like one of those worms in the Amazon that swims up your dick. When it takes hold, you can't get it out. Okay?"

"Okay."

A crew member opened the door allowing a rectangle of orange sunset into the cabin, Dapp a disappearing silhouette.

Ash went after him.

The big man was striding across the apron of the airstrip toward a black car parked near the small terminal building.

Dapp opened the driver's door and took a remote from on top

of the sun visor. He popped the trunk and when Ash arrived he saw guns. A lot of them.

Dapp slammed the trunk and got behind the wheel, revving the engine. Ash had to scramble into his seat as the Charger peeled off across the parking lot toward Baltimore.

FORTY-FIVE

Scooter sat at the table by the window watching for the cleaner. The skinny guy had clattered away in the truck a few hours ago.

Scooter had spotted a black trash bag in the rear of the pickup, so he guessed the man had headed into some town to dump it. And maybe to buy food and drinks and stuff.

Was the note Scooter gave him torn up and tossed in the garbage in that bag? In amongst the squashed eggs and soggy toast and chunks of sausage?

Scooter tried to keep himself calm, but he felt his throat choking. He went to the door and turned the knob, even though he knew he was being dumb.

At lunch time, the woman had brought him a plate with a wrinkled apple, a slice of dry bread and a can of Coke. The plate stood untouched on the table. When she'd left, she'd locked the door.

Scooter heard the sound of an engine and he ran back to the window.

Not the truck. An old green car came into view, trailing dust. It stopped near the kitchen door.

The big blond asswipe walked out, pointing a pistol. Holding it with two hands like he was in some action movie. He said something that Scooter couldn't hear.

The passenger door opened and a golden-haired boy not much older than Scooter stood up and smiled and waved. Scooter couldn't see the driver.

The big man lowered the pistol and went over to the car. He walked like he had boils in his armpits.

The boy lifted a gun and shot the blond man. It was a machine gun. Scooter heard a loud chatter. The bullets spun the man and he fell to the dirt.

Scooter saw the woman who'd been Holly come out of the side of the house, shooting her gun. One of the side windows of the car shattered.

The driver of the car must've fired a weapon too because the woman dropped facedown in the dirt, and then started trying to drag herself back to the house.

The boy followed her and stood over her. He put the machine gun to her head and pulled the trigger.

Scooter shut his eyes.

When he opened them he saw the boy looking up at him. The boy smiled and waved the gun and walked into the kitchen, disappearing from view.

Scooter lunged for the window and tried to lift it.

It's nailed shut, numb-nuts.

He heard footsteps on the stairs.

Scooter grabbed the chair and swung it at the window. The glass cracked but it didn't break.

A hand rattled the door handle and a voice said, "Hey, Scoot, buddy, how ya doin?"

Scooter swung the chair again, and the window cracked a little more.

The weapon chattered and bullets flew through the door into the room.

Scooter's mom was in his head, shouting something.

He swung the chair with all his strength and the glass burst out in a rain of shards. Not caring if he cut himself he jumped through the window, landing on the sloping roof. He slid until he came to the edge and nearly fell, grabbing the gutter, legs dangling.

He looked up and saw the light-haired boy at the window raising the machine gun.

Scooter let go and fell to the ground. Winded, he got up, and his knee hurt as he tried to run. Arms grabbed him and he fought, pedaling his legs, lashing out, but he was overpowered and smothered.

FORTY-SIX

Ash stood beside the Charger watching John Dapp, who leaned on the roof of the car, staring down at the farmhouse through a nightscope. They were parked on a rise that offered a view of the house that, ominously, was in darkness. Gibbous clouds hurtled past a moon as big as a dinner plate. A cold wind blew up from the valley but Ash was sweating.

"See anything?" Ash said.

Dapp didn't reply, scanning the terrain. When he was done, he laid the scope on the roof and put his hands in the pockets of his windbreaker.

"There are two bodies lying outside the house." He shrugged. "I can't be certain, but they both look like adults."

"Fuck. Let's get down there." Ash ducked into the car.

Dapp slipped the scope into his windbreaker and opened the trunk of the car and lifted out an assault rifle.

"We're going on foot," he said.

Dapp was walking away through the scrub, stones rattling as he descended the slope.

They came to a fence, silver in the moonlight. Dapp stopped and raised a hand. Then he walked toward the gate that stood open. As they neared the gate he stopped again and crouched, motioning for Ash to join him.

He took the scope from his pocket and stared through it.

Lowering it, he put his mouth close to Ash's ear. "Another body. A man's." Dapp pointed. "I want you to go through the gate first. Do it at a run and take cover in the scrub."

Ash stared at him. Dapp had taken up a kneeling position, weapon raised.

"Go."

Ash felt a spike of paralyzing terror, then he thought of his son and he ran. Heart smashing at his rib cage, he hurtled through the gate, expecting a hail of fire. But when he dived into the bush, there was only the sound of his own ragged breathing.

Shoes on gravel and Dapp was beside him. "Okay, my instinct is that whatever happened here is over. But, we watch our asses."

He stayed off the road, and Ash followed him through the corn toward the house.

They came to an empty barn. Dapp sheltered behind a wall and scanned the farmhouse with the scope. He stood and walked forward, the rifle extended. Ash shadowed him.

They came to the first body. Dapp knelt and took a flashlight from his pocket, shining it at the man's face long enough for Ash to see a stranger with matted blood in his blond hair.

"Know him?"

"No."

They moved across to the second body, lying prone near an open doorway. A smaller shape, and Ash felt sick dread. Dapp clicked on the beam, revealing a woman's gray hair scraped back into a bun.

Dapp grabbed hold of the hair and lifted the woman's face, most of the left side shot away.

Ash turned his head.

"This her? This Zima?"

Ash nodded, bile in his throat.

Dapp stood and went into the house, rifle ready. They were in a kitchen. The low hum of a refrigerator and the drip of a tap. Broken glass under their feet.

Dapp handed Ash the flashlight. "Walk."

Ash walked, Dapp at his shoulder.

A living room. Sofa. Two chairs. A coffee table and a TV set. Three mugs on the table. Across the corridor a foul-smelling toilet with a trickling cistern.

Dapp motioned to the stairs and Ash climbed, hearing the boards creak.

A bathroom. Two bedrooms. The first with twin beds and male paraphernalia littering the room. The odor of sour socks and cheap deodorant.

Another room across the corridor. A single bed. Neat. A woman's hairbrush and a couple of Tums lying on the table. Ash superimposed this on the bohemian clutter of Holly Howells's bedroom and understood the magnitude of Grace Zima's deception.

The last room was at the end of the passageway. The door stood open, shredded by gunfire.

Ash had to put a hand to the cold, damp wall.

Dapp took the flashlight from him and went into the room.

Ash was startled by a voice. He realized it was his own. He was mumbling some half-assed prayer.

"Okay," Dapp said, and Ash moved into the doorway.

The big man swiveled the beam of the flashlight. A narrow

bed. A chipped closet. A table by the shattered window. Ash stepped forward and felt something underfoot and leaned down and lifted a red hoodie.

Scooter's.

Dapp called him to the window and shined the torch through onto the sloping roof. A wooden chair, one leg broken loose, lay trapped by the gutter. Dapp brought the beam back to the window frame. Nailed shut.

"He smashed the glass and went out onto the roof," Ash said.

"Looks that way."

"Then where is he?"

Dapp didn't reply. He was out of the room thumping down the stairs.

Ash followed him through the kitchen door. Dapp stood under the roof of the room where Scooter had been held. He played the flashlight over the ground.

The beam showed a footprint etched into the soft sand. A kid's footprint. The sole of a sneaker.

"He jumped," Dapp said.

He walked on, the beam of the flashlight probing the ground.

"A vehicle took off right about here. At speed, wheels spinning." He directed the light at a pool of blood drying on the sand. Moved it a little farther and the beam found a shoe.

A cheap women's pump, scuffed and peeling.

Dapp hunkered down and lifted the shoe. "Doesn't come from Zima. I'm guessing here, but I think this woman was run over. Badly hurt or killed."

"Another woman?"

"Yes," Dapp said.

"And Scooter was in that vehicle?"

"I'd say so."

"And the driver?"

Dapp stood. "Yeah, the driver."

He ran the flashlight over the walls of the house and across to an empty garage. Panned the light then moved it back to a locked door.

Dapp was walking, and Ash hurried to catch up with him. The big man pointed the flashlight through the window next to the door, into a small bedroom.

He stepped back, raised his foot and kicked the door just beside the lock, sending it splintering inward.

Ash watched as the room was revealed by the beam of the flashlight. A bed with sharp edges, military-style. A desk, empty but for a ballpoint pen set at right angles to the corner.

Dapp found a switch and a florescent flickered and cold light washed the room.

The big man opened the single drawer of the desk. Another couple of pens and a Walter Mosley paperback. *A Little Yellow Dog.*

He crossed to the narrow closet. A few pairs of sweatpants and T-shirts folded in a neat stack. Overalls and a pair of gloves.

"The cleaner," Dapp said. "The cleaner lived here."

Dapp squatted and ran the flashlight under the bed. He reached in and pulled out a small trunk, locked with a padlock.

"Bring that," he said to Ash.

Ash lifted the trunk. It wasn't heavy. He followed Dapp out of the room.

"Put it down," Dapp said gesturing with the rifle barrel. Ash dropped the trunk to the ground.

Dapp threw the flashlight to Ash.

"Get back and shine it at the lock."

Ash moved away and held the beam steady. Dapp walked five paces and aimed the rifle and fired twice. The broken lock fell to the dirt.

Dapp held out a hand for the flashlight, then opened the trunk. He removed a big brown envelope. Inside were X-rays and wads of medical test results.

"Lance Corporal Uhuru Bakewell, US Marine Corps. Retired." Dapp said, reading. He flicked through the pages. "Soon to be dead."

He dumped the envelope and dug further and found military discharge papers and a pair of dog tags on a ball chain.

Dapp lifted out two medals and dangled them in the beam of the flashlight.

"A Purple Heart and a Silver Star," he said. "We got us a goddamn war hero here."

He went back into the trunk and found a photograph. A skinny black guy in uniform with his arm around the shoulders of a big white man wearing sergeant's stripes.

"Okay, this is how I read it. Your son somehow gets this guy"—Dapp tapped the face of the smaller man—"the cleaner, Bakewell, to send you that email. He goes into town to do it. Probably has errands to run. Comes back into the middle of a firefight. Takes your boy and gets the fuck out of here."

"And goes where?"

Dapp shrugged. "Wherever an ex-jarhead goes when he's balls deep in the shit."

FORTY-SEVEN

Dave Dolan had to self-surrender day after tomorrow and start a ten-year stretch up in Lewisburg. He'd been busted with a trunk of heroin cut with carfentanil, an elephant tranquilizer. Driven the shit across the state line from Ohio straight into a combined Homeland Security / State Police goatfuck. His third bust since he'd been given an Other-than-Honorable discharge from the Corps two years back. Thrown out on his ass just a few months short of his twentieth anniversary, which meant he'd lost both his pension and his VA benefits.

During sentencing, the judge had sat with his chin propped in his hand and listened to Dolan's attorney detailing the dumpster fire that was the ex-marine's life. The judge had sighed and, acknowledging Dolan's service to his country, given him a month longer out on bond to bring some order to his affairs before he started his time.

But here he sat, two days to go, drinking beer and smoking weed in his trailer, everything as fucked up as it had ever been.

He shared the double-wide with his wife, their six-year-old twin daughters, and his dead brother's retard teenage girlfriend and her infant son. When his brother had OD'd a few months ago, what could Dolan do but take in the girl and her ailing baby?

He uncapped another longneck and stared at the tube and tried not to hear the two women yelling at each other by the stove.

His wife, Belinda, hated the girl, and accused Dolan of screwing her.

Which was untrue.

Well, almost.

There'd been that afternoon not long after Kevin died, when Belinda took the twins to Walmart and Dolan had comforted Danielle. There had been whiskey and oxy and weed and one thing had led to another.

Fuck.

He drank his beer and stared blankly at CNN and wished he were back in Helmand Province eating dust and taking fire. Keeping his boys safe.

Or trying to.

A violent, brutal life, but a life that he'd understood. With rules he could comprehend. He'd been respected. Admired. He'd felt a sense of purpose.

Until he'd fucked it all up.

Back here, he was a nothing. A nobody.

And now he was going away for a decade and he had no fuckin money. Last cash siphoned by legal fees. Belinda was out of work. Danielle had never worked and was mentally deficient, truth be told. And the baby boy, his face a tiny replica of Kevin's, needed some kind of heart surgery, and there just wasn't the dough.

Dolan'd had the genius idea of shifting a lot of product before he surrendered, and leave Belinda set up. But, surprise fuckin surprise, nobody would supply him. Nobody would take his calls. Only person *might've* supplied him he owed a boatload of money to, and Dolan was avoiding him like a dose of the clap.

Fuck, nobody would even have a beer with him down at Jack's Bar. They were all scared shitless he was wearing a wire. That he'd been given the self-surrender in exchange for incriminating others.

That he'd cut some kinda deal.

Christ knows he woulda done it, too, if it had been on the table.

But it had not.

Dolan stood up and left the trailer, left the shouting bitches and walked out into the night. He was a tall man, still lean and sinewy, but his face kinda sunken in and hollow, and his muscles going slack.

He found himself on the main drag of Haynesville, a sad-ass town in southwest Pennsylvania, with its boarded-up storefronts and potholes and piss-yellow street lights. Looming over the town was the dark silhouette of the abandoned steel mill. He remembered when the blast furnaces were torn down in the midnineties. It was the only time he'd seen his father cry.

Dolan was outside the Dollar General when his cell rang. He thought it was Belinda, ready to bust his balls, and he nearly ignored it, then he saw Unknown Number and he hit the green button.

"Yeah?"

"Sarge?"

He stopped on the sidewalk, seriously spooked. He'd just minutes ago thought of Afghanistan, and here was this voice from back then, like he'd done some magic trick.

"Sarge?"

"Yeah, who is this?" Dolan said, even though he knew damn well who it was.

"It's Hoo, Sarge. Uhuru Bakewell."

"Jesus, Hoo, I thought you were dead, man," Dolan said, stepping around a massive woman who was pawing through a rack of ugly dresses outside the dollar store.

A laugh. "Hell, no. Still this side of the grass."

Dolan had a piano tuner's ear for trouble and he wanted to kill the call and keep walking but he said, "Something wrong, Hoo?"

A beat. "Sarge?"

"Yeah?"

"I'm a just a few hours away. Wonderin if I can maybe drive on up and impose on you for some advice?"

What do you say to the man who saved your life—even if you have gone and royally fucked that life up?

"You bet, bud, I'm right here," is what you say.

FORTY-EIGHT

The thrumming of the tiny Mitsubishi's wheels on the road was lulling Scooter to sleep. He forced himself to sit up and wiped his eyes.

"Sleep, boy. I got this," Hoo said, taking his eyes off the interstate for a moment.

That's what he'd told Scooter to call him: Hoo. Like something out of those Dr. Seuss books his mom used to read him when he was little.

Scooter pushed away the memory of his mother and stared through the windshield at the moonlit countryside.

No way was he going to sleep.

Hoo said, "You hungry?" Scooter shook his head. "Thirsty?" He nodded. "Okay, next gas station, I'll stop. Right?" Another nod.

Hoo went quiet, and they drove in silence.

They'd been on the road for about an hour.

After they'd fled the farm in the pickup, the blood from the old woman they'd run down still on the cracked windscreen, Hoo had driven fast and hard, checking his mirrors. After a few miles he'd pulled the truck off the road and hid it behind some trees.

"Come on, boy," he said and started walking across a wheat field.

Scooter fell in beside him, and as they walked, he began to shake. Not because he was cold. 'Cause the fear had finally hit him. His teeth were chattering.

Hoo stopped and crouched and put his hand on his shoulder.

"You scared, right?" Scooter nodded. "So scared you could damn near mess your pants?" Another nod. "Nothin to be ashamed of. I was a marine, me. Over there in them dumbass wars. I got real scared too. Fact, I done it once." Scooter looked at him. "I messed my pants. For real." He squeezed Scooter's shoulder. "So, be scared. Means you're alive. And that's a *good* thing."

They set off again and the shaking slowed as Scooter fell into the rhythm of walking.

"I ask you a question?" Hoo said and Scooter nodded. "You silent by birth or silent by choice?" He squinted down at the boy. "I'm goin with choice. Right?"

Scooter nodded again.

"Okay, that's cool. Too much damn noise in this world. But anytime you wanna talk, I'm here, okay?"

They walked on through the field, the only sound the wheat whispering in a slowly stirring breeze and an orchestra of night creatures tuning up. After maybe ten minutes, a clapboard house rose square from its neatly tended yard.

The lower floor was in darkness. One light burned in the upper floor, behind a drawn blind.

Hoo hunkered down in a clump of bushes and Scooter joined him.

He pointed. "See that?"

The little red car, shiny as an M&M, was parked under a carport beside the house, lit by a strip light.

"That there is an old lady car. No other car in sight, so my guess is she lives here alone." Hoo's finger moved to the upper window. "And old ladies, they go to sleep real early."

He was right. Within minutes the bedroom light went out.

"Now, you wait here, boy," Hoo said and disappeared into the shadows.

It took a moment for Scooter to see him near the carport and then the strip light flickered and died. A dog barked far away and, for a fearful moment Scooter imagined the beast, a big, muscled thing, coming at him out of the dark.

But all he heard was a low whistle and he saw that the car was rolling silently away from the house.

Scooter ran to the car. Hoo was pushing it, steering through the open door.

"Get in," he said and slipped behind the wheel, stopping the car.

Scooter got in the passenger side and closed the door softly. Hoo pulled some wires free from under the steering wheel and did something with them and the Mitsubishi started and they drove to the road without headlights.

"What I'm doin is wrong, okay?" Hoo said. "It is not cool to do this. I'm only doin it because this is a life-or-death situation, you gettin me?"

Scooter nodded.

"I don't hold with no stealin."

The boy nodded again.

"Okay, then." They were on the road, heading into the night, and Hoo switched on the lights. "This bein an old lady's car, I'm pretty sure she won't see it's gone till mornin. By which time, we'll be far away."

Hoo took them onto the interstate and for a while he was tense, checking the rearview. Then he relaxed a little.

"You're probably wonderin where we goin?" Scooter looked at him. "Maybe think I should be in touch again with your daddy?" Scooter nodded. "I sent that email and look what happened. I'm thinkin that secret email address ain't so secret no more."

Lights came up behind them and Hoo sat up straighter, watching his mirrors. A muscle car growled by, and Scooter heard a snatch of rock music, and then the car was gone.

"So," Hoo said, "we gonna go pay a visit to an old army buddy of mine. Best man I ever known. He's up in Pennsylvania, just a few hours away. He's a smart guy. He'll have thoughts on how to deal with our predicament. And he's more your complexion. Case you haven't noticed, you and me, well, let's say nobody gonna accuse us of bein family."

He laughed, and Scooter smiled for the first time in a long while.

FORTY-NINE

John Dapp sat in a window booth of a Taco Bell off I-95, washing down his steak Doubledilla and chips and salsa with a can of Mountain Dew Kickstart.

He could see the Charger parked outside in the dark, the eatery's purple bell reflected in the car's windshield. Danny Ash was asleep in the passenger seat. They hadn't gotten two miles from the farm before he'd clocked out. Dapp figured it was some kind of stress-induced narcolepsy.

Dapp pushed his plate to the side and lay the photograph of the two marines on the table. He shot a picture of it with his cell phone, getting the faces as sharp as he could, and emailed it to the obese hacker, along with the information on Lance Corporal Uhuru Bakewell's dog tags.

He stowed the phone and the photo. As he continued eating, he saw Ash leave the car and look around, confused. He rubbed his eyes and scratched an armpit then hurried into the restaurant.

"I was asleep, man," Ash said, sliding into the booth.

"I noticed."

"What are you doing?"

"I'm eating," Dapp said.

"What are you doing about finding my son?"

At that exact moment, by some quirk of synchronicity, images of the farmhouse appeared on the wall-mounted TV behind Ash's head, and Dapp, riding a wave of sleep-deprivation, grief, and some kind of numb terror, had to bite back a laugh.

He waved his half-eaten tortilla at the screen. "Well, there's that."

Ash swiveled in his chair, jiggling his legs. He did that a lot, the jiggling.

Dapp ate and watched the CNN bulletin. Cop cars in the night. A coroner's truck. The news anchor saying that there had been a shooting at a farm in Maryland that was rumored to be a safe house used by Homeland Security.

Dapp had called the cops and CNN simultaneously to alert them to the events at the farmhouse. Then, via his proxy Jimmy Mung, he'd engineered the Homeland rumor. Had Mung lob it into the slavering maw of Twitter, Facebook, et al., and—as these things had a way of doing—it was now finding itself regurgitated by the mainstream media.

The anchorman said, "The farm is believed to be where the ten-year-old son of terror suspect Daniel Ash, also known as Mohammed Ashraf, was being held. More as the story develops."

Ash pulled his cap lower, slumping in his seat, even though he looked nothing like the millennial douche whose face had just appeared on the screen.

The news bulletin moved on to a report of a hostage situation at a Duluth abortion clinic and Ash turned to Dapp.

"No mention of Victor Fabian."

"The nexus between Fabian and these events will evolve."

"*Nexus? Evolve?* Jesus, who even speaks like that?"

Dapp said nothing, staring at Ash as he chewed.

Ash held up a skinny hand. "I'm sorry. I'm freaking out. I'm terrified."

"You would be." Dapp wiped his mouth on a napkin. "Breathe."

"Breathe?"

"Yeah, breathe."

He sipped at his Kickstart. "You were never known as Mohammed Ashraf, were you?"

"No. That was my father. He was born in Yemen. Came here and changed his name to Ash."

"Why did you go there?"

"To Yemen?"

"Yes."

"My father died when I was three. I never met any of his family. Then two years ago, somebody reached out to me on Facebook, saying my father's brother, his only surviving relative, was on his deathbed. That he wanted to see me. So, I went."

"And while you were there, the civil war broke out?"

"Yes."

"And then the plane thing?"

"And then the plane thing."

Ash looked out the window, hoping to end this thread. It wasn't something he spoke about. Ever. He'd shut down Jane whenever she'd tried to talk about it. Dismissing her pleas that he get help. Retreating into himself, becoming ever more distant. And in response she'd started spending a lot more time in China.

"You're not fucking *here*, Danny," she'd said on one of her increasingly infrequent trips home. "So, I might as well be away too."

Away with Victor Fabian.

"So what happened?" Dapp said. "With you and that plane?"

Ash looked at him but said nothing.

"It's okay," Dapp said, "you can tell me to butt out. Just my old spook curiosity."

Ash tapped the tabletop. Jiggled his leg. Then he shrugged.

"I ate some bad food the evening before. Spent the night puking. Didn't sleep. I took some medication at Sanaa airport that poleaxed me and I passed out in the departure lounge. Missed the plane. Only woke up after ..."

"After the bomb?"

"Yes."

"Jesus."

"What do they say about the worse luck your bad luck saved you from?" Ash said.

"Fucking A." Dapp went to work with a toothpick. "Nobody ever claimed responsibility for downing that plane, right?"

"Right."

"As I recall, speculation at the time was that the target was some Shia Imam?"

"Ali bin Al-Huthi," Ash said. "He was flying to an Islamic conference in Kuala Lumpur. He was traveling with his son, Hussein."

Dapp narrowed his eyes. "Let me guess. You spent time studying the passenger manifest?"

Ash nodded. "I did. Obsessively." He stared at a spot above Dapp's head. "The captain was Bader Hamed. The first officer was Abdullah Karman. The senior flight attendant was Fatima Basha. The oldest person on board was Naseem Lahum, eighty-nine, and the youngest Isra Hirsi, three months. I can still name a dozen or so of the other passengers."

Dapp sucked his teeth then said, "Luck's not a fucking zero-sum game, Danny."

"Meaning?"

"You got lucky. Doesn't mean you deprived somebody else of theirs. Luck's random. There's no greater order to things, man."

"I know. But …"

"But it's still quite the thing to live with?"

"Yes." Ash looked out the window again. "I thought that was it for me. That the one totally wild, reality-warping thing that was ever going to happen to me had happened. That the rest of my life would be happy monotony." He turned back to Dapp. "Then this …"

"Yeah, this," Dapp said.

Ash swiped a hand across the table, picking up nonexistent crumbs. "What's your reading on what went down at that farmhouse?"

"I suspect people close to the presidency outsourced the kidnap of your son to a private crew. Fabian would have been party to that. But something has happened, and I'm not sure what, that has caused Fabian to turn up the heat." He paused.

"Go on," Ash said.

"Okay, you understand that, at most, these are theories not slam-dunks?"

"Yes. Speak."

"Fabian uses a couple of contract killers. A young man and an old woman."

Ash stared at him. "The shoe?"

"Yes. The shoe."

"You know these people?"

"Yes," Dapp said, "I know them. They killed my wife."

"Jesus. And they …?"

"I believe he sent them to kill your son."

"Why?"

"Maybe Fabian figured if your boy was dead, you'd have nothing to lose. You'd become visible. Easy to eliminate."

"Who's to say they didn't take Scooter?"

Dapp shook his head. "Not their modus. They're killers not kidnappers." He drank and burped into his fist. "No, Bakewell's got him."

"Got him where?"

Dapp shrugged. "I'm casting out the net."

Ash wiped the table again. "These killers …"

"Yeah?"

"They're still out there."

"At least one of them, yes. The boy."

"You think he's a danger?"

Dapp shrugged. "As a duo, they were batting a thousand. They got the job done, no matter what. But if the woman's dead or wounded, that has to impact the boy's commitment to complete. It's tough to call." He drained his Kickstart. "Anyway, your son's in another arena."

"You're sure?"

"I am. Yes."

"The waiting is stressing me out."

"We won't be waiting long." Dapp sat forward and laced his fingers. "We're gonna have to take the fight to Victor Fabian."

"So we're going to DC?"

"We're going to DC."

"To see the daughter?"

"Yes, to see the daughter."

FIFTY

Nicola, dressed in gray sweatpants and a white T-shirt, sat on the bed in the spare room of her father's house, her hands on her knees. She stared down at her bare toes flexing on the stippled beige carpet that resembled the pelt of an animal.

Her father had left the clothes for her folded over a chair. They were too small to be his. Who they belonged to was a mystery.

Their conversation in the living room had been cut short by the trill of his cell phone. He'd stood and walked off into the kitchen, where he'd spoken for perhaps two minutes. She could hear none of his words, but the rumble of his voice was freighted with anxiety.

When he returned, he made a great show of bonhomie, but she could see how gimcrack it was and that pleased her. She could suddenly glimpse the old man beneath the satyr's fleshy carapace.

"How about a bite at the Palm?" he said.

She was sure that he was gambling on her refusing and out of spite she almost accepted his invitation, keen to see how he'd deal with being dropped into that shark tank of Washington's power elite in this unusually weakened state.

But exhaustion had won out and she'd demurred, and he'd walked her up to the spare room, where the clothes had awaited her.

No sooner had he wished her sweet dreams and departed than the terror had slipped into the room like fog off the Potomac.

Nicola scratched at her arm and continued scratching until she'd raised a wheal and drawn a thin trickle of blood. She forced herself to stop, literally sitting on her hands. When she could trust herself again, she reached for her phone, which lay on the side table with her McEwan novel and an unopened pack of tampons.

She ran a finger across the face of the iPhone to rouse it and tapped to activate the video camera, holding the phone at arm's length.

Nicola blinked at her image on the screen, cleared her throat and said: "Note to self: Despite my resolution to the contrary, being here with my father has plummeted me into a state of self-perpetuating anxiety. I find myself visualizing the worst thing that could happen to me, but as soon as I'm sure that I have it, I think of something even more fucking terrifying. So, hard as I try, I can't seem to top out on just what that worst thing would be."

FIFTY-ONE

A gas station, like a lightship in the night, swam out of the darkness. Uhuru nudged the turn signal and left the interstate. The pumps were deserted, and there was one old pickup parked outside the convenience store.

He stopped the little moon buggy near the truck and pulled one of the ignition wires free, stilling the engine.

"Best I go in there alone, okay?" he said. Scooter nodded. "You need the john?" Another nod. "Wait till I get back. Yeah?" A twitch of the kid's head.

Uhuru left the car and walked into the store, blinking at the bright light.

The only other customer was a chunky white guy in overalls, down by the fridges. He gave Uhuru that special look that crackers reserved for him, kinda narrow and suspicious.

Uhuru grabbed a basket and dumped in chips and candy bars.

The white dude carried a six pack of beer across to the counter where a young Latino with a complicated hairdo watched MTV on the wall-mounted TV.

Uhuru crossed to the fridge and put a few cans of Coke and a bottle of water into the basket.

The white guy took his beer and went out, stopping at the ATM that stood by the entrance.

Uhuru walked over to the cashier. As he placed his basket on the counter a state trooper's patrol car drove up and came to a halt beside the Mitsubishi.

The Latino was taking his time, scanning each barcode more than once until he got a reading, Uhuru counting every beep.

The trooper stood up out of the vehicle, wearing his striped pants and Smokey the Bear hat.

***

Scooter saw the cop car in the Mitsubishi's side mirror and he slid down low in his seat. The cop, who resembled the one who'd hassled him and his father that day on the mountain, left the cruiser and walked toward the store.

As he passed the front of the Mitsubishi, he stopped and stared at the car. He turned and came closer, unclipping a flashlight from his belt.

Scooter wormed his way between the seats into the back, crouching on the floor just as the beam raked the front of the car.

Scooter waited for the beam to find him, but he heard the cop say, "Sir, you see the driver of this car?"

From where he was huddled Scooter glimpsed a man in overalls getting into the pickup parked near the Mitsubishi.

"There's a nigger inside. Might be his," the man said, slamming the door.

The truck rattled to life, reversed, and drove away.

***

The cop stood looking toward the store.

Uhuru stepped away from the counter. The scanner was still beeping. He moved fast, pushing through a door that said Staff Only. Walked past a couple of lockers and a storeroom and came to another door. Bolted. Worked the bolt loose and opened the door onto the night and the stench of trash.

Uhuru sprinted past a dumpster full of garbage toward a broken fence and bush and trees beyond.

He heard a noise and turned and saw it was the boy, falling in beside him. They made the trees and stopped running. The kid went behind a Virginia pine and Uhuru heard a drizzle of piss.

When the boy was done they walked for a half hour across some kind of pasture. They found a farmhouse where Uhuru stole a beat-up Ford truck. This time he took the old highway heading north toward the state line, the small towns strung on it like charms on a bracelet, left for dead by the interstate.

FIFTY-TWO

Orlando Peach sat behind the wheel of the Chevrolet at the drive-in, his mother at his side. Her shattered head rested against the passenger window, her thin hair matted with blood.

As he stared at the blank, shredded screen, a lone tear welled up in Orlando's right eye and trickled down his cheek. He captured it on his forefinger and brought it to his mouth, the salinity sharp to his tongue.

He sat for a few more seconds and then he turned to his mother. "It's time, Mama. It's time."

Orlando clicked on the headlights, the beams falling on canted rows of rusted speaker poles. He opened the car door and stepped out, standing for a moment with his hand on the roof, trying to still the voices that possessed him again, their buzz saw screech almost deafening.

Orlando shook his head, as if that would quiet the voices, and walked around to the passenger side. He cracked the door, reaching inside to stop his mother from tumbling out.

Very gently he lifted her and carried her away from the car, their shadows flung far by the headlights. He set her down on the cratered asphalt and brushed her hair from her ruined face and straightened her clothes, pulling down the hem of her dress. When he reached her feet, he paused. One of her shoes was missing, her naked sole callused and bloodstained, toenails long and yellow.

He pondered a moment, then removed the other shoe and placed it beside her.

Orlando stood and went to the rear of the car and opened the trunk, lifting out a jerry can. He returned to his mother and stood over her, unscrewing the cap. He doused her in gasoline. Then he walked backward, emptying the can, leaving a glistening trail on the blacktop that reflected a slice of the moon and the scudding clouds.

He took a book of matches from his pocket and struck three together, their red sulfur heads melting into one, and dropped them into the gasoline. The blue flame rushed toward his mother, and her body ignited with a suck of oxygen.

Orlando stared as the fire consumed her, and then he returned to the car and drove away.

He watched the flames in his rearview until he went over a rise and he could no longer see them.

FIFTY-THREE

The bawling of the sick baby woke Dave Dolan. He'd fallen asleep in his chair in front of the TV, and now weak gray light leaked in through the window of the trailer. His mouth was dry and he felt like shit and his head ached. A cocktail of whiskey, weed, and blues had finally knocked him senseless around 3:00 a.m.

CNN was still muttering and mumbling. He muted the TV and stood, suddenly chilled in his undershirt and sweats. His skin was a mess of tattoos: a skull atop an hourglass on his right forearm, an eagle on his shoulder, "Death before Dishonor" in fancy script on his left forearm.

The infant lay crying in its little crib by the sofa where Danielle was passed out, mouth open, drool trickling down her pimply chin. Dolan raised his bare foot and prodded her ribs with his toes. Her head lolled but her eyes didn't even flicker.

At the sink he looked for a bottle and baby formula but found only dirty dishes.

Belinda and the twins were in the bedroom, door closed. But the noise would wake his wife, and she'd be out soon, snarling and hating, her words like blows to his body.

Just one more day, he thought. One more day and I'm gone.

Maybe it'll be a fuckin relief.

Then he looked at the little baby version of his dead brother and thought of his sleeping girls and didn't know how they were going to make it while he was away. Jesus, they'd be sixteen when he was released. Wouldn't even know him. His bitch wife already told him there was no fuckin way she would be bringing them up to Lewisburg to visit.

He grabbed a jacket and pulled on his work boots without socks, laces untied, and went out into the morning. Walked around the trailer out of sight of his neighbors, miserable deadbeats to a man, and drilled a stream of piss into the mud, splashing his boots.

Done, he lit a Lucky and stood and smoked and tried to think of nothing at all.

His phone rang and without looking he knew who it was. Fuck. As if he didn't have enough worries.

He answered. "Yeah?"

"Sarge," Uhuru Bakewell said.

"You here?"

"Yeah."

"Where you at?"

"Some kind of iron bridge over a river."

"I know it. What you drivin?"

"Old Ford F-150. Used to be blue, I reckon."

"Wait there, okay?"

Dolan patted his jacket for his keys and walked round to where his '71 Olds 442 was parked. Like most things in his life, the muscle car had gone to hell. Rusted and faded, soft top ripped and peeling. He'd bought it ten years ago, on leave, splurging his reenlistment bonus. Belinda had thought he was hot shit back then and had blown him zealously while he'd sped them to nowhere and back listening to Iggy Pop.

Belinda came out onto the step of the double-wide and started shouting. Dolan fired up the 442, the V-8 and shot mufflers drowning out even her, and took off in a spray of mud.

He drove through the dying town. The sad, sagging houses. The boarded-up buildings. This shithole and the deserts of the Middle East had been the backdrops to his life. Only time he'd seen the ocean was from inside a transport plane.

He left Haynesville behind and came to the old truss bridge that spanned the stagnant river, the steel catching the brown sunlight that broke through a layer of cloud. He'd heard that the town council wanted to sell it for scrap and reroute the road.

It took Dolan a moment to spot the Ford, parked off the bridge in the shade of a stand of white oaks. He coasted the 442 to a halt and cut the engine.

The door of the truck opened and Uhuru Bakewell stepped down. Never a big man, he looked even smaller than Dolan remembered.

Dolan found a smile and walked forward, embracing his one-time comrade.

"Hoo, you bastard."

"Sarge."

"You look like shit."

"Yeah, what can you do?"

The passenger door of the Ford creaked and gravel crunched as a kid climbed out. The boy took a step forward into the sun.

Dolan knew he'd seen the boy's face and flashed back to

the torrent of news he'd ingested along with the alcohol and chemicals through the night.

He felt the same sick fear that he'd felt going into battle and turned to Bakewell and said, "Fuck, man, tell me this isn't who I think it is."

FIFTY-FOUR

Ash sat on the bed of the motel in Northwest DC. He knew if he lay down, he would fall asleep, would retreat again into the oblivion of unconsciousness. Would then have to fight his way back to reality and reassemble himself like a broken mosaic.

John Dapp lay on the other bed, staring at the news on TV. Another school shooting.

Ash stood. "I'm going to get ice."

"There's ice in the fridge," Dapp said.

"I need a lot. I want to soak my feet." Dapp stared at him blankly. "It's just a thing I do in the morning." Dapp shook his head and switched from CNN to NBC.

Ash left the room and walked down the stairs to the graffiti-besmirched pay phone that stood between the ice machine and a broken Coke dispenser.

His first prayer, to hear a dial tone, was answered.

He found change in his pocket and fed the phone, then dialed a number from memory. His second prayer was that he'd got the number right. For an atheist he was praying a lot lately.

The phone rang a long time. While he waited, Ash read from the wall that Muhammad eats dick and that black lives don't matter.

At last a voice said, "Steve Root."

Ash said, "It's me."

A sharp inhalation. "Where are you?"

"Have you heard anything about my son?"

"Just garbled stuff. About some farm in Maryland."

"He was held there. He got away. I don't know how. And I don't know where he is now. Do you know somebody called Victor Fabian?"

"Vaguely. Some vulture capitalist. Why?"

"My wife was working for the CIA in China. Victor Fabian sold her—and a whole crew of CIA assets—out in exchange for a business deal with the Chinese government."

"Whoa, hold on now."

"No time. Fabian had her killed. He's done what he's done to me and my son as part of a cover-up. The administration is connected. Check out a front company called Executive Protection Services. Got that?"

"Wait—"

"And I also need you to check out somebody called John Dapp. D-a-p-p. Claims to be ex-CIA. Last based in China. Says Fabian murdered his wife in California yesterday. I need to know all you can find out about him."

"Listen—"

"I have to go."

"Wait."

"I'll call you later."

Ash hung up the phone and was halfway up the stairs when he realized he was empty-handed. He went back down and filled a bucket with ice.

When he returned to the room Dapp was still on the bed, staring at the screen. Crying parents and children. Emergency vehicles.

Ash went into the bathroom and emptied the ice into the bathtub. He sat on the edge of the tub and removed his shoes and socks.

Dapp entered and without embarrassment unzipped and drilled a stream of piss into the toilet bowl.

Ash shoved his feet into the ice and bit down on a yell.

"You wax too?" Dapp said.

FIFTY-FIVE

Victor Fabian sat behind the walnut desk in his office watching as Dr. Banks took the chair facing him and folded his legs, fussily arranging the crease of his suit pants. He was sallow and bald, with a ludicrous comb-over.

Banks cleared his throat and stretched his neck like a turtle. "I have reviewed the results of the tests we did last month and, in combination with your anecdotal reports, I believe I have diagnosed your condition."

"I have a *condition*?"

"Yes."

"And does this condition have a name?"

"No. This is largely uncharted territory."

"I see. What can I expect?"

"It presents as a major neurocognitive disorder. In some cases, the process is gradual. In others, it manifests almost overnight, especially if there is an incident of significant stress to trigger it."

"Stress is my lifeblood."

"Be vigilant, Mr. Fabian. Monitor yourself." Banks uncrossed his legs and smoothed the creases of his pants. "What do you know of your ancestry?"

"Nothing."

"Nothing?"

"Is this relevant?"

"It could be. Our genetic material is our crucible, after all."

Fabian looked away and ran a hand through his thick hair. "I was bought from an orphanage in Antwerp when I was still mewling and puking and smuggled into America." He turned to Banks. "Since the monsters who procured me were not my blood, I will say no more of them."

"Understood."

"This degeneration … it's inevitable?"

"Yes."

"An inevitable descent into dementia? Madness?"

"Let's say you will experience increased decompensation."

"And there's no treatment?"

"Palliative only."

"So no miracle drug? No incisive laser?"

"No."

"Well."

"You're free to solicit other opinions."

Fabian shook his head and clipped and lit a cigar. The match trembled only slightly. Soon he was shrouded in a veil of smoke.

"Leave me," he said.

Banks nodded and withdrew.

Fabian smoked a while then left the cigar in an ashtray and walked through to his bedroom and sat on the bed, hearing the springs moan. He opened the bedside drawer, revealing the Ruger within.

He looked at the pistol and thought about his life. Thought about how he had left marks behind him like a snail.

He closed the drawer.

FIFTY-SIX

Why'd grown-ups think that just 'cause you didn't speak you couldn't hear?

Ever since he'd taken his vow of silence, Scooter had noticed it. His father sometimes did it, and almost all the adults he came into contact with were guilty of forgetting he was listening. Holly, when she'd still been Holly. When she hadn't been dead. Even Hoo and this guy Sarge.

Talking in front of him like he wasn't right there with them in this scuzzy hut in the woods, roof falling in, walls peeling, windows broken. Sarge saying it was his brother's place, that he was away.

There was no electricity, and when Scooter'd gone to take a pee, he'd almost spewed. The toilet was backed up and reeking.

But he'd found a phone in the john, lying under a porno magazine. An ancient Motorola. Scooter had stuck it in his pocket. Didn't even know yet if it was charged.

Earlier, Hoo and Sarge had hidden the truck behind some trees by the bridge, and Sarge had driven them over here in his old car, Scooter scrunching down in the little back seat.

Even though he knew better—his pop drove a Nissan Leaf—Scooter found the car kinda cool. Skanky and noisy.

But cool.

And these men—these *guys*—they were as different as he could imagine from his father.

It wasn't just that his pop was kinda small. Hoo was even smaller, but he looked real hard. And he had taken charge. Saved Scooter's life.

Now Hoo and Sarge sat in this filthy place, drinking beer, smoking, talking like Scooter wasn't right there, lying on the stinking sofa, its innards spilling out like beer froth.

"What were you thinkin, Hoo? Takin this kid?" Sarge said.

"They were gonna kill his ass, Sarge. What the fuck could I do?"

"Shit, you already got your fuckin medal, man. And you ain't gonna get no medal for this. You'll get a fuckin bullet and a shallow grave." Sarge shook his head. "You're the bravest son of a bitch I ever met, Hoo."

"Sarge."

"No, this has to be said. You saved my ass. And the others."

"I just done what any of us woulda done."

"Bullshit, you're a genuine fuckin American hero. But that doesn't mean you ain't dumb as a goddam rock."

"Word."

They laughed and opened more beer.

"So, what's your plan?" Sarge said.

"I figured it's time to go to the media."

"The *media*?"

"Yeah. Like the *Washington Post*. Or the *New York Times*. Maybe CNN."

"Oh, you just gonna walk in there? Say, hey, I got you guys a scoop? Gonna win you a fuckin Pulitzer?"

"No, I was thinkin you would."

"*Me*?"

"Look, Sarge, let's not fool each other now. Brother like me goes anywhere with that white kid, only one way things gonna end: in a fuckin hashtag."

"Or a toe tag."

"Church."

"Yeah, but *me*?" Sarge said.

"Decorated marine vet? Sure."

Sarge got real quiet and tore the label off of his beer bottle. "I was discharged, Hoo. Other than Honorable."

Hoo stared at him. "Bullshit."

"God's truth."

"What you do?"

"Ah, it's gone, man."

"No, I need to hear."

Sarge drank and wiped his mouth with the back of his hand. "You know those Afghani militia fuckers and their thing for little boys?"

"*Bacha bazi*. Boy play. Scumbags."

"Afghani woman comes to me. Desperate. Says some commander's got her nine-year-old kid chained to a bed in his room in the compound. Had him for a week."

"Jesus."

"Woman's all beat up 'cause she tried to free her boy."

"What you do?"

"What could I do, man? I go over there. I see the kid. Christ."

At this point they remembered Scooter and looked his way, and he quickly shut his eyes and pretended to be asleep.

Sarge finished his beer and opened another. "I tell the fucker to let the kid go. He laughs in my face. I put him in the hospital. Damn near killed him. Freed the boy though."

"But your ass got kicked out the Corps?"

"Yeah. They give me a choice: take the OTH or our Afghani *allies* would push for a court martial. I said fuck it and came home."

"Cryin fuckin shame."

"Like I said, Hoo, doin the right thing isn't always the *right* thing." Sarge looked across at Scooter, who was still faking that he was asleep.

"So what *have* you been doin?" Hoo said.

Sarge shook his head. Looked everywhere but at Hoo. "Ah, man. I've done some shit I ain't proud of." He sat quietly for a while then said, "Truth is, Hoo, my brother ain't away."

"Where he at?"

Sarge drank and stared at nothing, then he looked at Hoo and said, "He's dead, Hoo. OD'd three months back. Fuckin heroin. Died right there, man." Sarge pointed toward where Scooter lay. "Right there on that fuckin sofa."

Scooter levitated like he'd been cattle-prodded, and what could the two men do but laugh?

"Guess you ain't sleepin now, huh, kid?" Hoo said.

The laughter dried up and Scooter went to the window and looked out at the gloomy forest. The men sat in silence for a while. Smoking. Drinking.

After what seemed like forever, Hoo said, "I'm sorry, Sarge."

"Ah, it was a fuckin wake-up call, man. I'd been dealin some of that shit myself. After Kev died, I said no more. No more of that shit."

"Good for you."

"Yeah."

Sarge chugged back his beer and stood.

"Look, let me give all this some thought, okay? I wanna help you, man. I wanna help you."

"Thanks, Sarge."

"I'll be back later with some supplies." They walked to the door. "You packin, Hoo?"

"Nope." He looked at Sarge. "Should I be?"

"Nah, it's cool, nobody comes up here. Just listen for my car, okay?"

"Can't miss that."

"Beautiful, huh?"

"If you're a damn cracker." They laughed and Sarge left, and Hoo locked the door.

By the time Hoo came and stood by the window beside Scooter and watched Sarge get into the rusted old car and drive away, he wasn't laughing anymore.

FIFTY-SEVEN

Nicola Fabian had a sore toe. She'd left her father's house that morning on the pretext of buying new clothes—perfectly believable given that her baggage was still missing in action. Fabian had been huddled in his office with the Uriah Heepish Ricky Pickford and had seemed distracted and not at all sorry to see her go.

The fear that had plagued her the night before still lingered, and it was a relief to escape the house, even though her mission brought with it its own set of anxieties.

John Dapp—who was steering her toward some very hush-hush assignation—was of the belief that her father was having her watched, so Nicola went down to the K Street area and trawled the boutiques. She bought jeans and tops and a quite fetching pair of high-top espadrille boots. On a whim, she decided to wear them out of the store.

She was punished for this gauche behavior when the right boot began to chafe, leaving her small toe throbbing.

As she shopped, she wore the earpiece of her iPhone, and fielded a series of calls from Dapp.

He issued curt commands. "Turn onto L Street. Walk for ten

seconds then do a one-eighty and head back the way you came."

A minute later: "Go into Nordstrom. Look around and come back out almost immediately."

Then he ordered her to get on a bus, a great, stinking, panting thing that carried her out into those endless, faceless American suburbs that scared her on some primal level.

After fifteen minutes, he'd called her and told her to leave the bus, and as she made her way onto the sidewalk, trying not to limp, her phone rang again.

"Black Dodge Charger at six o' clock," Dapp said. "Get in the back."

She looked around, panicking, for her knowledge of American cars was nonexistent, and she suddenly went blank trying to conjure a clock face. But the Dodge was impossible to miss, low and feral, as if it had driven out of a video game, growling up beside her like it wanted to bite a chunk out of her arse.

She opened the back door and was still sliding in when the car accelerated. Was it possible for a car's engine to have an American accent?

Well, this one did.

The driver was big with a cop's blunt haircut. The passenger was slight, wearing a plaid shirt and a mesh trucker cap. His black hair screamed dye job.

She caught the driver's eye in the mirror. "You're John Dapp?"

"I am."

"And who's he?" She nodded at the passenger.

"His name's Danny Ash. Mean anything to you?"

"No. Should it?"

"Only if you watch the fucking news."

Nicola blinked and shook her head. "I've been on planes."

Dapp maneuvered through the traffic, driving carefully, keeping to the speed limit, checking his mirrors.

"Okay," he said, "let's present our credentials. I'm an ex-CIA case officer. Last post Shanghai. Your father caused the death of twenty-seven of my assets. You know what assets are?"

"I've read le Carré," Nicola said.

"Bitchin." He switched lanes, then found her eyes again in the rearview. "And two days ago your daddy sent hired killers to murder my wife in California. They succeeded."

She stared at him in the mirror and felt her mouth moving but words wouldn't come.

At last she said, "God."

Danny Ash turned in his seat and looked at her. "My wife was one of Dapp's so-called assets." His hipsterish drawl was at odds with the redneck shirt and cap. "And when I tried to initiate an investigation into her death, your father kidnapped my son and had me branded a jihadist. So, now I'm a fugitive."

Ash was staring at her with his tragic eyes, and she felt John Dapp's gaze in the mirror.

"Well, bloody hell," she said, "I'm not going to apologize for the old bastard. After all, he did have my mother killed fifteen years ago."

"Okay," Dapp said, "so we're all motivated to bring Victor Fabian down."

"My priority is my son," Ash said.

"One and the same thing," Dapp said, as he turned into the parking lot of a Dairy Queen.

"Where are we going?" Ash said.

"To get ice cream."

Dapp pulled up beside a billboard-sized menu and an

intercom mounted on a pole. When the intercom squawked he ordered a large Blizzard and a Kickstart. He looked at Ash and then at Nicola in the mirror. "What'll you two get?"

Ash said, "I'm good."

Nicola just shook her head. Dapp shrugged and drove to the cashier's window and collected his order, paid, and steered the car across the lot. He parked facing the street and killed the engine.

Dapp opened the bag and revealed what looked like a freshly laid turd.

"Dear God, what *is* that?" Nicola asked.

"Oreo cookies, soft serve with a fudge center. Only thing I missed in Shanghai."

Nicola said nothing, staring out the window at the drabness while Dapp tucked in. He was a noisy eater.

With his mouth full, Dapp said, "Okay, we need to deconflict a few things about who is doing what."

"Do you always talk this way?" Nicola asked.

"He does," Ash said. "He's like an outtake from *Men in Black*." She laughed. Dapp didn't.

"Okay, then," she said, "why don't you go ahead and mansplain?"

Danny Ash's turn to laugh. Dapp, again, was unmoved. There was something about his implacability, not to mention his reassuring bulk, that she found curiously comforting. Attractive even, God forbid.

He wiped away a mustache of vanilla ice cream and said, "You're your father's Achilles' heel. Because of his feelings for you."

"I'm not so sure of that."

"Sure of what?"

"That he really cares about me. I sometimes feel like a prop that he moves around for his own amusement."

"Even truly evil people want something good to hang on to. To prove to themselves that they're human."

"And I'm that something good?"

"Yeah, like Hitler's dog," Dapp said.

"Hitler's dog?"

"Blondi," Ash said.

"Yeah," Dapp said, stuffing his mouth. "He loved that thing. Really loved it. Cried like a baby when it was poisoned in the bunker."

"Didn't he love Eva Braun too?" Nicola asked.

"Nah, that was weird and sexual. The dog thing was pure."

"Okay, so I'm Daddy's German shepherd." She looked at Dapp. "And, what, you're going to poison me?"

"No, Nicola, I'm not going to fucking poison you." Dapp licked fudge off his fingers, his lips making a smacking sound. "I'm going to kidnap you."

FIFTY-EIGHT

As Dave Dolan stepped into his trailer he took a blow to the ribs that felled him. Winded, he lay on the dirty linoleum floor and saw Harley Comfort sitting on the sofa, his arm slung along the back, Belinda and the twins at his side.

Belinda had blood on her mouth and the girls were weeping. Danielle sat on a chair clutching the baby, staring at Dolan through raccoon eyes.

Four of Comfort's goons stood in the cramped living area. One of them held the baseball bat that had dropped Dolan.

Comfort, a compact man dressed in pressed jeans, clean white Nikes, and a Lacoste golf shirt, said, "Dave."

"Harley." Dolan got to his knees and the guy who'd hit him raised the bat but Comfort shook his head.

"Know why I'm here?" Comfort said in his Pennsyltucky slur.

"Yeah, I know why you're here."

"Okay, then, Dave. Make me whole."

"I can't."

"You can't?"

"No. I'm sorry."

"You're sorry?"

"Yeah."

"I don't think so, Dave. I don't think you're sorry. And I done writ the book on *sorry*."

Comfort put his hand on the leg of Jenny, the younger twin by four minutes.

The child flinched and Belinda said, "Get your hand off of her, you cocksucker."

Comfort laughed but didn't remove his hand. "Quite the mouth this bitch has on her, Dave. You need to keep her in line."

"Harley, please, man. We go back a long way," Dolan said.

"Sure we do, Dave. Sure we do. Which is why I expected you to honor a deal. Pay me for the product you done already sold."

"I'm tapped out. I ain't got that kinda cash."

"So, you about to head off to your three hots and a cot and leave me hangin?" Comfort squeezed the child's leg, and she yelped. When Belinda lunged at him, one of the men backhanded her across the face.

Dolan tried to get up, but the man beside him pushed him down with the bat.

"Stay on your knees, Dave. Where you're headin you'll need the practice." Comfort hitched his jeans and sat forward. "Okay, this is how it's gonna go. You get me my ten Gs before you start your stretch. If you don't, I'll be sure and come and pay frequent visits to all these nice little ladies when you're gone. And they'll be *conjugal* visits. Gettin me?"

Dolan nodded. "I'm gettin you."

Comfort stood. "You know where I am, Dave."

He walked out, the double-wide rocking as his men followed. They weren't even out the door when Belinda launched herself at Dolan, nails raking his face, fists pounding him.

"You useless motherfucker! Is there no end to the shit you'll rain down on us?"

Dolan blocked as best he could and bolted from the trailer, making a run for his car. He sped away, heading for the road.

He saw Harley Comfort's old blue Eldorado bouncing slowly toward town, like a waterbed on wheels, and turned the other way.

Dolan drove aimlessly, sniffing, wiping at his nose, which was bleeding from one of his wife's punches.

He found himself up by the abandoned furnace, rusted and overgrown with ragweed and scrub.

He stopped the car and lit a Lucky and stared down at the town. At the cramped rowhouses, the boarded-up buildings, the rutted streets, the abandoned warehouses, the railroad tracks like scars on the landscape.

After a while he flicked away the smoke and reached for his cell. He dialed and waited and said, "Yeah, operator, connect me to Homeland Security. Pittsburgh office."

FIFTY-NINE

"Is it a grief thing?" Ash asked as he watched Dapp demolish a triple Baconator in a Wendy's in downtown DC. "All the food?"

"No," Dapp said, licking ketchup off his fingers.

"Really?"

"Really."

But the little dweeb was right. Dapp had always liked to eat—Shanghai had been heaven for him with its cornucopia of street food—but since the murder of Yingying, his appetite had been insatiable, and it didn't take a shrink to know that this was displaced grief. He gained weight easily, and could already feel the pounds packing themselves on, his gut folding over his belt like a concertina.

Ash jiggled his leg and scratched at his stubble and cleared his throat.

He wasn't eating. He'd ordered a coffee that he'd barely touched, the top already wrinkled and scummy.

"You're really going to kidnap Nicola Fabian?" Ash asked.

"Maybe," Dapp said belching into his fist.

"Think it'll help us find Scooter?"

"Perhaps."

Dapp got busy with a toothpick, and Ash regarded him with distaste.

"Or maybe I should just kill her." Dapp spoke around the toothpick. "What can I say? I'm an 'eye for an eye' kinda guy."

Ash stared at him. "What you are is a self-absorbed asshole."

He pushed out of the booth and headed for the restrooms.

Dapp sat a while and looked out at the traffic and DC's low-rise skyline.

"What we have here," he said to himself, "is a textbook case of fucking mission creep."

His mission was to get Victor Fabian. The kid was just collateral. If he got saved, all fine and dandy. But now that he'd been wrested from Fabian's clutches, his value had diminished exponentially.

Dapp needed to refocus.

One of his phones chirped, and he knew by the ringtone that it was Jimmy Mung.

"Yeah?" he said.

"Hey, Henry. Piece of cake to track down the guy in the photograph. Name's David Dolan. He was Bakewell's platoon sergeant for three years over in Afghanistan. He's retired now and lives in Pennsylvania. Got a pen?"

"Wait," Dapp said and fished a ballpoint from his shirt pocket. He took a paper napkin from the dispenser on the table and flattened it. "Okay."

He wrote down the ex-marine's name and address.

"Later," Mung said and hung up.

Dapp folded the napkin and put it in his jeans pocket.

When Ash returned from the head, Dapp said nothing about the call.

SIXTY

Victor Fabian sat in his office smoking a cigar, using a remote to surf his way through the news channels.

What he saw didn't cheer him.

The debacle at the Maryland farm had taken on the incendiary momentum only possible in these days of the twenty-four-hour news cycle, the fires fed by rumor, innuendo, and gossip gushing in from social media.

It was now taken as gospel that Danny Ash's son had been held at the farmhouse. The three bodies had been linked to Executive Protection Services, which in turn had been revealed to have close links to Fabian—styled by CNN as "a shadowy vulture capitalist who has served as a close advisor to the president"—and a succession of photographs of him were flung onto the screen.

He was unused to this. Good God, he was allergic to it. His was a flower that bloomed in the dark.

When a photograph appeared that showed Fabian lurking in the background as the POTUS gripped the hand of some Asian potentate, he sought momentary respite on Fox News. A toothsome bimbo with dead eyes wished the whole thing away as "yet another desperate attempt by the liberal media to discredit the president."

Pickford appeared in the doorway. Fabian shut down the TV and stood, jaw jutting.

"Something from our man in Homeland," Pickford said. "A fix on the Ash boy."

"It checks out?"

"Yes. It seems he's up in Pennsylvania. An ex-marine comrade of the cleaner's has sold him out for a reward."

"Semper Fi." When Pickford looked at him blankly Fabian said, "Is Homeland on pause?"

"There's a window."

"Then brief the Peaches."

"I think it's singular."

"What?"

"Peach not Peaches. Reports from the farm indicate that the woman may be dead."

"So let the son handle it." Pickford said nothing. "You have a problem with that?"

"It goes to his state of mind, sir. Without the woman, I feel he may lose his compass."

"What choice do we have? We're asking for a ten-year-old child to be murdered. That's not something you can put on Craigslist."

"Point taken, sir."

Fabian began the ritual of pruning and firing a fresh cigar. Pickford hovered.

"There's something else?" Fabian said.

"There has been a back-channel communication from the presidency, sir," Pickford said.

"Yes?"

"They will not intervene on your behalf when the DOJ seeks an indictment."

"That's *when* not *if*?"

"I'm afraid so. The optics aren't good," Pickford said.

Fabian tried to remain calm, igniting his Cuban, but he felt dislocated and absurdly fragile.

"So, they'll just furrow their distinguished Caucasian brows and throw me under the bus?"

"The term lightning rod has been used."

"I prefer sacrificial lamb."

"There is the suggestion that you leave immediately, before the FBI arrests you. That you go to China and wait this out."

"Exile, is it?"

"Yes, sir. For a period of time."

"Do you know your *Lear*, Ricky?"

"As in the jet?"

Fabian laughed smoke. "No, *King Lear*. Shakespeare's greatest tragedy. When the old king is exiled, his daughter is slain by his enemies."

Then all humor left Fabian's eyes. He sighed and looked suddenly ancient. He folded into his chair and tears ran unchecked down his cheeks.

Pickford stared at him in horror. "Sir?"

Fabian sniffed and swatted at his damp face. "I can't risk anything happening to Nicola."

"No, sir."

"I want her with me in China."

"Will she go?"

Fabian wiped a smear of snot onto the back of his hand. "I won't give her a choice."

SIXTY-ONE

In Orlando Peach's hour of need, fate sent him a helpmeet.

He'd crossed into Pennsylvania, en route to Pittsburgh if the road signs were to be believed, when the migraine seized him. The voices had been incessant, maddening, since the night before, allowing him no sleep.

And now the migraine.

After he'd burned Mama, he'd driven the country roads aimlessly, waiting for a message. Waiting for guidance. None came, and darkness gave way to a gray dawn and then uncertain sunlight.

At last the telephone call had come, directing him to the man who had killed Mama. Orlando had struggled to filter the caller's voice through the wall of hisses and screams and wails, but he'd managed to scribble the name of a town in Pennsylvania and map coordinates on a scrap of paper.

The GPS was a mystery to him, and the coordinates may as well have been hieroglyphics. Navigation and planning had always fallen to Mama.

As he drove along the interstate, lights began to pulse behind his eyes and pain seized him at the temples. Mama had tended him when he'd been so afflicted. Settling him down in dark rooms. Placing cool cloths across his forehead. Laying her hands on him.

No pain medication could tame the migraines.

Only Mama's ministrations had made him well again.

He felt bile in his throat and he blinked through sweat, close to fainting, the lines on the road shifting out of register and multiplying.

A sign in mustard colors flowered from the farmland: an exit to a gas station and a convenience store.

Orlando took the exit and battled the car into a parking bay outside the store.

He opened the Chevy door, something requiring enormous effort, leaving him panting. Getting out was almost beyond him, and he clung to the roof and then willed himself on.

The inside of the minimart was mercifully arctic, and Orlando felt slightly restored. The voices were momentarily muted and the redness of the pain faded enough for him to see a grubby girl who may as well've had "runaway" tattooed on her pimply forehead.

She was about sixteen, chubby, dressed in dirty jeans, sneakers, and a denim jacket. A pack hung from her one shoulder. He was close enough to read the button she had pinned to the pack: It's a *Hunger Games* Thing—You Wouldn't Understand.

Too true.

But what he did understand was that she was perfect.

Orlando, feigning interest in a car magazine, watched as she scuttled down the aisle like a cockroach, her black hair a greasy curtain over her eyes.

The girl stopped at a selection of junk food and her eyes skimmed over Orlando to the fossil behind the cash register, who was busy fighting the shakes as he tried to hang up strips of jerky. She shoved two packs of Oreos into the pocket of her jacket and hurried out, her pack bouncing on her back.

Orlando dropped the magazine and followed her outside, feeling a renewal of strength now that he knew what he must do.

"Miss," Orlando said, touching the girl on the arm.

She spun and stared at him in terror. Backing away, she said, "What you want?"

"I believe you took a couple of items from that store without paying."

"What the fuck's it to you?"

Orlando didn't hold with profanity, but he calmed himself and smiled his most radiant smile. "Please, I mean you no harm. I think we may be able to help each other."

She looked at him through narrowed eyes. "Yeah? How?"

"Can you drive?"

"Sure I can *drive*. Why?"

He pointed to the Chevrolet. "That's my car over there. I'm tired and suffering from a migraine. I need someone to drive me to a town near Pittsburgh."

"What's in it for me?"

"Shall we say a hundred dollars?"

"Where's a kid like you get that kind of money?"

"I'm not as young as I look."

She squinted at him. "No, you ain't, are you? You're not some kinda prevert now?"

"No. No, I'm not." He reached for his wallet, found a fifty and held it out to her. "Shall we say half now, half when we arrive at our destination?"

She snatched the money from him and tucked it into her jacket.

"Okay," she said and they walked toward the Chevy. "That thing have a stick shift?"

"No, it's automatic."

"Okay, 'cause I don't do no stick." As they neared the car she said. "And let's be clear on something."

"What?"

"Any other services come extra, okay?"

He shook his aching head and regretted it. "There will be none of that."

She laughed and slid in behind the wheel of the Chevrolet, adjusting the seat to accommodate her short legs. He handed her the key and she started the car, reversed, and took off toward the interstate. Surprisingly she was a careful driver, merging smoothly with the sparse traffic.

"You know how that works?" he said, pointing at the GPS.

"Duh, yeah. Don't you?" She gave him a sidelong glance.

He didn't reply, just read her the coordinates from the scrap of paper and she punched them in.

"You not Amish, are you?" she said. Then she laughed and answered her own question. "No, I guess not. Or we'd be ridin in a fuckin buggy."

Orlando closed his eyes and retreated from the smell of her sweat, from the pain and the voices. Retreated into a safe space, focusing on the work ahead.

The work that was everything.

SIXTY-TWO

Toe throbbing, Nicola climbed the steps to her father's house and knocked at the door. She had not been entrusted with a key. After a few moments, Ricky Pickford opened the door and gave her one of his blank looks.

Carrying her shopping bags, she walked through to the living room, Pickford at her heels like a lapdog.

Her father watched her from his club chair, drinking cognac and smoking a cigar. Posed, as if he were sitting for a portrait.

The room was gloomy, oppressive with the smell of tobacco and men. A clock ticked tiredly. It took her a moment to see the third man, sitting on the sofa, dressed in a black suit. What remained of his hair was combed in dark quills across his waxen skull.

"Nicky-Nicks," her father said, rising, holding out his arms.

Reluctantly she walked into his embrace and caught that curdled tang again.

"Been shopping?" he said.

She set the bags down. "Yes. A little."

"Good." He turned to the man on the sofa. "This is Doctor Banks."

Banks rose and inclined his head. He stayed standing, his hands clasped behind his back.

"Are you ill?" Nicola asked.

"Oh no, nothing like that," Fabian said.

She noticed the tremor in his hand as her father lifted the cigar to his mouth.

He exhaled. "Let's just say I've suffered a slight reversal of fortune." He tried a smile that didn't quite take. "It's temporary, but it requires a strategic withdrawal. I'm flying to back China. Wheels up in an hour."

"This is very sudden."

"Yes."

"What's happened?"

He shrugged. "Darling, sometimes we can see a fragment of the *what* of things, but nothing at all of the *why*."

"You're being very cryptic."

"I apologize. I'll explain everything, I promise. In Shanghai."

"Shanghai?" she said. "But I—"

The rest of her question was choked when, astonishingly, Pickford came up behind her and held her in a surprisingly powerful grip.

The doctor was at her side, a hypodermic in his hand, and she felt a needle jab her arm.

As she slid into a place that was suffocatingly dark, Nicola thought, "John Dapp, you won't be able to kidnap me, because I've already been fucking kidnapped."

SIXTY-THREE

When Dave Dolan stepped into the trailer, he thought it was deserted. No screaming baby, no yelling kids. No Danielle. And best of all, no fuckin Belinda.

He'd just allowed himself to relax when he heard his wife's voice from behind him.

"Dave."

Belinda stood in the doorway of the bedroom. Her mouth was swollen.

"Where's everybody?" he said.

"I took the twins to my mom's. They were freakin out. When I got back, Danielle was gone with the baby. Dunno where and don't fuckin care."

He nodded, waiting for the tirade. It didn't come.

"What we gonna do, Dave?"

"I'm fixin it, Bel."

"Yeah? How?"

He shook his head. "Better you don't know."

"Fuck you, Dave." But she said this without rancor.

Her arms hung limply at her sides. Like all her fight was gone. And that cut him. Made him feel worse than he'd felt in years.

Dolan walked up to her and moved a strand of dirty-blonde hair from her face. He put a finger to her swollen lip.

"Sorry, baby."

"Yeah, well, I never could keep my trap shut."

They looked at each other, and then they were kissing hard, even with her sore mouth. It got hot fast, and they were in the bedroom tearing off their clothes and fucking like there was no tomorrow.

Which there pretty much wasn't.

Afterward, Dolan lay on the bed smoking. Belinda snored softly beside him.

He said, "Two birds, man. Two fuckin birds."

Dolan got and up pulled on his shirt, jeans, and boots. He walked out the front door and down the steps. He crouched and lay on his back and scooted under the trailer. A mess of soggy plywood and plastic pipes. He ripped some insulation loose and forced open a length of plywood and retrieved a rifle and a handgun cocooned in stretch wrap.

As he clambered out from under the double-wide, he saw Belinda, wearing a ratty robe, standing in the doorway, watching him.

"What you doin, Dave?"

"Something that's either real smart or real fuckin dumb."

"Dave ..."

He stared at her. "I don't walk back in that door later, I guess it was dumber than all hell."

Dolan put the weapons in the trunk of his car and drove away without looking back at his wife, still standing in the doorway.

When he reached the road he took out his phone and dialed.

"What?" Harley Comfort said.

"Harley, I got your money."

"Yeah?"

"Yeah."

"Fuck me, that was fast."

"You're a good motivator."

Comfort laughed. "I am, ain't I? So, bring it on over."

"I'm seen with you, I'll be in breach of my bail."

"Who gives a fuck? Ain't you surrenderin tomorrow?"

"I don't want to be arrested now, man. I still got things to fix before I go." Dolan drove out of town, into the woodland. "Meet me at Kevin's place in an hour."

Dolan could hear Comfort lighting a smoke. "Dave, you fuckin with me?"

"I ain't fuckin with you."

"'Cause that would be walkin down the wrong damn road."

"Your dough's right here, Harley."

"Well, okay then. I'll see you at Kev's."

SIXTY-FOUR

A silver Lincoln Navigator cruised up to the Gulfstream that was parked on the apron of a private airstrip in northern Virginia. The SUV was followed by an ambulance.

Ricky Pickford stepped down from the passenger seat of the Lincoln and opened the door for Victor Fabian. A chill wind blew in over the airstrip and lifted Fabian's hair, wrapping his pants around his legs.

Fabian stood with his hands in his coat pockets and watched as the rear doors of the ambulance were opened and his daughter was stretchered out. Two burly men in paramedic garb carried her up the stairs and into the jet. Fabian followed.

Inside the plane, he looked on as Nicola was lifted into a reclining chair, her head lolling. A young woman in a nurse's tunic appeared, carrying a medical bag. One of the paramedics brought a drip stand, which he set up beside Nicola.

The nurse suspended a drip bag from the stand and set about inserting a catheter into Nicola's hand and taping it down. She took her pulse, raised her eyelids, shone a flashlight into her eyes, and listened to her chest with a stethoscope. The nurse attached a pulse monitor to the tip of Nicola's index finger and clicked on a portable monitor that displayed her vital signs.

"Is she well?" Fabian said.

"Oh, yes, sir. Perfectly." The woman smiled and took the seat beside Nicola's.

Fabian seated himself where he couldn't see his daughter. The sight of her made him squeamish, not out of guilt for what he had done, but because she was a reminder to him of what awaited him. A decline into gape-mouthed imbecility. His wasting body tended to by a succession of these brisk, young medical mercenaries.

"Sir?" Ricky Pickford was standing at Fabian's side. "Everything's in order."

"Thank you, Ricky."

"Then, I'll say bon voyage."

Fabian stared up at him in confusion. "What does that mean, Ricky?"

"It means have a good trip."

Fabian said, "Jesus Christ, Ricky, I know that. Why aren't you buckling yourself in?"

"I'm not going to China, sir."

"What?"

"I'm afraid I can't."

"You *can't?*"

"We have no idea how long you'll need to be there, sir. I have a family."

Fabian blinked. "You have a *family?*"

"Yes, sir. Two sons and a daughter. And a wife, of course."

"I had no idea."

"No, sir, of course you didn't."

Fabian lifted his chin. "Are you taking a *tone* with me, Pickford?"

"No, sir. Merely stating a fact."

Fabian, astonishingly, was at a loss for words.

Pickford raised a hand in salute and turned and left the aircraft.

A uniformed young blonde woman with the ludicrous heel-toe gait of a ramp model appeared from the cockpit and closed the hatch. The jet started to taxi onto the runway.

The blonde stood over Fabian and said, "Need any help with your seat belt, sir?" Her smile indicated that her help would not necessarily end at the management of his belt.

Fabian shooed her away with a flick of his hand and stared out the window as the plane hurtled along the runway and flung itself into the sky like a bolt from a crossbow.

SIXTY-FIVE

Ash followed the lumbering figure of John Dapp along the corridor toward the motel room. The big man stopped and dug in his pants pocket for the room key. He found it and was about to slot it into the lock when he lifted his hand and stepped back.

He threw the key to Ash, who almost fumbled the catch.

Ash looked at him blankly, and Dapp put a finger to his lips and jerked his head toward the door.

Ash stepped forward and opened the door. As he was crossing the threshold Dapp shoved him hard in the back and Ash lurched forward, falling into the room. Ash heard a sound like a rubber mallet striking a drum. As he hit the floor he saw Dapp coming in with a gun in his hand.

There were two men in the room. One of them, Ash now realized, had shot at him and missed, blowing a hole in the bathroom wall. Dapp shot the man in the head with his silenced pistol.

The other man, who was standing by the bed, raised his weapon, and Dapp shot him twice in the abdomen. Dapp ran at him and wrestled the pistol from his grip, sending it skidding across the carpet to where Ash knelt.

"Shut the fucking door," Dapp said.

It took forever for Ash to gain control of his body. He lurched to his feet and made it to the door and slammed it closed. He stood with his back against it, gasping.

Dapp was over the wounded man, pressing the gun barrel to his skull. He looked up at Ash.

"What the fuck did you do?" Dapp asked. Ash just shook his head. "Fucking answer me!"

"I made a call," Ash said.

"From the pay phone downstairs?"

"Yes."

"You fucking dickhead." The bleeding man writhed and Dapp hit him in the neck with a ham-sized fist. "Who did you call?"

"A journalist."

"Jesus. Who?"

"Steven Root. At the *New York Times*."

"You call him on his cell phone?"

"Yes."

Dapp shook his head. "You didn't think that a guy like that is under surveillance? That all his calls are monitored? You sent out a gilt-edged fucking invitation for these assholes to come and get us."

"I'm sorry."

"*Sorry* doesn't quite fucking hack it."

Dapp stood and grabbed the wounded man by the ankle and dragged him toward the bathroom. He lifted him and flung him into the bathtub, the man's head striking the tiles, his blood splattering across the stained enamel. He stared at Dapp, his face waxen, his breathing shallow. He had thinning hair and his skin was grooved with wrinkles.

Ash stood in the doorway. "What are you doing?"

"I'm going to ask our friend a few questions," Dapp said. "My methods may offend your delicate sensibility, so I suggest you wait outside."

Ash withdrew and closed the door.

He looked at the dead man sprawled on the floor between the two beds— a young man, dressed in khaki chinos, boat shoes, and what had been a white cotton shirt, now soaked red with blood.

Ash sat on one of the beds and glimpsed himself in the mirror. He didn't much like what he saw. He shifted, the bedsprings creaking, until he was looking at a warped print of the Lincoln Memorial.

He heard wet slaps and moans coming from the bathroom and the low murmur of Dapp's voice. A scream was smothered into a gurgle. More slaps. Then the sound of running water, then coughing and crying, and water running again.

Ash tried to tune it out. He thought of Scooter. Thought, for no good reason, of the time, years ago, when he'd taken him camping. He hadn't been able to pitch the tent, Scooter whooping with laughter as the canvas and poles collapsed around Ash.

Humiliatingly, another camper, a husky fellow with an outdoorsman's beard, came to Ash's rescue and got the tent fixed in a minute.

He'd been sweet, though, and had said, "Hey, no shame, man. Took me a long time to figure this stuff out." Then he'd gently punched Scooter's arm and said, "You're a lucky kid to have a dad who spends time with you. Have fun, guys." And he'd ambled off to where his unwashed-looking girlfriend sat smiling at them through meaty barbecue smoke.

A shove on the shoulder nearly toppled Ash to the floor. Dapp stood over him, drying his hands on a towel.

Ash looked toward the bathroom.

"Gone," Dapp said. He wiped his face.

"Who were they?"

"They worked for Executive Protection Services."

"And?"

"And nothing. They were bottom-feeders." Dapp threw the towel on the bed and started gathering his few belongings. "Gotta move."

"Where are we going?"

"Uh-uh. Not we. Me." Ash stared at Dapp. "Time to adios the buddy movie. I'm going after Fabian alone."

"And what about Scooter?" Ash said.

Dapp dug in his pocket and found the crumpled Wendy's paper napkin. He handed it to Ash who unfolded it and saw a man's name and the name of a town.

He looked up at Dapp who was walking toward the door.

"That's the guy who was in the picture with Bakewell," Dapp said. "If I were you, I'd get my ass up there pronto."

Ash couldn't find anything to say.

Dapp paused a moment then lifted his coat and unholstered a pistol. He tossed it onto the bed beside Ash, and it bounced once and lay there gleaming darkly.

"Ever use one of those?"

"No."

"Pick it up," Dapp said.

Ash hesitated before he lifted the weapon. It was surprisingly heavy.

"When you want to fire it, release the safety."

"How?"

"On the left side of the weapon, just above your thumb, there's a switch."

Ash saw the safety catch and moved it down with his thumb. There was a little click.

"Now cock it," Dapp said.

Ash looked at him.

"Take the rear of the weapon in your left hand and pull it back."

Ash obeyed and heard it rasp as it was cocked.

"Now all you do is point and shoot. Meanwhile, put the safety back on."

Ash felt the grooved switch beneath his fingers and slid it home.

"Time to man the fuck up, Danny," Dapp said and he opened the door and was gone.

SIXTY-SIX

Dapp was speeding away from the motel in the Charger, still buzzed on the adrenaline rush from the gunfight, when one of his phones rang.

A phone that hadn't rung in years.

He pulled over, checking his mirrors, and then took the phone out of his jacket and stared at its blinking face, listening to the cricket chirp.

At last he lifted it to his ear.

"Yes?"

"John."

The voice triggered a tightness in his chest. "Yes."

"Black Escalade to starboard. See it?"

"Yeah."

"Why don't you come aboard?"

Dapp sat a while, contemplated lead-footing it out of there, but instead he cut the Dodge's V-8 and walked over to the SUV with the tinted windows. A young guy as blank-faced as an android stood by to usher him inside.

A man was alone in the back. A man with gray hair and gray skin, dressed in a gray suit, the funk of decades of nicotine seeping from his pores. He occupied a position in the CIA so august and rarefied that Johnny-come-lately directors deferred to him if they were wise.

"What do you want?" Dapp asked as the SUV accelerated down Wisconsin Avenue.

"What you want: Victor Fabian shut down."

"Do you speak for the presidency?"

"No, I speak for the Agency. And lately our views and the presidency's seldom align."

"Yes, but surely the presidency also wants him silenced?"

"Well, they chose to exile him." Dapp blinked and the gray man nodded and a light fall of dandruff floated to his shoulders. "Yes, he's gone. Got on his little jet and flew into the sunrise."

"China?"

"Yes. And he's taken his daughter with him. Against her will."

"I see." Dapp felt himself gripping the door in an attempt to anchor himself. "Why are we having this conversation?"

"We can get you to China."

"I can get myself to China."

"Sure you can. But we can get you there more swiftly. And more quietly."

"And what would you want me to do over there?"

The slightest of shrugs. "Whatever you want to do."

"You want me to kill Victor Fabian?"

An inclination of the gray head.

"I'm not an assassin," Dapp said.

"No, you're much too nuanced for that."

"Nuanced?"

Another shrug.

"Why don't you want Fabian to speak about the presidency's role in what happened?"

"This presidency is a runaway train. It will jump the tracks with or without this. But Fabian knows too much about too many good people."

"There are good people circling this clusterfuck?"

"There are always good people." An emphysemic sigh. "And sometimes good people do bad things."

"That's catchy." Dapp folded his arms across his gut and stared at the Gothic spires of Washington National Cathedral visible through a row of cedars. "So you're offering me a plane ride?"

"And any assistance you may need with your cover."

"I've got that down, thanks."

"We're also offering you the reassurance that whatever you may do over there would be in the national interest."

"I don't need that reassurance."

"Not now, perhaps. But when your blood has cooled it may be a balm for a man as *nuanced* as yourself."

They drove a while in silence, and then the gray man said, "You're on the side of the angels, John."

"No."

"And for what it's worth, I'm sorry that you've suffered so."

"You're a Catholic, aren't you?" Dapp looked at the gray man.

"Long lapsed."

"Well, I'm here to tell you that suffering is not ennobling," Dapp said. "It is not the gateway to some kind of enlightenment or salvation. But it has taught me something really profound."

"What?"

"That to a nail everything looks like a fucking hammer."

The Escalade stopped at a light. Dapp stepped down, slammed the door, and walked away without looking back.

SIXTY-SEVEN

The Chevrolet bumped over the railroad tracks that carved a gash through the forest. The narrow road, its surface a lunar landscape of potholes and cracks, wound up an incline, the tree canopy almost obscuring the leaden sky.

The girl drove slowly, the GPS intoning that they were almost at their destination.

Orlando had to focus hard to separate the GPS's electronic voice from the others that filled the inside of his skull like buzzing bees.

He wanted to scream, but he shut his eyes and pressed his thumbs to his temples.

"You okay?" the girl asked.

She chewed gum and the headphones connected to her cell phone dangled from her ears. She'd listened to music the whole way, her head and shoulders undulating like a camel's, her fingers tapping the steering wheel.

Annoying, but infinitely preferable to conversation.

He had no need of another voice.

A dirt track snaked into the trees, up to a hut that was barely visible in the foliage.

When the GPS grew ever more insistent Orlando reached across and muted it.

Suddenly, now that he was where he needed to be, the voices were little more than a whisper, like the sound of a breeze in the leaves of a tree.

He exhaled, quieting his mind. Finding his still point.

"Drive on," he said.

"But we're here."

"Drive on past the next bend and pull over."

She obeyed, accelerating. "When do I get the rest of my money?"

"I need to deliver a package, and then we'll go down to the town and I'll pay you."

"You gonna need any more drivin?"

Orlando smiled at her. "Perhaps. You're a very good driver."

"My grammy taught me. She's passed now."

"Stop here," Orlando said and the girl pulled onto the berm, the scrub brushing the side of the car.

"Pop the trunk," he said. "There's a lever by your seat."

She fumbled and found the lever and pulled it.

Orlando opened the door and stepped out.

"I need your help," he said.

"With what?"

"With the package."

The girl cut the engine and climbed out of the car. Orlando walked to the rear of the Chevy and raised the lid of the trunk. The girl joined him and glanced inside then gave him a confused look.

"It's empty."

He got behind her and pushed her down so that her torso was in the trunk. She tried to fight him, but he took the knife from his pocket and slit her throat, holding her close as she died, feeling the convulsions as her meager life left her.

Orlando heard the sound of a vehicle approaching. He grabbed the girl's feet and flung her into the trunk, slamming the lid closed before an old blue Cadillac bumped up, a quartet of inbreds sliding their eyes over him as they drove by.

SIXTY-EIGHT

Dave Dolan crouched in the pine trees and dogwood above the hut, binoculars to his eyes, watching the road that wound up from town. He'd left his car way down the hill, hidden from the road. Far enough away for Hoo Bakewell not to hear its distinctive gargle.

He thought of Hoo in the hut with the kid.

Then Dolan thought of that day back in the rural badlands of Afghanistan when he'd led six men on a bait patrol. Going into a contested area, hoping to draw out the Taliban.

They had.

Hiding behind a maze of low dried-mud walls on a vast plain stubbled by corn stalks, they were peppered with fire from a PK machine gun, rifles, and rocket-propelled grenades. A grenade exploded near Dolan, and he went down, tasting his own blood. Beside him, a nineteen-year-old kid from Kansas lay with his guts spilling onto the sand. Dolan tried to move.

Couldn't.

Another grenade incoming, and the rifle fire getting closer. Two men near him were hit.

Then he felt someone dragging him. Hoo Bakewell, getting

him behind a higher wall. Going back for the other two, little guy lifting and hauling men nearly twice his size.

Then going out on his own.

Dolan later learned that Hoo had flanked the enemy, taken out the PK gunner, and killed eleven Taliban. He'd run out of ammunition and killed the last man with a baseball-sized rock, pulping his skull.

Then he'd returned to the squad and opened the dead corpsman's bag and set up IV lines and tied tourniquets and pressed down on compress bandages, talking to his comrades, swearing he'd hunt their white asses to hell if they fuckin died on him. Keeping them alive until a chopper had arrived, throwing up a cloud of red dust that had clogged Dolan's throat and tasted just like honey.

Fuckin Hoo.

Glassing the road, Dolan said, "It's not too late, man."

Not too late to get Hoo and the boy out of there.

Then he caught the flare of sun on a windshield and saw the Caddy bumping through the potholes.

It was on.

Whatever the fuck it was that he was doing, it was on.

***

Uhuru felt it. Felt the trouble coming. Felt that prickle on his skin like a cool breeze had touched him. Same feeling he'd had over there in the desert when some bad shit was about to go down.

He took the boy by the shoulders and pushed him under a table in the middle of the room, away from the windows.

"You don't move, hear?"

The kid, eyes big and scared, nodded.

Uhuru had searched the house and found an old hunting knife with a rusted blade in the stinking bedroom. He gripped it, standing with his back to the wall by the front door, feeling the chill of the brick, waiting.

He heard a fall of stones and a rustle coming from the back of the house, and he moved fast to the one rear window, glass cracked and dirty.

Movement toward the hut. Not an animal. A man.

Then a whistle. A short, sharp bleat. Uhuru knew that whistle. Heard it too many times on night patrol to forget it.

He edged forward and saw Sarge scrambling toward the back door.

Uhuru opened the door. Sarge was carrying a rifle. Sweating. Fighting for breath. Not what he used to be, no sir.

"Hoo."

"Wassup, Sarge?"

In reply Sarge gave him an old Colt .45. One of those handguns that were better to throw at somebody than to shoot, they were so inaccurate.

Sarge was at the front window, peering out.

"They found the truck, Hoo."

"The cops?"

"Yeah. And your name was on the news. They've connected you to me. They come round my trailer askin questions."

"What you tell 'em?"

"What you think I told 'em?"

Uhuru nodded.

"Got to get you and the boy outta here, okay?"

"Yeah, Sarge. Okay."

Then Sarge took another look and said, "Fuck."

Uhuru peeked out the window and saw four men walking up the path toward the hut.

"Them ain't cops," he said.

"No. Worse."

"Yeah?"

"That's Harley Comfort and his crew. He's into everything bad in this county. Owns the cops. He's after the reward money, Hoo."

"Reward?"

"You don't know?" Uhuru shook his head. "Half a million. That'll buy a shitload of go-go juice. You best cover the rear."

Uhuru stared at Sarge who had crouched and slid the barrel of the rifle through the open window.

"Anything you wanna tell me, Sarge?"

"Yeah. Make your shots count. These fuckers don't play."

***

Dolan wiped sweat from his eyes and took a bead on Harley Comfort as he walked up the pathway, hands in the pockets of his pressed jeans, saying something to one of his men. Always the mouth, Harley.

Dolan shot him straight through the heart and swung the rifle and shot the man next to him.

He winged the third man, who was diving for the trees.

The fourth man peeled off around the side of the house.

"Two comin your way, Hoo."

Dolan smacked another clip into the rifle and went to the rear window, staring out. He saw nothing.

***

Orlando Peach ran through the trees toward the gunfire, moving with an animal grace, the voices stilled now.

He counted the shots.

Three.

A rifle. High caliber.

Then quiet.

He saw the bodies lying by the front of the hut. Two of the four men from the Cadillac.

Orlando stayed under cover, waiting, listening. The drone of a fly. The rolling call of a red-bellied woodpecker. Then he heard a man moving through the trees.

He went toward the sound of moaning and weeping. Fresh blood gleaming crimson on the green leaves.

Orlando found the wounded man on his hands and knees, gut shot, one hand pressed to his abdomen, holding himself in.

He looked up at Orlando and said, "Help me, son. Help me."

Orlando took the knife from his belt and helped the man to his reckoning.

He lowered the body and waited.

Another rustle. A man trying to move quietly. Doing a miserable job of it.

Orlando, wraithlike, moved through the trees until he saw the man.

This one wasn't hurt. Just terrified. Panting, swinging his handgun at shadows. Orlando waited until the gun jerked away from him then he moved in fast and cut the man's throat.

He retreated into the bush, taking up a position where he could watch both entrances of the hut, unslinging his rifle, lifting it to his eye.

It took maybe five minutes then the back door opened and a

tall, thin man came out, rifle held combat style. He had the look of a soldier home from the wars.

Orlando shot him through the head, and the man fell flat.

Orlando panned the rifle toward the house and glimpsed a face moving away from the window.

The face of a savage.

Orlando saw the man driving the truck straight at Mama, who was out of the car, trying to reload her automatic. Saw her flung into the air, her head starring the windshield, her body falling to the dirt, the man's truck fishtailing away under the cold moon.

Orlando breathed deeply. Then, keeping to the trees, he moved in on the hut.

***

When Uhuru saw Sarge go down he stood with the pistol pointed at the door and said, "Boy?"

He risked a quick look over his shoulder.

"Boy, you light out through the front door and you run, you hearin me? You run till you can't run no more."

The boy hesitated, staring up at him from under the table.

"Go!" Uhuru said and he grabbed the rear door and flung it open, flattening himself against the wall.

Nothing.

He waited, sweat filling his eyes. He wiped his face.

Waited.

***

Scooter watched Hoo. Watched him standing with his back to the wall by the open door.

Then Hoo ran out into the light, shooting the gun.

He was struck by a burst of fire and staggered and dropped.

Scooter sobbed and sprinted for the front door. Tripping. Falling. Getting to his feet he ripped open the door and ran, ran past the dead men and into the forest.

***

Orlando stood over the savage. Even though the mud man was dead, Orlando smacked another clip into the rifle and emptied it into him, tearing him to pieces. Mincing him. Feeling flesh and blood and bone spray up onto his face, and it was good.

When he was done, he stood a while and sniffed the air and walked into the hut. He saw the open front door and walked through it, reloading the rifle, moving toward the leaves that still trembled from the boy's passing.

SIXTY-NINE

Ash drove the Toyota Camry along the interstate through northern Maryland toward Pennsylvania. He kept to the speed limit. He drove carefully. He couldn't be pulled over.

He'd stolen the car.

No, he'd fucking *jacked* the car.

Walked out of the blood bath in the motel room carrying the handgun and watched John Dapp speed away in the Charger.

Gone down the stairs and crossed the parking lot until he came to an intersection and, without knowing what he was doing until he'd done it, walked up to where the Toyota was stopped at a light and pointed Dapp's gun toward the middle-aged man at the wheel, the guy pleading and raising his hands and falling out of the car in his haste to hand it over.

Ash saying, "I'm sorry. I'm really sorry," as he drove away.

Leaving DC, as he'd programmed the GPS and obeyed the digital voice, he'd waited for the shakes to come.

Waited for the panic.

Waited for the reality of what he had done to hit him.

Nothing.

He was totally numb and Ash realized how radically the last few days had recalibrated his understanding of terror.

Even when, just as he'd crossed the Mason-Dixon line, a cop car grew large in the rearview and Ash waited for the blaring voice to tell him to pull over, he felt no fear. Which meant he'd probably shoot the cop.

But the cruiser passed him and disappeared.

Ash listened to the news on the radio. The rote recitations of the world's slaughter, mayhem, and carnage didn't touch him. He was interested only in news of his son.

There was none.

"He's safe," Ash said aloud. "He's safe."

And he kept on saying it, like a mantra.

SEVENTY

Scooter plunged through the woods, undergrowth tearing at his skin, a branch whiplashing him across the cheek, drawing blood. Pain took him under the ribs and his lungs were raw.

He stopped and listened, heard nothing but his own sawing breath. He limped on, coming to the railroad track that curved off into the woods.

***

Following the boy was easy for Orlando. Broken twigs. Scuffed soil. A shred of fabric spiked to a branch where the child's shirt had snagged.

As he closed in he heard the boy crashing through the woods. And then silence.

Orlando picked up his pace and arrived at the railroad track. He looked up the silver rails and saw the child, hunched with cramp, dragging himself around a bend, disappearing.

Orlando adjusted his stride and walked along the railroad ties, rifle slung from his shoulder, his breath smooth and easy, every muscle, every fiber, every cell at one with his task.

***

Scooter's shoe snagged on the splintered wood of a tie and he tripped, sprawling, flinging his hands out to break his fall. He tore his palms on the crushed gray stones.

Ballast. They were called ballast, these stones, he remembered. Dumb, useless information that stuck like fluff to his Velcro brain.

He stayed down, gasping for breath. Crying silently.

Then he sensed something and looked back and saw somebody walking toward him.

At first, when he saw it was a kid, he thought he was safe. Then his eyes narrowed against the glare and he realized that it was the boy from the farmhouse.

The one who had shot the woman and the others.

The kid raised a hand and shouted, "Hey, Scoot, wait up."

Scooter forced himself to his feet. The embankment, raw soil overgrown with scrub, was too steep to climb. The only way was forward along the tracks.

He fell into a limping run, but when he looked over his shoulder, the killer kid was almost upon him, smiling as he sprinted, rifle in his hand.

And then he was close enough to reach out and shove Scooter, sending him sprawling, facedown.

"On your knees," the kid said.

Scooter didn't move.

"Listen to me, now. Kneel."

Scooter obeyed, kneeling on the stones.

The kid lifted the rifle and pressed the barrel against Scooter's left temple. It was hard and cool.

"Your mama and daddy teach you to pray, Scoot?"

Scooter shook his head.

"No?"

Scooter shook his head again.

"Well, sorry, little buddy, but then yours shall not be the Kingdom of Heaven."

The rifle made a coughing sound as they kid racked it.

Scooter closed his eyes and thought of his mother. Saw her smiling, the wind tugging at her hair. Thought of his father and wondered if he was dead too.

Waited.

Nothing happened and he heard the kid laughing and the rifle barrel was withdrawn.

Scooter opened his eyes and saw him lower the weapon.

"Well, Scoot, somebody's looking out for you. Damnedest thing—the rifle jammed. First time that's ever happened to me. Course, I could just unjam it and finish my task, but I'm thinking, no, Orlando, this is some kind of message. This child's life is being spared as part of a greater plan, the intricate design of which will surely be revealed in the fullness of time."

Orlando slung the rifle over one shoulder and reached down and hoisted Scooter over the other, as if he weighed nothing at all, and walked back the way they had come.

After what seemed like forever the man—up close Scooter saw that he just looked like a kid—cut through the forest and they came to the road, where an old car was parked.

Orlando stood for a while in the trees, listening, then he carried Scooter to the rear of the car and unlocked the trunk and popped it.

Scooter saw the dead girl inside and screamed.

Screamed even louder when Orlando dumped him in on top of her and slammed the trunk lid closed.

SEVENTY-ONE

Ahmed Ashraf was cavity searched. Stripped naked and forced to bend and spread the cheeks of his backside while the guards shoved their gloved fingers up his anus. The dark ones were the worst. The *abeed*. The unclean. A violation of him as a man and a Muslim, having their black hands on him.

Then the guards watched as he dressed in his orange jumpsuit and took him to the basement of the Metropolitan Correctional Center. He was handed over to three federal marshals, who shackled his ankles, chained his waist, and cuffed his wrists.

A remote-operated electronic door buzzed open and they hop-marched him along a tunnel forty feet below Pearl Street in lower Manhattan. The heathen fools walking above, talking on their phones, hurrying to their offices, had no idea what or who was beneath them.

Ahmed, heavily bearded, was a big man, and he was exhausted, panting, sweat pooling under his arms and at his groin, by the time they had passed through the second door at the north end of the tunnel.

They stood and waited for the prisoner elevator to clatter down, the doors shuddering open. Ahmed was locked inside a cage for the ride up to the cells of the Daniel Patrick Moynihan

Courthouse. The court for the Southern District of New York.

Before entering the courtroom, he was unshackled long enough to remove his jumpsuit and dress in sweatpants, a T-shirt, and track shoes. Then he was chained again.

He was led to the defense table where his lawyer, a young Jew in a rich man's suit, nodded at him. Ahmed ignored him and sat. One of the marshals tethered the chain of his shackles to a bolt in the ground. The chains were wrapped in vinyl tape to stop them rattling like alms in a beggar's bowl. The table was skirted in fabric, black as a woman's abaya, to hide that he was fettered like a beast.

The prosecutor, a yellow-haired whore in an immodest blue skirt and high heels, did not look at him, pretending she was making notes.

The judge—an old man with a speckled bird's egg for a head—came in, and Ahmed had to rise into a crouch, hobbled by the chains.

The judge sat. He cleared his throat, stared out over his glasses, and said, "I have considered a plea by the defense to suppress emails linking the accused with Muslim extremist groups because they were obtained under the provisions of Section 702 of the Foreign Intelligence Surveillance Act. The defense contends the Fourth Amendment rights of the accused were infringed because these emails were obtained while he was on American soil. I am denying this plea since Mr. Ashraf is not an American citizen. However, he is constitutionally entitled to due process. Therefore he will have his day in court. The jury trial will proceed at a date to be determined."

They had to stand again when the old man left the room. Then Ahmed's chain was loosened from the bolt and he was taken away, to dress in his orange jumpsuit and hop like a jerboa back to the MCC.

Back to 10 South, the isolation wing.

Back to his small cell, with its frosted windows and its hard fluorescent lights that were never dimmed.

Ahmed was alone in this room for twenty-four hours a day. His one-hour recreation privileges had been withdrawn because he had dared to stand by the wall and mutter "assalamu alaikum" to the man in the cell beside his.

A man he had never seen.

He showered in this cell and was watched by cameras when he performed his ablutions and his prayers.

He was forbidden television and radio, and newspapers were delayed and censored.

He had been here for five months and had spoken to nobody but the guards and his lawyer.

Ahmed sat on the bed and thought, as he had many times before, about killing himself. Martyring himself. Removing himself from the clutches of the enemy. But he knew it was impossible with the unblinking eyes of the video cameras trained on him every second of the day.

The slot in his door rattled open and a newspaper slapped the floor of the cell.

The *New York Post*. Days old. Whole pages were missing and others had chunks cut out of them. But there was enough left for him to see the face of the man staring at him from below the fold on the front page.

The face of Daniel Ash.

SEVENTY-TWO

Ash stepped out of the Toyota onto the cracked sidewalk of what was left of downtown Haynesville. The car's GPS had lost its signal, and he needed to ask for directions.

Above the rundown buildings, he could see some kind of abandoned factory up on a hill. A foundry, he guessed.

He walked past a legal disability clinic, an off-track betting parlor, two shuttered stores, and turned into a minimart.

The shelves were nearly depleted and one of the two refrigerators at the rear was dark and empty. Ash looked for bottled water and couldn't find any, so he bought a can of Sprite that he had no intention of drinking. He crossed to the counter, where a sallow man with dirty hair and Coke-bottle glasses was watching *People's Court* on an old portable TV.

A handwritten sign was taped to the cash register: Smoothies, Slushies, and Fountain Pops Cannot Be Bought with Food Stamps.

Ash paid for the Sprite and laid the napkin Dapp had given him on the counter and said, "Can you tell me how to get to this address?"

The man looked at the napkin and then he stared up at Ash.

"You lookin for Dave Dolan?"

"Yes."

"Ain't you heard?"

"Heard what?"

"He's dead, man. Dave Dolan's dead."

Ash gripped the counter. "When?"

"This mornin."

"What happened?"

The man shrugged and turned back to his TV. "I look like fuckin CNN, buddy? Go ask the cops."

Ash left the Sprite on the counter and ran for the Toyota.

***

Scooter was totally freaking out in the pitch dark. Yelling, beating at the trunk lid, kicking. All he was doing was hurting his hands and getting himself covered in the dead girl's blood. It was tacky. Like strawberry jelly.

He nearly spewed. His mouth filled with puke, and he had to fight not to barf. He forced himself to swallow the vomit. It burned his throat like acid.

He had to calm down.

Had to think.

First, he moved himself so that his back was to the lock of the trunk, and he used his feet to push the girl as far away as he could. There was no way to avoid contact with her, but at least now he wasn't lying on top of her, feeling her squidgy flesh and picturing that rip in her throat.

He breathed to calm himself but the ripe stink of blood and poop got him gagging again.

There had to be a way to open the trunk.

Scooter lay there, feeling the car rattling along the road, and tried to recall anything useful from all the random crap that his mind had absorbed from the internet over the years.

Nothing.

He started to freak out again and had to grab hold of himself.

Heard his mother say, "Come on, Scoot. You've got this. Come on."

And, just like that, he remembered seeing something on YouTube. A video clip of some asswipe locking himself into his car trunk and jerking a luminous pull tab to activate the interior latch that popped the lid.

Scooter felt around the lock. Nothing. Remembered the asswipe saying these latches only came standard in newer cars. This Chevy was what? Thirty years old? Forty? Scooter had no way of telling.

Anyway, no pull tab.

The car hit a bump and his ass bounced and landed on the phone in his jeans pocket.

The phone.

The freakin cell phone.

***

The GPS had recovered its signal, and Ash let it guide him through the narrow, potholed streets, empty of life. He took a corner too fast, and the exhaust pipe of the Toyota scraped the cobbles, but he didn't slow down.

The houses thinned, and he passed an abandoned warehouse, and the pitted asphalt turned to dirt, and ragged old trailers appeared through the stunted trees.

The GPS told him he had reached his destination.

Ash parked under a tree and opened the glove box and took out the pistol. He checked the safety was on and slipped it into the inside pocket of his jacket. It dragged the jacket down and he shrugged to try to correct the hang. He opened the door and tugged his cap a little lower and set off along the muddy road toward the trailers.

***

Scooter Houdinied his hand into his pocket and pulled the cell phone out. Felt for the power button, pressed it, and the small face lit up, gray and dull. Not all bright and jazzy like a smart-phone. He saw that the battery was low. He tried to use the phone as a flashlight, moving it around the trunk lock, but the beam was too feeble and it was growing dimmer, the battery dying.

He turned the phone toward him and punched in 911.

No service.

He remembered hearing that texts sometimes go through even when bandwidth is too low for a call.

Thumbs flying he typed: *Im 10yr old boy abducted & locked in trunk of old green Chevy near Haynesville PA.*

He had a sudden flash of the license plate as the man called Orlando had slung him into the trunk.

Virginia plates.

Scooter typed 911 in the address line and had just hit send when the phone died in his hand.

SEVENTY-THREE

Ash stopped walking when he saw a police car parked outside one of the trailers. A small group of people stood near the double-wide, rubbernecking. Edging forward, he spotted two more cop cars and a black SUV terrifyingly reminiscent of the one driven by the men who had abducted Scooter.

The fear Ash thought had been cauterized from him kicked in now, big time, and his balls sucked up tight, and he wanted to turn and run, but he thought of his son, wounded, even dead, and he moved forward.

Two uniformed cops were standing outside the rundown trailer, talking to a guy in a suit. The door of the trailer was open and Ash could see more uniforms inside. No ambulances.

A good sign? Maybe they had been and gone.

Ash hung back and watched. His eye was drawn to a skinny woman in a Steelers T-shirt and no coat, despite the chill. She wore jeans that had been frayed and torn by hard living and not by machinists in a Cambodian sweatshop. Her hair stood out in uncombed spikes, and she smoked, cupping her right elbow in her left hand, her arm moving like a metronome to and from her mouth, a speech bubble of smoke dragged from her face by the wind.

She fluttered like a magpie through the group of onlookers, smoking and talking. People turned their backs to her. One heavy teenage girl went as far as shoving her away.

Ash drifted to the edge of the group, toward the woman, who stood alone now, scratching her scalp.

She looked at him and said, "Real fuckin shitfest, huh?"

"What's happening?" Ash tried to coarsen his voice, but only managed to sound like he had a head cold.

The woman narrowed her eyes. "Where you from?"

"Pittsburgh," Ash said.

"Yeah?"

"Yeah."

"Got a smoke for me?"

He patted his pockets and shrugged. "Sorry."

"Help me with a sawbuck, mister. I need to buy baby formula." She smiled at him. Meth had eaten most of her teeth.

Ash took change from his pocket. About six dollars. He handed it to her. She looked at the money in disappointment before pocketing it, about to wander off.

"Wait," he said.

"For what?"

"Walk with me and I'll give you a twenty."

"You wanna blowjob?"

Ash looked at her ruined mouth and felt sick.

"No, I want you to tell me what went down here."

She stared at him. "What's your interest?" Then she stabbed a finger with chipped nail polish at him. "You a journalist, right? One of them media fuckers?"

Ash shrugged.

"What the hell, your money's green." She held out her hand, palm up.

He took a ten from his pocket and gave it to her. "Let's talk and you'll get the rest."

She led him behind a thicket of trees into a field strewn with Filet-O-Fish wrappers and Keystone Ice empties.

She pointed to the trailer. "That's Dave Dolan's place. Lives there with his wife, Bel, and his sister-in-law and some kids. Meant to self-surrender up at Lewisburg tomorrow."

Ash stared at her blankly.

"Start a prison stretch, man. Dealin. Now, word is that there was some kinda shootout round an hour back, up by his dead brother's cabin. My sister's friend works dispatch for the state police, and she says Dave's dead. And so's Harley Comfort and three of his crew. And some nigger."

"And a boy?" Ash said, battling to find his voice. "A kid of around ten years old? Anything about him?"

She shook her head. "Nope, nothin about no kid. Woulda heard."

"You're sure?"

"Sure, I'm sure. Kids is news."

"And who's this Harley Comfort?"

"Drug dealer. Just about the meanest son of a bitch ever walked God's earth."

"How do I get to the cabin?" Ash said.

She shrugged her bony shoulders. "Shit, I dunno. Never been up there."

Ash turned and started back toward the Toyota.

"Hey, wait," she said.

"Yeah?"

"You owe me a sawbuck."

He gave her the money, and she showed him those teeth again. "Sure you don't wanna go to my trailer?"

Ash walked away.

SEVENTY-FOUR

Orlando drove the Chevy along a narrow, pitted road that wandered through farmland. At a derelict barn with a faded American flag painted on its splintered wooden door, he came to a T-junction, and, for no good reason, turned right.

As if this were some invisible cue, the voices returned, like a radio in his head that was cranked to full volume. Screeching and hissing and cursing. Spewing filth and then quieting down and whispering. Whispering to Orlando that he was done for. That he was finished. That he was a dead man.

Above the whispers, he heard the siren of a police car as it came up behind him, fast, lights flashing, a metallic voice joining those in his head.

And then, like magic, the voices were gone, with a last snaking snigger that echoed and then dissolved into the cold air.

Orlando clicked on the blinker and took the Chevy onto the gravel shoulder of an empty stretch of road.

He ran a hand through his hair and found his most beatific smile, watching in his side mirror as the cop fixed a hat to his head, walking up with a hand on his unclipped holster.

***

Scooter, his skull vibrating against the carpeted floor of the trunk, heard the siren, heard the amplified voice yelling for Orlando to pull over.

He wanted to bang on the trunk lid but he stopped himself.

Wait. Wait for the right moment.

At first, he thought Orlando was fleeing, but the car slowed and bumped to a halt, settling on its springs, groaning. Scooter, his face pressed to the taillight, heard the police car stop and the smack of a door and the sound of boots on gravel.

Now.

He pushed back and kicked and punched at the trunk as hard as he could and shouted until he thought his lungs would burst.

***

As the cop neared Orlando's door, the boy started make a racket in the trunk, his feet clanging against the metal like a dervish was trapped inside.

The policeman had his SIG P227 pointed at Orlando.

"Hands on the wheel," he said.

Orlando placed his hands on the steering wheel at ten and two.

The cop reached forward with his left hand and opened the door a few inches, then stepped back.

"Get out the car. Real slow now."

Orlando released his hands, swiveled, and started to slide out, locking his eyes to the cop's like a snake charmer.

Then he dropped his right hand and lifted the sawed-off from the seat beside him and emptied both barrels into the trooper's chest, blowing the man backward.

As he hit the ground, the cop fired two shots. They pierced the car door, one passing by Orlando harmlessly, shattering the side window. The second round took him in the left shoulder.

Orlando kicked the door open and fired again, blowing the trooper's face off.

He closed the door and reached over into the glove box and found the travel pack of Kleenex Mama had always kept in there. He wadded the tissues and shoved them under his shirt, the paper sticking to the blood.

Leaving his left arm to hang limp, he clicked the car into gear and drove, breathing away the pain.

***

Scooter heard the gunfire. Then the Chevy started up, the exhaust rattling beneath him, and the car rolled away, picking up speed.

Scooter kicked and yelled and beat his fists on the metal until they bled.

He found himself lying up against the dead girl and recoiled in horror.

Exhausted, he drew his knees up to his chin and hugged himself and bawled like a baby.

SEVENTY-FIVE

Driving away from Haynesville, Ash found a regional news station on the radio. He listened to a sports roundup until the top of the hour. Then he heard a version of what the woman had told him, about a shootout in a cabin outside of town.

Nothing about Scooter.

Which meant nothing.

Then the newsreader said, "This just in. A state policeman has been shot dead at a traffic stop outside Haynesville after responding to a 911 call about an abducted child. Police are looking for a young man driving a green 1980s Chevrolet with Virginia license plates. It's believed that he was involved in the earlier shooting incident in the town that left six people dead."

As he passed a derelict barn with a faded Stars and Stripes painted on its door, the report moved on to an update on a local election and Ash clicked the radio off.

SEVENTY-SIX

John Dapp wasn't hungry. Following the mistress dispeller through the stalls on Shanghai's Chenghuangmiao Old Street, he was immune to the heady scents of the street food, the cooked blood, ginger, soy, and five-spice powder floating from the woks.

The food he had dreamt of lying in his bed back in anemic Birdland: crispy pot stickers, soup dumplings, eel noodles, fried pork pancakes, and radish fritters.

His appetite, for the first time in days, had evaporated when his eyes had found the giant Shanghai Tower across the Huangpu River, rising through the smoke and the pollution over the ornate roofs and wooden pagodas.

The mistress dispeller, a compact, handsome man in his midthirties, ate without cease as he walked, moving from stall to stall, weaving effortlessly through the crowds. Dapp, the bulky *laowai*, felt like a linebacker in Lilliput, as he so often had in the years he'd lived here.

Dapp'd learned the language and decoded many of the customs, but his sheer American bulk had set him forever apart.

His companion spoke Mandarin to Dapp as they strolled, switching to Shanghainese when he ordered from the stalls or answered one of the five phones he kept in his pockets, each with a different love song ringtone.

The man, during Dapp's sojourn in Shanghai, had been useful to him. Never exactly an asset, he had been Dapp's go-to guy when he'd needed goods and services too opaque to acquire conventionally.

He'd been a computer salesman, studied psychology, taught tai chi and worked as a private detective. And now he was a mistress dispeller. Hired by wives to scare away their husband's mistresses, or "Little Thirds."

A very Chinese occupation in a country that placed a high social value on matrimony, a country where women were still yoked and subservient, and seldom considered divorce.

"A secondhand woman is like a secondhand car," the mistress dispeller said, eating oily black eels with his fingers. "Once it has been driven it is not worth a fraction of its original selling price. But a secondhand man, on the other hand, is like renovated property here in Shanghai: his value merely appreciates."

"So how do you do it?" Dapp asked, only because it was required of him to observe some etiquette. "How do you get rid of these mistresses?"

The man shrugged. "There are different methods. In my latest case I got close to the Little Third. Befriended her."

"Seduced her?"

"No, no." He waved a pork pancake. "Not me. Never. In any case, it wasn't necessary. I took her walking on the river promenade and shot some selfies of us with our arms around one another. These pictures found their way to her lover." He picked something from his teeth. "In a jealous man's imagination a picture can speak ten thousand words. The adulterer ended the relationship and returned to his wife."

It sounded benign, but Dapp suspected that there were darker products of the mistress dispeller's art. Shame and humiliation. Extortion. Blackmail.

Even violence and murder.

His companion stopped, leaning on a railing, staring down at the canal.

Dapp, standing beside him, felt something nudge his ankles. A shopping bag from No. 1 Department Store. He looked around but couldn't see the minion who had made the delivery.

One of the man's phones rang. A song that Dapp remembered. A song of love and loss by the chanteuse Fish Leong. It had been popular when he'd started sleeping with Yingying, and she'd sometimes sing it to him as she scrubbed his hairy back in the bathtub.

The mistress dispeller, talking on his phone, nodded to Dapp and walked away, disappearing into the crowd.

Dapp opened the bag and saw the pistol inside, wrapped in colorful rice paper.

The song was still playing in his mind, and he saw Yingying's face as he made love to her in his apartment off Hunan Road.

Then he saw her lying dead in the blood-drenched room in California, and his eyes were drawn again to the gleaming glass facade of the Shanghai Tower, drawn to its highest floors.

To the lair of Victor Fabian.

SEVENTY-SEVEN

Nicola was twelve years old. She was on the bed with her mother and Finn, drugged, trying to speak, their mouths and bodies smothering her.

Trying to say, "No. Please. No more."

Nicola felt a hand on hers and she screamed and drew in on herself like a salted slug.

"It's okay, Miss Fabian. It's okay."

An American voice.

Nicola opened one eye a slit and saw the smiling face of a young woman hovering over her. She had blonde hair tucked under a cap and wore a white tunic.

The past slithered away like a snake into a hedgerow as Nicola remembered what had happened at her father's house. Remembered the needle that had sent her plunging down a rabbit hole.

"Where am I?" she said, her voice a croak.

She sounded like her mother on the backend of a bender, God forbid.

"Mr. Fabian's home," the nurse said.

"In Washington?"

"Oh, no, Miss Fabian. In Shanghai."

Shanghai.

Nicola tried to compose herself and sat up, the young nurse darting in like a terrier to plump pillows behind her.

"And where *is* my father?" Nicola asked.

"In the living room," the nurse said. "Shall I tell him you're awake?"

"Yes, why don't you do that?"

The woman left the room, closing the door after her. Nicola swung her legs off the bed and had to stop a moment to slow her spinning head. She stood, using the wall for support. It was covered in some kind of flocked wallpaper that felt, horribly, like skin.

Her bare feet disappeared into an arctic expanse of carpet. The room was huge and extraordinarily bland, the sprinkle of chinoiserie doing little to lend it distinction. A room furnished by checkbook.

She kept a hand on the wall and made for the curtained window. It seemed to take forever, and she had to pause more than once.

Finally her fingers were on the silk drapes and she lifted them away from the floor-to-ceiling glass, blinded by sunlight.

When her eyes adjusted to the glare, she was struck by vertigo. She was looking down on Shanghai from an impossible height. The city was shrouded in smog, a serpentine river and an endless sprawl of skyscrapers floating away into the miasma.

"Nicky-Nicks."

She turned to see her father striding into the room, wearing white trousers and a cotton shirt with frog buttons and a mandarin collar.

Nicola said, "If you ask me if I slept well, I'll fucking geld you, I swear."

He smiled, but there was something counterfeit about it. He had dark rings under his eyes, his widow's peak was untamed, and he'd shaved poorly.

"You're angry. Let me explain."

"Please do."

"I brought you here for your own protection."

"You kidnapped me. You fucking *shanghaied* me!"

"I had to. You wouldn't have come voluntarily."

"No. No, I wouldn't've."

"Please understand that there are very dangerous people aligned against me. In my absence, they'd think nothing of striking out at a loved one to wound me."

"A loved one?"

"Yes. You, darling."

"I shudder to think of what you do to people you don't like. Oh, wait, I know. You fucking *kill* them."

Fabian walked across to her and raised a hand. She shrank from him.

"Do. Not. Fucking. Touch. Me."

He dropped his hand. "You need some time to adjust."

"I want to leave here. I want to go home."

"I'm afraid that's impossible."

"So what am I? The princess in the tower?"

"If you like." That imposter's smile.

"And what do I do? Rot here?"

"No, no. I have great plans."

"Oh, you do, do you?"

"Yes. I want to give you that job you asked for."

"Doing what?"

"I'll show you. Tomorrow."

She stared at him. There was something unhinged, fanatical, in his gaze.

"I've built a city, Nicky-Nicks. A fabled city. A place of wonder. Quite literally a modern-day Xanadu. And, in the morning, I'm taking you there."

SEVENTY-EIGHT

The Chevy stopped. Scooter lay in the dark, holding his breath, listening. After a minute the driver's door creaked, the car lifted on its springs, and he heard footsteps. The key scuffed in the lock and the trunk lid was raised, offering him a view of Orlando silhouetted against a low, gray sky.

"Get out," Orlando said.

Scooter blinked and sat up. He tried not to look at the girl as he dangled his feet over the trunk and then slid down to the gravel. He was stiff and his legs felt like Play-Doh.

The car was parked on a dirt road in the middle of a field, the corn whispering in the breeze.

As his eyes adjusted to the light, he saw that Orlando had blood on his left shoulder and his arm hung at his side. He held a sawed-off shotgun in his right hand.

Scooter had seen those guns in the movies his pop didn't like him to watch.

Too violent, his father had said. A distorted vision of humanity.

How the frig's *this* for distorted, Pop?

"Close the trunk," Orlando said.

Scooter was happy to obey, shutting away the poor girl.

He had her blood on his shirt and on his hands. This made him feel sad now, rather than sick.

Orlando motioned to the side of the car with the gun barrel. "Open the fuel flap." Scooter did as he said. "Unscrew the cap."

It was tight and Scooter had to use both hands to open it.

He let it drop and it dangled on its little tether, clanking against the body of the car. The sharp smell of gasoline reached his nostrils.

"Open the rear door. There's a rag on the floor. Lift it out."

Scooter saw a length of white cloth and reached for it.

"Hang it in the gas tank."

Scooter fed the cloth into the dark mouth. Orlando lifted a foot and rocked the Chevy, the sound of gasoline washing the sides of the full tank. He set the shotgun down on the roof of the car and took a box of matches from his jacket pocket and threw them at Scooter.

"Light the rag."

Scooter stared at Orlando. The man lifted the shotgun and said, "Do as I say, boy."

Scooter struck a match and the wind blew it dead. He struck another and shielded the flame with his body. He set fire to the soaked cloth and heard a whoosh as the fuel ignited, flame chewing toward the tank.

"Move," Orlando said, pointing into the field, and Scooter walked quickly, the wounded man following him.

After half a minute the tank blew, and Scooter felt a draft of heat on his back. He looked over his shoulder and saw the Chevrolet in flames.

He thought about the girl in the trunk and wondered if he'd live to know who she had been.

SEVENTY-NINE

Ash was parked at a gas station on a country road somewhere in rural Pennsylvania, watching crows perched on a power line.

He had a prepaid cell phone in his lap, bought at the gas station's 7-Eleven.

He shut his eyes and sat a while and when he opened them nothing had changed. Maybe a few less crows on the wire.

He punched in a phone number and when he heard Steven Root answer he said, "Give me a landline where I can call you in one minute."

Root hesitated, then rattled off a number and Ash ended the call.

He wrote the number on a scrap of paper, waited long enough for an old bus to shudder by, then dialed.

"Yes?" Root said.

"It's me."

"Listen, have you heard?" Root asked.

"Heard what?"

"Victor Fabian's skipped the country. Flown to China. With his daughter. He was about to be indicted."

"Fuck."

"Good news is his little flunky, Ricky Pickford, has been pulled in by the FBI."

"Okay."

"And my sources tell me that Pickford is being very cooperative."

"Yeah?"

"Uh-huh. One of the topics is you and your son. How you've been framed."

Ash sat up straighter. "And?"

"Let's just say that there has been a reassessment."

"A reassessment?"

"Yes. The feds know that a media shitstorm is about to break and they want to contain it as much as they can."

"How?"

"They want you to come in."

"To hand myself over?"

"Yes. They say they want to help you. And they want to find Scooter."

"You believe this?"

"I do. I do believe it."

"Your source is reliable?"

"Very. The feds are keen to distance themselves from the whole mess."

"So?"

"Where are you?"

Ash hesitated then said, "Pennsylvania."

"Where?"

"Not far from Pittsburgh."

He heard the sound of tapping on a keyboard. "Okay, I can

be in Pittsburgh in under three hours. I'll get you a lawyer lined up, and we'll go with you to the FBI's Pittsburgh office."

"I dunno."

"Why?"

"Jesus, all I've got is your word."

"Which is worth shit, right?"

"These days, yes."

"Look, I totally get it. I do. But what are your choices? How the fuck else are you going to find your son? Clock's ticking, man."

Ash watched the last of the crows swoop away, leaving the line quivering. "Okay. I'll call you in three hours."

"Don't bail on me."

"I won't."

EIGHTY

Ahmed Ashraf sat at a steel table in an interview room at the MCC. His legs were shackled and his handcuffs were chained to the table.

His lawyer, the young Jew, came in carrying a briefcase and sat down opposite him. The Jew wore another very expensive suit. Ahmed's father had been a tailor in Yemen, and he recognized the quality of the fabric and the skill of the stitching. Knew, also, that this man could not afford such clothes on the salary of a public defender.

So, he came from wealth and privilege.

Ahmed could see him with his white whores. Drinking, telling of his exploits. Having them hanging on his words as he described his heroic defense of animals such as Ahmed. Using these tales to grease his passage into their beds.

"Ahmed?" The Jew was speaking.

Ahmed blinked. "Yes?"

"I expected the judge to deny my plea. But what it did was allow me to get a look at aspects of the government's case." He ran a hand through his perfumed hair. "Things aren't looking great. The prosecutor's tough, with a very good track record. She has the emails between you and your handlers in which you state that you planned to target Manhattan subway trains at rush hour. And state that you bought explosives and tested them."

"But I did not do it. The attacks."

"Only because you were apprehended first." The lawyer lifted a printout from the table. "This email, Ahmed, how do you think it'll play with a jury?" He read, "'We are marching toward them with turbans that will become their burial garments. Their blood will be spilled generously. Looking forward to death in large numbers.'" He dropped the paper and it whispered as it fell to the tabletop. "You, Ahmed, are looking at forty years to life. In solitary confinement. Unless you can give the DA something."

Ahmed sat silent for a long time. Long enough for the Jew to start to shuffle his papers together.

Then Ahmed said, "I can. I can give her something."

"What?"

"I can give her information on Daniel Ash."

The lawyer stared at him. "The fugitive?"

"Yes. He is my cousin. The son of the brother of my father."

"Okay. But what can you give her?"

"He missed a plane. Ash. A plane that was bombed. Everybody on board, they were killed."

"That's common knowledge."

"Yes, but his baggage, it was on that plane." Ahmed sat as close to the Jew as his shackles would allow. "And the bomb it was in his suitcase. And Daniel Ash, he put it there. The bomb."

"How do you know this?"

"I was there. I was there at the airport in Yemen with Daniel Ash."

EIGHTY-ONE

Ash drove on the interstate toward Pittsburgh, surfing channels on the radio to try to find news of Scooter.

He heard nothing more about his son or the man in the green Chevy, but he heard a lot about Victor Fabian. Reports telling of how he had fled arrest by the FBI on charges ranging from tax evasion to money laundering.

Newsworthy only because of Fabian's close connection to the president.

A business associate. An advisor. A friend.

All of this lending credence to what Steven Root had told Ash.

About forty miles outside Pittsburgh, he stopped for gas at a Chevron station.

While he was filling the Toyota, the TV above the pump spewed a barrage of commercials at him: Pepsi, Tide, Michelob, Doritos, Skittles. An assault of noise and garish colors. Then the ads ended and CNN came on and suddenly he was looking at that old DUI photograph of himself.

His picture shrank to half-screen size and was joined by a photograph of a bearded face that he didn't immediately recognize.

Then he saw beyond the beard and he knew who it was.

Ahmed. His cousin Ahmed Ashraf.

Saw Ahmed turning to him, saying, "Hey, Danny, do for me a solid and get me a cup of coffee, man."

They were at Sanaa airport in Yemen, waiting for their flights out. Ash to Malaysia, en route to the US, Ahmed to Pakistan. The place was wild, swarming with soldiers and police. In the early hours of that morning, the airport in the city of Aden, a few hours south, had been attacked by the Houthi rebels who were trying to seize control of the country. Similar attacks were expected up here in the capital.

Ash looked at the frightened people, at the tense soldiers, and wanted to stay where he was. But Ahmed—bulky, sweaty Ahmed, with his stubble, his bling, and his grating Americanisms—had managed the impossible and organized Ash a seat on a Yemenia flight to Kuala Lumpur, where he'd get a Delta connection to Seattle via Tokyo.

So Ash stood, leaving Ahmed with the cart and their baggage, and pushed through the throng to where he'd seen the snack shop.

As he walked, the power went out, the overhead lights flickering and dying. Sunlight still flooded through the windows of the departure hall, but coffee wasn't going to be an option.

Ash turned back, and as he approached his seat, he saw that Ahmed was talking to a swarthy man in jeans and a T-shirt who was crouched over a suitcase that lay on the floor, unzipped.

Ash's suitcase.

EIGHTY-TWO

As they walked through tall trees that littered orange leaves onto the ground, Scooter got ready to bolt away from the wounded man and lose himself in the woods. He must have signaled his intent because Orlando prodded him with the barrels of the sawed-off hard enough to make him stumble.

"Don't even think about it, boy, or I'll blow you in half."

Orlando was panting, his face pale and damp with sweat. He drove Scooter ahead of him with the shotgun, their shoes crunching on the dried leaves.

The trees thinned, and Orlando nudged him again with the weapon and said, "Wait now."

There was a clearing ahead and then a road leading to a steel bridge over a river. A couple sat at a wooden table in the clearing, eating and drinking. Their car, a new Prius, was parked on the shoulder.

Orlando leaned in close. Scooter could feel the warmth of his breath and smell its staleness.

"You just keep on staying quiet, okay?" Orlando said.

Scooter nodded, and Orlando hid the shotgun under his jacket.

He draped his good arm around Scooter's shoulder and said, "Walk now."

They stumbled into the clearing, Orlando leaning on him, locking him in with his arm.

The woman, young with pale hair, looked up at them and her mouth fell open.

The man, thin with glasses, stood. "Are you boys hurt?"

Orlando said, "My brother and I have been in an accident, sir. We could use your help."

The man hurried toward them and Orlando lifted the shotgun from under his jacket and shot him in the face. The woman barely had time to scream before Orlando shot her too. She toppled from her seat onto the leaf-strewn ground.

Orlando was panting and weaving. He pointed the shotgun at Scooter.

"Check his pockets for his car keys."

Scooter stared at Orlando.

"Do it!"

Scooter didn't want to look at the man, with half his head blown away, but he knelt beside him, weeping, and patted his jeans until he felt the smart key.

He removed it and held it up.

Orlando looked at the small black box. "You messing with me?"

Scooter shook his head.

"Toss that thing by my feet and take hold of his ankles."

Scooter sobbed, wiping snot from his face.

He felt the coldness of the barrels on the back of his neck.

"Stop being a little girl and haul him into the trees."

Still sobbing, Scooter grabbed the man's ankles and pulled

him toward the woods. He nearly spewed when he saw the trail of hair and brain that was left behind on the ground. The man was skinny but it was almost beyond Scooter's strength to drag his body. He stumbled and dropped the man's feet and gasped for air.

Orlando was shadowing him and he showed Scooter the barrels of the shotgun.

The boy took hold of the dead man again and towed him until he was hidden.

"Okay, now the woman," Orlando said.

Scooter crossed to her and saw the hole in her chest. Then he saw she was still alive. Blinking. She gazed up at him.

"Help me," she said in a whisper, blood running from her mouth.

Scooter looked at Orlando, who shot her again.

Scooter started to run and heard that racking sound. He stopped and stared down at the leaves.

"Come back now and get rid of her," Orlando said.

Scooter obeyed.

After he'd hidden the woman's body his hands were red with her blood. He took a water bottle from the table and washed them, wiping them on the napkins that flapped in the wind. There was still blood on them.

They walked across to the car and Orlando made Scooter get in first. Then he levered himself in behind the wheel, grunting with pain, his shirt drenched with sweat. He took the smart key from his pocket, staring at it in confusion.

He blinked and looked at the Prius's dash as if he were looking at the flight deck of a spaceship.

"You know what to do here? And don't even think of lying to me."

Scooter reached forward and pressed the ignition button.

Lights blinked and the car started silently.

Orlando clicked it into gear and they pulled away in electric mode.

He coughed a laugh. "Car's like you. Lost its tongue."

Then the gasoline engine kicked in, and they bumped across the bridge and drove down toward the small town in the valley below.

EIGHTY-THREE

"Danny? What the fuck?" Steven Root said, the babble of airport announcements in the background. "The right-wing echo chamber has jumped all over this plane thing."

"Jesus, Steven, it's total bullshit," Ash said, parked at the roadside, talking on the burner phone, staring out over a massive landfill. A nagging wind carried the stench his way. "My suitcase wasn't even on that plane. You know airlines remove the baggage of no-show passengers."

"Sure, under normal conditions. But this was in the middle of a civil war."

"So what are you saying, Steve? That I blew that fucking plane out of the sky?"

"I'm not sure, Danny. I'm not sure what I'm saying. Is this Ahmed character really your cousin?"

"Yes. The son of my father's brother."

"The son of the guy you visited in Yemen?"

"Yes."

"And now he's up on terror charges?"

"Steve—"

"Was he with you? At the airport?"

Ash watched a truck disgorge its cargo of trash, scores of birds boiling up from the filth. He remembered reading somewhere that New York exported its garbage to Pennsylvania each day by truck and train.

"Danny?"

"Yes," Ash said, trying to corral his scrambled thoughts, "we were there together, briefly. He was flying to Pakistan. I was flying home."

"You can see how this looks, right?"

"Yeah, I can. And can't *you* see he's grabbing at straws, man? Using these lies about me to leverage some kind of deal?"

"Sure." Root didn't sound convinced. "Anyway, this can be straightened out. Let's stick with the plan. I'm just leaving Pittsburgh International. Meet me at FBI headquarters."

"You're crazy. No way."

"Danny, you have to come in. If you don't, it's tantamount to an admission of guilt."

"No, they'll crucify me."

"Then how are you going to find your son?"

"I don't know. But I do know I'm not going to find him if I'm arrested by the fucking feds."

Ash ended the call. As he drove away, he threw the phone into the field of heaped trash.

EIGHTY-FOUR

When they were close to the town, Orlando said, "Look for a pen and paper."

Scooter opened the glove box and rummaged inside amongst the jumble of cosmetics that made him think of his mother. Beneath a pack of wipes he found a small notebook with a ball-point jammed in the spiral and lifted it out. A loose photograph was wedged into the pages. A photograph of the dead couple holding a baby, smiling at the camera.

Scooter wanted to cry again, but he forced the tears back.

Turning in his seat a little, he folded the photograph and put it into the front pocket of his jeans. He didn't know why.

"Write this down," Orlando said. "A pair of latex gloves. A bottle of hydrogen peroxide. A pair of scissors. Rolls of gauze, bandage, and surgical tape. You got that?"

Scooter nodded as he wrote.

***

Orlando found the drugstore in the sad main drag, most of the buildings boarded up. He parked outside and stowed the sawed-off under his jacket and levered himself out of the Prius, keeping his eye on the boy. Together they entered the pharmacy, a bell gargling as Scooter pushed open the door. An old man reading a newspaper stared at them from behind the counter.

There were a couple of rows of sparsely stocked shelves and a closed door to the side marked District Nurse. A handwritten sign said Back at 2 p.m. There were three scuffed orange plastic chairs beside the door. One of them was occupied by a very thin woman with a lived-in face. A battered stroller stood beside her, a baby with a dirty mouth strapped inside.

Orlando sat beside the stroller and pulled Scooter close.

He gave him a fifty-dollar bill and said, "Take that list up to the old man. Do anything dumb, and I will shoot this child, you have my word on that. Do you understand?"

Scooter nodded. Orlando released the boy and watched him approach the counter.

***

The druggist took the note and held it at arm's length.

He peered over his glasses at Scooter and then looked down toward where Orlando sat. He seemed about to say something, but then he turned and rooted through shelves behind the counter.

There was one of those big round mirrors up near the ceiling, and Scooter could see Orlando sitting beside the woman and the baby, staring at him.

Hiding his hand with his body, Scooter slipped the photograph of the dead couple from his pocket. He unfolded it and laid it facedown beside the cash register and checked the mirror again.

***

A big clock with black hands on a white face hung in the corner and Orlando listened to it tick. He felt his eyes drooping closed and shook his head, blinking.

Orlando waited for the voices, but they didn't come. He almost missed them. At least they forced him to stay alert.

The baby mewled, and the woman rolled the buggy back and forward with her foot. The brat needed a diaper change.

Scooter came back carrying a plastic bag.

"Get everything?" Orlando said.

The boy nodded and Orlando used the chair to lift himself to his feet. The room yawed and he nearly fell. He put his arm around Scooter's shoulders.

"Move."

They went out onto the sidewalk, and Orlando made the kid open the driver's door and crawl across to the passenger seat.

Orlando slumped behind the wheel and hit the ignition button, his finger skidding off it, he was sweating so heavily.

The car started and he pulled away, forcing himself to stay conscious, heading toward the motel he'd seen on the way in.

***

Scooter stared out at the empty streets and the boarded-up stores. A man sat on the sidewalk with his hands hanging between his legs, watching them blankly as they passed. Orlando was hunched over the wheel and Scooter sat waiting for him to pass out so that he could run. But his kidnapper stayed conscious.

Scooter thought of grabbing the wheel and turning it, making them crash.

But the wounded man sat up straighter and gripped the wheel hard with his good hand.

Scooter saw a motel sign ahead over the trees. It was gloomy enough for the jerky little neon star to flash yellow against the gray sky.

EIGHTY-FIVE

Ash drove south through Pennsylvania on the interstate. He had no destination in mind. He was waiting. For what, he didn't know.

He had the car radio set to scan—an audio montage of music and talk shows and commercials and then a female newsreader saying, "Fugitive terror suspect Daniel Ash has been accused of bombing a plane out of Yemen two years ago that left all two hundred ninety people on board dead."

Ash—blind to the passing landscape of shuttered buildings and derelict factories—was back in the airport in Sanaa, Ahmed looking up at him as he approached, saying something to the man who'd been messing with Ash's suitcase. The stranger stood and hurried away, disappearing into the crowd.

Ahmed closed Ash's case and replaced it on the cart.

"You okay, cousin?" Ahmed said.

"What's going on?" Ash said.

"What you mean?"

"What were you doing? With my suitcase?"

Ahmed tried a smile. Brown teeth. "Nothing, man. Just to repack the cart."

"No. He was putting something into it. That guy."

As Ash reached for the suitcase, Ahmed grabbed his arm. He easily forced Ash into a seat.

"Cousin, you listen and you listen very careful okay?" Ash stared at him. "You will forget this and check your suitcase on board, do you understand?"

Ash shook his head. "No. Fuck this."

He tried to stand. Ahmed pushed him down.

"Please, cousin, better to do as I say."

"No. I'm getting help." Ash was peering around the chaotic departure hall.

"Do you want your wife and son to die?" Ahmed said.

Ash looked at him.

"Do you? That is what will happen. People, they are already outside your house in Pearson. Maple Lane number two three four. If you don't do exactly like I say, they will kill Jane and kill Scooter."

Ash shook his head

"You think I shit you? That this will not happen to your family? Don't take that chance, I warn you."

"This is madness," Ash said.

"No. No. This is jihad." Ahmed stared at him. "Give to me your phone. Come." He held out a thick hand.

Ash looked around. He saw a soldier watching them. An officer in a crisp uniform and a red beret, a pistol in a buffed leather holster at his hip. Ahmed saw him too.

"Don't be stupid, Danny. Laugh." Ash just gaped at him. "Laugh! For your family."

Ahmed laughed, and Ash managed a kind of a bark, and the big man slapped him on the shoulder, and the soldier turned and walked away.

Ahmed swallowed his fake mirth. "Now give to me your phone. Give it."

Ash handed over his cell and Ahmed stashed it in his jeans pocket.

Ash said, "What's in the suitcase?" Ahmed shrugged. "A bomb?"

"Better you don't know, okay?"

Ash put his face in his hands.

Ahmed leaned in close and his garlic breath washed over Ash. "Now listen, cousin, please. You will check in your baggage and get your boarding pass. You will go through security. I will be watching you for every second. If you are doing anything dumb, I will make a call." He put a hand on Ash's knee. "Don't worry, you will not get on the plane. You will be sick, in the toilet. You will miss it. Yes?"

"I can't do this." Ash was looking around again. "Jesus, Ahmed."

The big man had his cell phone in his hand. "You must choose, cousin. Some strangers or your wife and son. You choose. Now."

EIGHTY-SIX

They checked into a creepy Bates Motel kinda place just outside the town. The desk clerk, a fat man in a giant yellow onesie, was watching a game show with bare-assed people in it, and he hardly took his eyes off the screen.

He didn't seem to notice, or care, that Orlando looked like some mutant kid who'd just staggered out of *The Walking Dead*.

They took a room far from the road. There were no cars in front of the other rooms.

Orlando locked the door after them and stood with his back to it, then he slid down onto his haunches, the barrels of the sawed-off smacking the floor, blood falling from his arm in splatters. When he closed his eyes and his head slumped, Scooter began edging toward the window.

"Get over here." Orlando opened his eyes and gestured with the sawed-off and Scooter went to him. "Help me up."

Orlando wasn't big but he was heavy, and Scooter struggled to get him to his feet.

"Take me to the bathroom. Bring the medical supplies."

Scooter half carried Orlando into the stinky little bathroom. The wounded man sat on the closed lid of the toilet and panted like a dog.

"Cut away my shirt," he said. "Put on the gloves first."

Scooter wiggled his fingers into the gloves and found the scissors in the bag and tore them free of their plastic case. As he gripped the scissors, he had the idea to plunge the blades into Orlando's neck, but he couldn't do it.

He just couldn't.

Scooter lifted the shirt away from Orlando's body and cut the sleeve free. The blood had started to ooze around the sodden wad of tissues. Scooter pulled the tissues loose and Orlando made a whimpering sound and sweat dripped into his eyes.

"Clean the wound with the hydrogen peroxide," Orlando said, his voice soft and croaky.

Scooter opened the bottle and poured some onto cotton balls. The smell was sharp, and it made his eyes water. Tamping down his squeamishness, he wiped the blood away from the bullet hole.

Orlando gritted his teeth until white spots the size of dimes appeared on his jaws.

"Now cut some gauze and put it over the wound," Orlando said, voice thick with pain.

Scooter followed the instructions. Applied gauze and taped bandage over it.

"Make a sling from the bandage."

It took a few attempts for Scooter to get this done, and every time he touched Orlando the man moaned and muttered. At last the arm was in the sling.

Orlando sat back on the john and breathed long and hard.

"Clean up the mess and throw it in the bag."

Scooter did this, putting the blood-stained gloves in last. He knotted the top of the bag. He looked at his hands. They were still stained with the blood of the dead woman and the girl before her.

Orlando gripped the sink and heaved himself to his feet.

"Get me to the bed."

He helped Orlando out of the bathroom and sat him down on the bed, which smelled of mothballs and something worse. Orlando paused a moment, breathing fast, then he put the shotgun down and used his good hand to remove two zip ties from his pocket.

"Lay down on the floor."

Scooter saw what was coming and shook his head.

Orlando kicked out, catching Scooter in the gut. He folded and Orlando pushed him down, pulling his hands behind his back. Using his one hand he looped one of the ties around Scooter's wrists and pulled it tight with his teeth. The plastic bit into the boy's flesh. Next Orlando secured Scooter's ankles.

Scooter couldn't see him, but he could hear him breathing.

After a minute, Orlando knelt beside him, holding a length of wadded bandage.

"Open your mouth."

Scooter clenched his jaws and shook his head. Orlando put the shotgun to his temple.

"You know I'll do it. Better you listen."

Scooter opened his mouth and Orlando stuffed the bandage inside.

For a moment Scooter panicked, believed he was suffocating, then he forced himself to breathe through his nose.

The bed creaked as Orlando lay down. The TV clicked on, and Scooter heard a jumble of sound fragments until Orlando settled on a religious program. Some old man who sounded like he had a mouth full of nails ranted on about Christ having died for our sins and rising from the dead.

Scooter saw his father laughing, saying at least kids outgrew their imaginary friends, while these pathetic inbreeds turned them into cash cows.

Pop, always so sure he was right about everything.

Scooter saw his father tapping away at his laptop in his room late at night, the silent boy sneaking out of bed to spy on him. Saw the blogs and newspaper articles online talking about "the husband who waged a lonely war to get the mysterious death of his wife in China investigated."

Scooter felt his fear turn to rage.

Fuck you, Pop.

Fuck you for kicking over a hornet's nest and then not knowing how to stop the fury you unleashed.

EIGHTY-SEVEN

Ash sat in the dark at the wheel of the Camry listening to the choir's uneven rendition of "What a Friend We Have in Jesus." He was parked under the cover of trees across from the church, a low modern brick abomination with a roof that looked like a witch's hat.

The church was in the woods on the threadbare outskirts of yet another town that lay dying in the shadows of the abandoned mausoleums of industry.

Ash'd driven through the sorry little burg and stopped at the church and just sat there.

He was shit out of ideas, as John Dapp may have said, speaking around a mouthful of carcinogenic swill.

Ash had loathed Dapp, but he missed him.

Missed his blunt certainty.

He seemed to have written his own rulebook that allowed him to operate free of consequence and guilt. It had been easy for Ash to be drawn into Dapp's slipstream, even if that had meant ending up blood-spattered and terrified.

But this numb state that he'd entered into was even more terrifying, because he knew that it was a protective mechanism, the equivalent of curling into the fetal position and sucking his thumb.

And what he was insulating himself from was the terrifying

realization that his son may already be dead. That the man in the green Chevy may have flung his body into some cornfield or dumped it inside the Giger-like maze of a derelict mill.

Sitting there, hearing the banal hymn, he envied those people inside that ugly little church, up on their feet, waving their praise hands. Their mindless faith at least some insulation against the hardships of poverty and deprivation and the knowledge that each day would be more brutal than the last.

Ash the atheist had no such security blanket.

No little cocoon of magical thinking to slip into when he felt karma tugging at him like a riptide.

Yemen.

Ash, powerless in the face of Ahmed Ashraf's threats, had made a choice at that airport in Sanaa. A choice to save his family.

And now Ahmed had returned to Ash's life. Shackled and chained. Extravagantly bearded, dressed in an orange jumpsuit. Eyes ablaze with fanatical fervor.

No longer the flabby, vaguely cartoonlike figure he had cut in Yemen, with his stubbly jowls and his hairy butt crack showing above his knockoff designer jeans.

Ash had taken a dislike to Ahmed the moment he'd met him in the dismal apartment in Sanaa. His cousin, eager to talk of the year he had spent in Newark working as a fabric importer. Or so he had claimed.

So different from his small, ascetic father. The old man, dying of some cancer that seemed to be scouring him from within, his gaunt face the color of parchment.

A face uncannily like the one in the single photograph Ash had seen of *his* father. The high forehead, the wide smile, the beakish nose.

None of these genes visible in Ash. He resembled his mother, with his small features and blondish hair. Ahmed, big and over-weight, always sweating and scratching, looked like nobody in his family. Looked like a thug.

The day before he'd flown out, Ash had been woken by a whispered argument. Lying on the narrow bed in a tiny bedroom in the apartment—the family insisting he stay with them rather than at a hotel—he'd heard his uncle's breathless hiss, his aunt's beseeching wail and Ahmed's low, implacable rumble. Then Ahmed's heavy tread and the front door slamming.

Had the dying man and the powerless old woman suspected something of their son's schemes?

Ash would never know.

On the day Ash left Yemen, Ahmed had taken charge The hulking man drove with him in the taxi through the tense city, dealing with the military roadblocks along the way. Using his heft and donkey bray to clear a path through the panicked people clotting the airport.

Leading Ash toward the bomb.

Once he had neutralized any resistance Ash could offer, he had walked him toward the check-in counter, the suitcase wobbling on a cart with a squeaky wheel.

Before they could check in, they had to pass through a security point manned by armed soldiers.

There were two lines. One for foreigners, one for locals and residents of Arab countries.

The baggage scanner wasn't working. The soldiers were checking the baggage manually. The bags belonging to Arabs were yanked open, contents tossed to the floor. Prodded at with rifle barrels. Women in abayas were weeping, men were arguing with the soldiers, children were bawling. Some men were being led off to be body searched.

The few Westerners had it easy. The check was perfunctory. Ash showed his American passport and his suitcase wasn't even opened, the soldier just waved him through.

Ash looked back at Ahmed who was mired in the chaos, the contents of his backpack strewn across the tiles.

Ash walked across to the Yemenia desk, wheeling his suitcase. The last chance to stop this.

Then Ahmed was at his side, mouth-breathing, sweating.

"Go. Check in. Go."

Ash did as he was told. The computers were down and the harried check-in attendant handwrote his boarding pass in barely legible English.

He watched as his suitcase was lifted by a man in overalls and passed through a hatch covered by flaps of rubber.

"Come, hurry," Ahmed said, leading him to another security checkpoint at departures. This was more perfunctory, and he went through to the lounge.

Ash saw his plane out on the apron, with its red-and-blue tail. Saw a vehicle towing a baggage-laden trailer toward it.

He looked around at the other passengers. Women. Children. Families.

Two hundred and seventy-nine passengers and eleven crew. He would learn these figures later. And they would be branded into his memory.

Now, at the squat Pennsylvania church, the hymn ended and people filed out of the church into the parking lot. An old bus rattled up and Ash saw a hand-painted banner tied to the side: We're Singing the Lord's Praises at the Hersheypark Choral Festival!

People were taking bags and packs out of the trunks of cars. Kisses and handshakes were exchanged as the choir, around twenty men and women, all white, many obese, trundled onto the bus. The door of the bus sucked closed and the vehicle clattered off. The congregants waved and then went off to their rusted cars and trucks.

The lights of the church were doused.

Five cars were left in the parking lot.

Choir members, Ash guessed, who were leaving them here while they were away.

Ash knew how vulnerable he was in the jacked Camry. He wished he could steal one of those cars hunkered down there under a yellow industrial light, but hot-wiring a car wasn't in his skill set.

He couldn't steal a car, but even he could steal a set of license plates.

Ash went around to the trunk of the Camry and opened it. The trunk was remarkably free of junk, unlike his Leaf back home. He lifted the carpet and revealed a molded plastic toolkit. He found a screwdriver and a flashlight and knelt by the rear of the Camry and snapped the license plate free of the holder. He flung the plate into the woods and went to the front and freed that plate and sent it sailing into the dark undergrowth.

Ash stood a while and listened. Heard only the mosquito whine of a motorcycle far away. He crossed the road to the church parking lot, keeping close to the trees. Heading toward a dented old Toyota with Pennsylvania plates, he crouched and popped the front plate. As he was rising to move to the rear he heard a door and ducked down.

A big man in a padded jacket emerged from the side of the church. He locked the door and walked toward Ash, who hunkered down and felt for the pistol in his jacket.

The man passed him and climbed up into a truck. The pick-up's engine coughed and clattered. Died. Clattered and died again. He could hear the man muttering. At last, the engine caught and the truck reversed, headlights raking the car Ash hid behind, and the truck growled away out of the parking lot, onto the road, and into the night.

Ash freed the second plate and ran back to the Camry.

With some effort he managed to seat the slightly larger plates, bending them, smacking them home with the beveled plastic head of the screwdriver.

Finally he was done, and he got into the car and drove out onto the road, letting the radio scan again from station to station. Mass shootings, police killings, sexually predatory politicians, and, on talk radio, the tragic howls of the forlorn and the forgotten in flyover country.

But nothing about his son.

EIGHTY-EIGHT

Lying in the dark, trussed and gagged, Scooter lost track of time. The only light in the motel room came from the flickering TV, still tuned to the twenty-four-hour religious station. Sermons, hymns, and, most crazy-making of all, some kind of Christian rock spewed out.

He'd watched the room dim and a little finger of weak sunlight retreat through the window.

Like ET's finger.

His mom'd loved that old movie. Watched it over and over again with him when he was a little kid. Weeping at the ending and then laughing and hugging him to her and kissing him.

That warm, safe feeling that was never meant to end.

Ever.

Orlando lay on top of the bedspread, unconscious, delirious.

He writhed and shook and sweated. He spoke in what sounded like gibberish. The only word Scooter could understand was "Mama."

Mama, Mama, Mama.

He flashed back on that old woman as her head smashed the truck's windshield in a spider web of blood.

Orlando went quiet, and Scooter thought he was dead. Then the man coughed and groaned and was quiet again.

EIGHTY-NINE

John Dapp prowled his room at the Marriott in Shanghai's Green Zone, talking on a burner he'd bought at an Alldays convenience store.

Jimmy Mung said, "So, I've been tracking your friend's phone and internet activity. Seems he's planning a little trip in the a.m."

"Yeah?"

"Yeah. Booked a Sikorsky S-76C. That's one sweet ride, or so I'm told."

"Destination?"

"Somewhere called Yellow River City. Heard of it?"

"Yes," Dapp said. "I've heard of it."

He ended the call and sat on the bed and looked at his hunched reflection in the TV. Then he lifted the phone and dialed a number from memory.

After a few seconds an American voice said, "Yes?"

"You know who this is?"

A beat. "Yeah."

"I'm calling in my marker."

"Okay. You in-country?"

"I am."

"*Shen*?" The local nickname for Shanghai.

"Yes."

"Where and when?"

"Yellow River City. Soonest."

"We're talking a chopper?"

"Yes."

"Only you?"

"Yes, only me."

"Okay. I'll have the details for you within the hour."

Dapp dropped the phone on the bed next to the Glock he'd gotten from the mistress dispeller and went and stood at the window and stared out at the blinking lights of the Shanghai Tower.

He hummed Fish Leong's syrupy love song until it stuck in his throat.

NINETY

"Note to self." In the absence of her phone, Nicola lay on the bed in her father's lair and spoke to the ceiling. "Kill him or kill myself. Or kill him *and* kill myself."

She tried to sit up, but she couldn't. It wasn't the cocktail of jet lag and anesthetic that held her, it was a deep, paralyzing terror.

She had her answer to the worst thing that could happen to her. This. Being held prisoner here.

Then a jolt of panic so intense that it robbed her of her breath carved through the torpor and had her standing, sucking the sterile, climate-controlled air.

Still in her nightdress she crossed the room and reached for the door handle, terrified that it would be locked. But it wasn't, and the door opened soundlessly.

She expected to find the nurse she had banished sitting outside, but there was no sign of her.

Nicola could see down the passageway to a slanted window. The moon, fat and heavy, hung like a gaudy yellow bauble in the sky.

The apartment was vast and soulless, lit with ceiling spots that left circles of cold light on the carpeted corridor that stretched like a runway before her. Making no noise, she walked down the corridor, the feel of the carpet unpleasant to her bare feet. It was cold and slightly clammy. Like it had been recently shampooed.

She passed a trio of closed blond wood doors then came to the living room.

Nicola heard her father before she saw him—that booming baritone.

"Of course, Mr. President. Of course you can rely on me. I'm no summer soldier." He laughed the bullying laugh that for decades had rung through the smoke-filled rooms of exclusive mens' clubs. "I understand, certainly, that my reputation has reached escape velocity in the US. Hence my escape!"

He laughed again.

She edged forward, silently, and saw him standing with his back to her against the giant window. He was speaking on a cord-less phone. The base unit was attached to the wall near where she stood, its sleek black case reflecting points of light.

Nicola blinked, taking a moment to understand what she was seeing.

The phone's power light was dark.

The mains cable from the base unit lay coiled on the carpet, unplugged. And beside it was a white landline phone cable, also unplugged.

"I'm glad to hear that, Mr. President. Rest assured that this witch-hunt will come to naught. Your foes will soon be forced to swallow their pride and beg for your forgiveness. In fact, they'll *choke* on their pride—they'll need the fucking Heimlich!"

More booming laughter.

Nicola felt an almost overwhelming urge to join in and had to put a hand to her mouth to muffle her giggles.

Her father wasn't talking to the president of the United States. He was talking to himself.

NINETY-ONE

Back on the interstate, Ash drove aimlessly. He saw flashing lights. There was a wreck, a semi on its side, goods strewn all across the road. Cops slowed traffic to one lane, funneling vehicles through the mess. Ash inched along. A cop with a flashlight looked at him and held up a hand.

Ash waited for the inevitable but the cop was allowing a tow truck through. He waved Ash on and the traffic crept forward again.

A minivan came up beside Ash. A little kid in the back, strapped into a car seat. A boy, maybe three years old, grinning at him, his face made garish by the flashing lights.

Ash looking at the boy, but seeing another child, a little Arab kid in a Minions T-shirt, peeking at him through the gap in the seats at Sanaa airport.

"You will wait here," Ahmed said, sitting beside Ash in the departure lounge. "Then when the plane it is boarding, you go to the toilet. And you don't come out until it is gone. Okay?"

"If I don't board, they'll remove my baggage."

Ahmed laughed. "Where you think this is, cousin? JFK? The computers they are down. Everybody is shitting in their pants because the rebels are coming. The pilots they just want to get in the fucking air. No, no. The plane it will take off without you."

"If I hadn't seen what you were doing with my suitcase you would've let me board, huh?" Ash said.

Ahmed shrugged. "You would have died a martyr's death. You still have the choice."

"Fuck you."

The little kid popped up again and stretched out his fingers and touched Ash's hand.

It was as if that touch woke Ash from some kind of trance.

He stood. "No," he said, "I can't do this."

He left his seat and walked toward the harassed-looking ground crew in a cubicle near the boarding gate.

Ahmed was at his side, putting a hand on his arm, Ash shaking him off, weaving through people toward the cubicle.

Ahmed grabbed him and Ash was ready to fight when the big man shoved his cell phone at him and he heard Jane's voice.

"Hello? Danny?"

Ash took the phone. "Jane?" he said. "Janey?"

"Dan, are you alright? Jesus, I've been seeing the stuff on the news about the war and your phone goes straight to voicemail."

"Service is pretty much down. I'm fine. I'm at the airport."

"Yes, I know. Yusuf told me."

"Yusuf?"

"Your cousin's friend. He drove out from Seattle to tell me you're trying to get on a plane."

Ash stared at Ahmed. "He's with you? This friend?"

"Yes. He's right here with me and Scooter. So kind of him."

"Yes. It's kind."

"When are you boarding?"

"In ten minutes."

"Okay. I love you."

"I love you too."

Ash hung up.

Ahmed took the phone. Ash turned and walked back to his seat.

NINETY-TWO

Lying in the dark, Scooter heard an occasional car passing the motel or the moan of a rig as it shifted gear. Once he heard the distant whoop of a siren and believed, for all of a few seconds, that help was on its way. That the druggist had gotten the photograph to the cops, or the Prius had been spotted outside the room. But the sound faded and he heard nothing but the call of an owl and Orlando's muffled snores.

Deep in the night, the dead people did a little show for Scooter. Hoo. Sarge. The woman who had been Holly. The old wind-shield woman. The girl with the gashed throat. The man with the top of his head blown off. The young woman looking up at him and begging him to help her before Orlando finished her.

Scooter cried for a long time before he fell into a restless sleep.

He woke in agony. His jaws ached from the gag. His arms and legs were cramped and his bladder was as swollen as a football.

Scooter tried to roll toward the bed where Orlando snored softly, but he couldn't find the strength to shift his body. He tried to kick the floor to make a noise. All he did was scuff the wooden boards with his sneakers.

The exertions caused him even more agony, the zip ties sawing into his flesh. He gave up and lay still.

He needed to pee. Bad.

Scooter tried to think of something nice, to take his mind off the pain.

Tried to picture his mother.

But all he saw was blood and flesh and bone and mess.

Saw the woman lying in the leaves, mouthing *help me, help me, help me …*

Scooter sobbed and just let go and hot pee washed the front of his jeans and ran down his pants leg.

He lay in his pee and it cooled and he shivered and it stank and he wished that he could die.

NINETY-THREE

Ash slept behind the wheel of the Camry, parked in a beet field behind a stand of pine trees.

He dreamt of a white-and-red jet tracing four contrails onto a deep-blue sky.

He dreamt of an explosion, an orange-and-black ball of boiling flame that ripped the plane apart.

He dreamt of a boy, still strapped into his seat, his hair and clothes flapping, screaming as he fell toward the earth.

Scooter.

NINETY-FOUR

Dirty gray light trickled between the closed drapes, and Scooter heard the sound of a car coming to a crunching stop at a room near theirs. He heard voices: a man and a woman and at least two kids.

He tried to worm his way toward the door in the hope of kicking at it and somehow attracting their attention, but he slid just a few inches in the puddle of pee.

He probed with his feet and felt a wooden chair and managed to topple it. The clatter it made when it fell was drowned out by the Christians belting out some hymn on the TV.

A door slammed and the voices receded and Scooter lay and closed his eyes.

"Hey. *Hey!*"

A shoe nudged him in the ribs and Scooter woke and stared up at Orlando standing over him. He looked pale and weak, but his eyes were clear.

"What kind of a man can't hold his water?"

Orlando went into the bathroom and Scooter heard him peeing and the sound of flushing and water running in the sink.

Orlando emerged at the same time the family from the other room went out to their car. They spoke loudly enough to hear that they were going to get breakfast at Mickey D's.

The car started and rattled away.

Orlando crossed to the door and opened it and looked out. He waited a while, then he went out and closed it after him.

A few moments later Scooter heard a soft bang and something like wood splintering. Within minutes Orlando returned, clutching some boys' clothes in his good hand.

He threw the clothes on the bed and knelt and cut Scooter loose.

Scooter flexed his fingers, clenching his teeth in agony. The zip ties had carved red dents into his skin. When his ankles were freed he tried to stand but couldn't.

He sat on the floor, biting back the pain, pulling the gag free of his mouth.

"Get yourself in the shower," Orlando said. "Hurry now. Then we're moving out."

Scooter took hold of the dresser and got to his feet and used the wall to walk into the bathroom. Orlando sat on the toilet with the shotgun and waited as Scooter closed the smelly curtain around the tub and stood under the tepid water.

After he washed himself, Scooter got dressed in the stolen clothes. Clothes so gross he would never have been seen dead in them in his old life. Then he had to clean and bandage Orlando's wound again and put his arm in the sling.

When he was done, they went out to the Prius and drove into the grim morning.

If Orlando knew where they were going, he didn't say.

NINETY-FIVE

The helicopter was ridiculous. It had puffy, oyster-colored seats and chartreuse carpets and a wooden cocktail cabinet. The Queen flew around in one of these, Nicola was certain.

The cabin was remarkably quiet. She could hear her father's breath as he sat opposite her, staring out the trapezoid window. His right hand lay on the arm of the chair, his fingers stroking the leather. His left hand worried at the frayed strap of the binoculars that lay in his lap. Little tics she had never noticed before.

She felt her own fingers touching the braille of old scars on the underside of her arm. Nicola had felt no desire to hurt herself these last few days. She decided to take that as a good sign.

They were alone in the cabin. Her father's ninja squad had evaporated at the airport. She supposed replacements were waiting at their destination, wherever that was.

Nicola stilled her fingers and took a calming breath and said, "There's something I need to ask you."

Her father turned his head and looked at her. His eyes were curiously vacant, like an empty slide projector throwing blank light onto a screen.

Then he focused on her and smiled.

"Sure, Nicky-Nicks. Fire away."

"Why did you have my mother killed?"

He stared at her. "You go right for the jugular, don't you? Your father's daughter." She sat watching him, waiting. He shrugged one broad shoulder. "I did it for you."

"You're lying."

"I think we've passed that point, darling. We're all about the truth now."

"Daddy, please. You wouldn't know the truth if it buggered you in the shower."

He laughed his seal bark, but she saw a flash of rage in his eyes. He was still sufficiently intact for that.

"She'd hurt you enough," he said. "I couldn't risk her hurting you again."

"But she was getting clean."

"Exactly." He lifted his palms to the roof. "She would have quit that clinic, heady with the belief that she was cured, and sailed back into your life with the seductive fervor of the newly reformed. She would have been penitent yet charming. You would have fallen for her. Of course you would've. Like a ton of bloody bricks. And then? Well." He swatted an invisible fly. "How long would it have taken before she'd slid back into her old ways?"

"Maybe she wouldn't've."

"Please, Nicky-Nicks. Please. I knew your mother."

"Yes, you did. You knew she was a junkie when you married her. But the allure of that title dazzled your hungry peasant eyes, didn't it?"

"Nicola," he said.

"You married damaged goods. That suited you fine. You had the entrée you wanted and you let her flame and burn. Waiting for the inevitable call that she was lying dead with a needle in her arm in some rancid Peckham squat."

Her father's fingers grabbed at the leather of his seat hard enough to tear it. One of his shoes was beating a military tattoo on the carpet. His poker days were over. She almost laughed.

"You know what I think?" Nicola said.

"No, why don't you tell me?"

"I think you were afraid that she *was* clean. Afraid that she would stay that way and start to make the financial demands on you that were her legal right."

"Now, that's just absurd."

"Is it?"

He looked out the window. The hard sunlight on his face showed the erosion of age.

"What's wrong with you?" she said.

He stared at her. "What do you mean?"

"You're ill, aren't you?"

"No. I've never felt better."

"What's that tame quack of yours say? Dr. Banks?"

He ignored the question, turning to the window again.

"We're all just flies, Daddy. Even you."

His watery eyes were back on her.

"You know your *Lear*, don't you?" she asked. "Just as boys kill flies, so the gods kill *us* for sport."

Her father gulped water from a crystal glass, his Adam's apple yo-yoing.

She almost felt sorry for him.

NINETY-SIX

Orlando drove one-handed. The sawed-off sat in the door bin beside him.

There was pain in his shoulder, but the fever was gone and so were the voices. He felt a kind of hard-edged clarity, like a frontiersman resolutely blazing a wilderness trail, and it took him a while to hunker down into this new persona.

Mama, an expert on his shifting moods and tempers, had often woken him in the morning asking, "And *who* are we today?"

We would see.

The boy coughed and sniffed. He was crouched on the floor, under the dash, invisible to other cars.

The Prius was a hatchback, which meant that the trunk was not secure enough to hold a person against his will. Orlando considered this vaguely un-American. In his line of work, a car was useless without a secure trunk.

He missed the Chevy. Built back when Reagan was president. A time of optimism and swagger, Mama had told him when she'd home-schooled him. A time when being an American was something to be proud of. Now those who espoused a muscular, battle-hardened, take-it-to-the-enemy brand of patriotism were in the minority.

Like this sniveling child and his effete, Islam-loving father.

Some unfocused sense of outrage had Orlando aiming a kick at the boy, his boot connecting with the child's skull.

The boy yelped and tried to cover himself with his arms.

"Why don't I just kill you?" Orlando said. "Why don't I just stop the car and shoot you and dump your body in the woods?"

The child peered at him from under his arm.

"I would very much enjoy doing that. You have brought me nothing but strife. But since I'm a man of my word, I must keep you alive, at least for the moment. I gave my word that I would kill your father and I intend to honor that promise. Some contend that the devil's in the details, but I believe that he makes his home amongst loose ends. And your father is a very loose end."

They drove a while through the woodland.

"Call me a completionist," Orlando said, "I don't care. I want this thing finished."

He nudged the boy with his boot and the child cringed.

"I want you to contact your father. Forthwith. Now, don't say you can't. You can. I *know* you can." He eyed the boy. "How do I know? I just know things. *Like what things?* you're thinking. Like I know that you call your father *pop*." He laughed at the boy's expression. "See, that got your attention. You're almost ready to speak, aren't you? To ask how I know that? It's okay, save your breath. I don't know how I know. I just do."

A twinge of pain from his shoulder had Orlando settling himself more comfortably in his seat.

"And I know you're going to do what I say. And that's not some vision. You're going to do it because if you don't, I'm going to hurt you real bad for a real long time. You believe me? Yes, you believe me." He reached into his pocket, found his cell phone and threw it at the boy. "So do it. Contact your *pop*."

NINETY-SEVEN

Ash was in an internet café in a strip mall off the interstate. The spiritual twin of the one he'd used back in his hometown.

This café was managed by a sizable brunette who sat in a lawn chair behind the counter reading a paperback called *Adios, America!* while she ate a dish of deep-fried Twinkies. Ted Nugent yelped out of blown speakers.

Ash kept his eyes on the floor as he walked to a computer, barely registering a shrunken old man in a faded blue shirt who was playing online poker at the adjacent PC.

Ash logged onto the Yahoo account. Held his breath.

No new mail.

He sat staring at the monitor and surrendered to the impulse to access the cloud where he stored years of photographs and videos of his son.

He watched Scooter in Jane's arms at the hospital. His first steps. Splashing in the ocean. Smiling an Alfred E. Neuman grin with a missing front tooth.

Ash shut his eyes.

"That your boy?" The old card player was looking his way.

"Yes."

"They take him from you?"

"Something like that."

"A damn shame." The old man coughed into the side of his fist.

"Yes." Ash quit the cloud.

"Happened to me too," the man said. "Well, truth be told, I was careless. I kinda misplaced my kids along the road, and now I don't exist for them. Understandable, I guess." He released a long pneumatic sigh that tailed off into a wet cough. "I spent my life diggin coal and chasin skirt and drinkin myself simple. I had a dream once of retiring down to Florida and seeing my days out wearing nothing but resort clothes. Now I've got the black lung, and my ticket's all but punched."

He coughed again and gasped for air. Standing, he gripped the back of his chair with a hand like a talon and leaned his grooved face toward Ash. His breath stank of medication and malt liquor.

"Now, son, you're probably in no mood for advice, but I'll give you some anyway. Do whatever it takes to get your boy back. Eat whatever shit they serve you and go back for seconds. The love of kin is everything to a man. Everything. The rest ain't worth a goddamn."

Hunched over, the old man shuffled off. He was wearing carpet slippers cut away from bunions the size off crab apples.

"See ya tomorrow, Carol," he said to the woman at the counter. She grunted a reply.

If only it were that simple, Ash thought. If only he'd lost his son in a custody battle. A situation that would take a lawyer and perhaps an act of contrition to put to rights.

But this. This was beyond him now.

As he watched the old man scuff into the parking lot, Ash saw a perky young woman and a big bearded guy with a video camera on his shoulder interviewing people outside the convenience store. Their white van wore the branding of a local news station.

Ash had passed them on his way in. The woman was asking questions about an upcoming local election.

And just like that, Ash knew what he was going to do.

He was going to go to the TV journalist and tell her who he was. Tell her what had happened to Scooter. How he had to be found. Ask her and her cameraman to go with him to the local cops when he surrendered.

The local cops weren't working for the presidency. They weren't about to pull a hood over his head and spirit him away in some ghost van, never to be seen again. And that wholesome girl journalist had "Go Viral" stamped on her forehead.

He stood and started to leave the store. Then he remembered he hadn't logged out of the Yahoo account and turned back to the PC.

As he was about to click the mouse, Ash saw that he had mail.

He opened the message.

Come and get me, Pop. Please.

NINETY-EIGHT

Victor Fabian dozed in his seat. An updraft caused the Sikorsky to yaw and he woke, startled. He wiped a trickle of drool from his mouth and looked across at his daughter, who sat staring out the window, ignoring him.

He set about reassembling himself. Through the filter of his nameless condition, this was a haphazard process. There were holes. The line between memory and delusion was blurred. Emotions that he'd once been able to quarantine effortlessly ambushed him with abrupt savagery.

He felt sorrow. Shame.

And fear.

Most of all, he felt fear.

When he found his fingers pinching at the leather of his seat, he commanded them to be still, sat upright, lifted his jaw and forced his reeling mind to be quiet.

He was not his condition. He would not be cowed.

Staring down at the glittering glass towers rising Shangri-La-like from the dunes of the Gobi Desert, Fabian convinced himself anew that this city would be his legacy, his crowning achievement.

He had been involved from the drawing board. Had personally

forged the deals that had seen iron ore shipped to the northern Chinese seaport of Dalian from Rio de Janeiro and Port Hedland, making him indispensable to the Communist Party planners in Beijing.

Fabian looked down as the chopper circled, seeing the wide streets and the maze of office towers. Seeing the suburbs rolling out across the sand.

A city built to house two million people.

His city.

Never mind these recent setbacks, this city would make Fabian rich as Croesus. The hogs in DC had already grown fat at the trough that reached down Pennsylvania Avenue to the White House itself.

And what if a few accommodations had been made to keep the 18th Politburo smiling?

Fabian watched as the green Astroturf of a sports arena rose to kiss the wheels of the helicopter.

He turned to his daughter and smiled almost convincingly and said, "Welcome to Yellow River City, Nicky-Nicks."

NINETY-NINE

John Dapp, perched high on a half-built skyscraper, the desert wind ruffling his hair like the hands of a comfort woman, watched through binoculars as the fat-bellied Sikorsky wallowed to the ground.

A Chinese man in a suit stood waiting next to a black SUV.

The helicopter powered down and the stairs were lowered and the copilot opened the cabin door. Nicola Fabian stepped out. Victor Fabian followed and took her by the elbow. She shrugged his hand away and walked toward the car, Fabian at her heels like a corgi.

As the SUV drove across the Astroturf, the chopper powered up again and lifted into the sky, banking and swooping off over the skyscrapers.

Dapp lowered the glasses and walked across the empty expanse of concrete to a stairwell and descended quickly. By the time the SUV nosed its way out of the stadium, Dapp was following in the beige Chana maintenance van he had hot-wired.

ONE HUNDRED

Scooter knelt on an iron grid floor that hung high above a tangle of humongous old rusted-metal pipes and vats. His hands were zip-tied behind his back and a stinky cloth gagged him. The mesh cut into his knees, and since Orlando had pulled the zips too tight again, his wrists ached and his fingers tingled from lack of blood.

It was like he was trapped inside some super-creepy cyberpunk video game, everything dark and grungy.

Behind him, a massive iron chimney soared into the open sky. The beating of wings made him look up, and he saw a flock of crows scatter toward the clouds.

Orlando, arm still in a dirty sling, hovered in the shadows like the worst PlayStation villain come to life. There was something jagged and lo-res and unformed about him, difficult to grasp, like he shape-shifted in front of Scooter's eyes.

Scooter moved to ease the pain in his knees and the grid shook and stones and junk rattled to the broken floor far below.

Orlando leaned forward and smacked the boy in the face with the stubby barrels of the sawed-off shotgun, and Scooter fell onto his side, blood on his cheek.

The creep stood over him, silhouetted against the gray clouds, making him stare up into the twin piggy nostrils of the gun.

"You keep still, hear? You keep still, or I'll reckon with you right here and now."

Then Orlando cocked an ear and held up a hand, listening.

Scooter heard it too.

Heard the whine of a car approaching up the gravel road.

ONE HUNDRED ONE

Nicola Fabian felt as if she were in a waking dream as they drove through the ghost city. The streets were free of cars, the office towers unoccupied. The SUV turned onto a wide boulevard flanked by endless black-and-white apartment towers, standing like rows of domino tiles. All were deserted.

The only sign of life was a worker in blue overalls standing in the basket of a hydraulic crane that rose out of the flatbed of a truck. He was changing the bulbs in an ornate streetlamp fashioned to resemble a tree with hanging fruit.

The man came to attention as they passed, staring off toward the desert that was visible beyond the vacant buildings.

"What is this?" Nicola said.

"As I said, Yellow River City."

"But it's empty."

"Not quite. There's a small army of cleaners and maintenance workers who are shuttled in and out daily."

"But where are all the people? The *inhabitants*?" Nicola said, as the car took a turn and they passed a massive sculpture of two war horses rearing up on their hind legs, stone manes aflap, braided tails dragging the ground.

"They will come."

"Come from where?"

"They'll be enticed here from their yurts and yaks. It's just a matter of time. It's grand, isn't it?"

"It's creepy."

"It's the future. The Politburo in Beijing plans to urbanize over one hundred million rural Chinese over the next five years alone, housing them in purpose-built cities like these."

They passed a row of storefronts. Nicola saw they were merely facades, supported by planks planted in the desert sand. It was like a Hollywood back lot.

She looked up at a row of skyscrapers, unclad, unglazed, motionless cranes hovering atop them like stick insects. Cement mixers and backhoes stood idle.

"Has construction stopped?"

"For the moment. Just a little hitch. Nothing to worry about."

They left the skyscrapers behind and came to an endless sweep of two-story tract houses, built hard up against each other. If not for their cursory nods to Oriental design (curled eaves, gabled roofs, stunted little pagodas sprouting beside the chimneys) these cookie-cutter homes could have been outside Las Vegas, Albuquerque, or Phoenix. Grass and shrubs withered in the sun, the relentless desert reclaiming the landscape. A landscape from which all humanity had been bled.

The SUV drew up in the short driveway of one of the houses.

The driver came around to open the door, and Fabian stepped down. He smiled at Nicola and turned and walked toward the porch, the wind flapping his gray hair.

She breathed through a spike of panic and followed.

***

Dapp sat in the Chana, parked a block away from the SUV, glasses to his eyes. He watched father and daughter walk into the house. The driver carried in their bags and then returned to the car and drove away.

There was no security detail.

The Fabians were alone.

ONE HUNDRED TWO

Ash, at the wheel of the Toyota, saw the chimney stack rising through the pine trees and the dogweed. The rutted road crossed a railroad track, long disused, ties scattered and broken, rails overgrown. A massive steel cylinder, once part of a blast furnace, lay rusting like an alien artifact in the weeds beyond a listing barbed wire fence.

A sheet-iron building that had fallen in on itself was to his right. He turned the Camry and bumped over the uneven ground and parked beside the derelict shell. Switched off the engine and listened to it ping. Listened for anything else. Heard birds and the wind whistling through holes in the sheet iron.

Ash had the pistol beside him on the passenger seat.

He lifted it and moved the little switch so that the safety was off. Gripped the weapon and cocked it the way Dapp had showed him. It made a glottal rasping sound, like a throat being cleared. His fingers were slick on the metal, and he wiped them on his jeans.

Ash put the gun in his jacket pocket, left the car and started walking through the weeds toward the chimney that rose black against the sky like some satanic mill.

***

Orlando stood with his back to the chimney, sniffing the air like a gun dog as he listened to Daniel Ash moving through the scrub. He swore he could smell the fear on that little man down there.

He heard Ash's shoes on the gravel. Heard the ring of one piece of sheet metal striking another as the clumsy fool blundered through the scrub. A city man. A soft man. A useless man. A man who, like so many of his ilk, had drifted far from what nature had intended.

Orlando looked over at the boy, who was kneeling again, also listening. He almost felt pity for him, that he'd been sired by such a pathetic specimen.

Orlando crossed to the boy and placed the twin barrels of the Remington to his temple and said, "You be still now."

ONE HUNDRED THREE

Nicola prowled the house. It was like a tastelessly dressed set. The living room was furnished with a brown faux leather suite of two loungers and a sofa, still covered in their showroom plastic. Three hideous prints of Chinese junks sailing into lurid sunsets hung on the walls.

Upstairs, in the main bedroom, the linen had beads of sand hidden in its folds like contraband.

In the en suite bathroom, the toilet seat was still sealed by a paper ring but smelled of mold. When Nicola flushed, it gurgled uncertainly, and the water rose so high she stepped back lest it drench her shoes, but it drained slowly away, surging and burping.

She turned on the faucet in the sink, and it groaned and rattled but no water emerged.

Nicola looked at herself in the mirror and couldn't help but laugh.

She could not have written a better ending for her father.

Deserted by both his mentors and his lackeys.

Bankrupt.

Half mad.

Exiled in a McMansion on the edge of the Gobi Desert.

It was delicious.

The only problem was fate had written her a guest role.

She went downstairs. Her father sat in a lounger staring out the window at his folly. She wondered what he saw.

Nicola sat on the sofa. The plastic squealed.

"So," she said.

He looked at her and smiled vacantly.

"The refrigerator is stocked. Can you cook?" he said.

"Barely. I don't suppose we can order in from the Mongolian BBQ?"

He laughed. "You're funny. Men like funny women."

"Do they now?"

"I always have."

"No, I think you liked your women pliant. If not comatose."

He said nothing, and his eyes were drawn to the window again.

Nicola sat listening to the smack of the kitchen clock and the nagging of the wind.

ONE HUNDRED FOUR

Ash followed the railroad tracks to the side of the furnace. Where once huge doors must have hung was a gaping black hole in the sheet iron and the crumbling brick that it clad. A sudden wind took hold of a strip of iron and banged it like a hammer striking a gong.

The wind threw dust into Ash's eyes, and he stopped and blinked and wiped his face.

When his vision cleared, he approached the maw in the side of the building. His feet found what had once been a brick floor, now in ruins. He stepped into the darkness and every primal impulse told him to run. He gripped the handle of the gun through his jacket, as if that would anchor him.

His eyes slowly adjusted to the gloom and the labyrinth of his fearful imaginings was made manifest—towering rows of rusted industrial vats, massive pipe flanges studded with bolts as big as bull's heads, and outsize valve wheels shedding paint and corrosion.

He stumbled into a dangling chain hook that swung and sounded against a hollow vat. Too late he grabbed at the hook to still it, and his hand came away red with rust.

Ash walked on, seeing a glow of gray sunlight above him. He looked up at the chimney though the lattice of a gridded steel floor.

He blinked against the sudden glare, then a shape above him

separated itself from the industrial forms. Somebody knelt on the grid.

"Scooter!" he shouted, his voice echoing.

He heard a blast and his left leg was taken out from under him. Raw pain as he dropped to the shattered floor, panting and sobbing.

Ash looked up at his son and the man who stood over him, his weapon leveled through a gap in the grid.

***

Orlando should have finished Ash. Sent him to his reckoning.

But an errant impulse stayed his finger and he said, "Do you see a ladder ahead of you?"

Ash nodded.

"Then why don't you come on up and watch me kill your son?"

ONE HUNDRED FIVE

Nicola heard footsteps on gravel and stood and walked to the window. She looked out and said, "What did Raymond Chandler say, Daddy? When it gets boring, have a man come in the door with a gun in his hand?"

She went to the front door and opened it and said, "Well, hello, John Dapp."

***

Dapp stepped into the room, the pistol held at his side.

Victor Fabian looked up from his chair. "You two know each other?"

"We've dined together at Dairy Queen," Nicola said. She looked as if she were enjoying this.

Dapp stared at Fabian, who said, "John, you're out of your bailiwick."

Dapp felt a rage so intense that he wanted to burst into tears. He could find no words. He raised the pistol.

"Shoot him if you like," Nicola said, "I don't care. But that may be altogether too merciful."

Dapp looked at her.

"I mean, think about it, John. He's broke. He's powerless. He's lost out here in the fucking desert. And he's going woo-woo." She put a finger to her head and rotated it.

"What do you mean?" Dapp said. He didn't lower the weapon.

"He's losing the old marbles, man. He won't admit it, but he is. Madness. Dementia. Tertiary fucking syphilis, who knows? But it's got him. Hasn't it, Daddy?"

Fabian clenched his jaws and grabbed hold of the arms of his chair, but he couldn't stop the spasms and the shaking that racked his body.

"You have transport?" Nicola asked.

"A car. And a helicopter on call," Dapp said.

"Okay then. Do whatever you feel is appropriate. I'll be outside."

She stood over her father.

Fabian said, "Nicky-Nicks …"

Nicola wiggled her fingers at him.

"Bye, Daddy," she said and walked out.

Dapp crossed the room and put the gun to Fabian's skull. Standing with his finger on the trigger, he heard the wash of the old man's breath.

ONE HUNDRED SIX

Scooter watched his father lie weeping and bleeding on the broken bricks. His pop tried to get up, but he cried out and fell back.

Scooter heard Orlando laugh and he tried to break free of the zip tie. Useless. Dumb. The plastic just cut into his flesh, and he felt blood on his wrists.

But the pain focused him and he calmed himself, breathing through his nose. Watching as his father got to his knees again and dragged himself toward the ladder.

***

Ash grabbed hold of a valve wheel and pulled himself to his feet. The shotgun pellets had taken him in the meat of his upper leg and the pain was immense. He was going into shock.

He breathed and pulled himself toward the ladder.

Taking hold of it, he stepped onto the first rung with his good leg, then he tried to put his weight on the leg that had been shot. He screamed and lost his grip and tumbled back to the floor.

***

It was agonizing to watch. Scooter looked on as his father dragged himself forward and grabbed the ladder, hauling himself upward. Scooter expected to see his pop fall again, this time from a height.

But slowly, inch by inch, he made it up the ladder, and his white, sweating face appeared through a hole in the floor. He stopped and looked at Scooter for a long time, sucking air.

Then he turned to Orlando and said in a stranger's voice: "Let him go. You have me. Let him go."

***

Ash gripped the ladder, his vision blurred by sweat and pain.

He blinked and saw his son. Saw that he had blood on his face, but that he was alive.

Ash dragged himself up one rung farther and gripped the grid, holding himself in position, fighting the pull of gravity.

He stared at the gunman and thought at first he was hallucinating.

This was a boy too. A boy not much older than his son.

Then the boy shifted into a beam of sunlight and Ash realized that he was wrong. The face was ancient in its evil.

"Let him go," Ash said again.

The man turned his weapon toward Scooter, placed the stubby barrels against his head and racked it, the sound hard and terrifying as it echoed in the cavernous space.

Ash didn't think. He plunged his right hand into his pocket and didn't even pull the weapon free, just stabbed at the trigger and felt the pistol buck as he fired through the cloth of his jacket. He saw the surprise on the man's face when the round took him in the abdomen.

As he folded over, the gunman discharged the shotgun, but the weapon had slid from Scooter's head and the buckshot flew harmlessly downward, ringing on the metal vats with a sound that was almost musical.

Scooter sprang from the floor and took off, the grid bouncing and clanking.

The man racked the shotgun, the stubby barrels tracking Scooter.

Ash fired again but missed, the round ricocheting off the chimney.

The gunman drew a bead on Scooter and, as he pulled both triggers, the boy disappeared, plunging downward as the rusted grid gave way.

At last Ash freed the pistol and emptied it into the man's torso. The lunatic stood and stared at him and seemed unmoved as he racked the shotgun yet again, panning it toward Ash. Then his face went slack and the sawed-off slipped from his grasp and clattered to the metal and he toppled forward onto the lattice, his blood dripping like rain to the floor below.

Ash hoisted himself onto the grid and grabbed at a railing and hopped forward, shouting his son's name.

He felt his strength ebbing and he tripped and lay on the mesh and couldn't move, eyes closing, darkness like a blanket thrown over him.

ONE HUNDRED SEVEN

Nicola stood outside the house framed against the empty sky-scrapers, her arms folded, her hair blowing across her face.

John Dapp came out of the front door and closed it after him.

"There's a sandstorm coming," Dapp said. "Let's move."

He walked to a little beige van and Nicola followed him and they drove away down the street, eddies of sand swirling in from the desert, patterning the cracked blacktop.

ONE HUNDRED EIGHT

Ash heard his wife say, "Danny. *Danny!*"

He opened his eyes and saw where he was, and he had no idea how long he had been out.

Terror spiked adrenaline into his blood and, using the rail, he hauled himself upright, dragging his wounded leg, screaming silently through the pain.

He came to where his son had disappeared and looked down through the jagged hole in the mesh at an open tank the size of a racquetball court. Scooter floated facedown in yellow water, hands tied behind his back.

He wasn't moving.

Ash looked for a way to get to him. He saw a chain with links wider than his head dangling toward the floor.

He lay on his belly and leaned through the hole and reached for the chain.

His fingertips brushed it but he was too far away.

He looked down at his son and heard a cry that he took a moment to realize was his own.

Ash lunged forward, hanging in space for an eternity before his right hand grabbed a link of the chain. His wounded leg slammed into the metal and he moaned and nearly lost his grip, swung, and clutched the chain with his left hand, and hung, gasping.

Then he stepped his foot into a link and supported himself and found a better grip and half slid, half rappelled his way down the chain until his feet found the hook and he had to let go and drop to the floor.

Red pain seized him and left him blind, and he was sure he was going to pass out but he got to his knees and crawled to the tank, coughing bile.

His vision returned, and he looked at the ladder bolted to the side of the vat and he knew that he would never be able to get up there.

He flashed on his son floating above him, lifeless.

Saw bodies floating in the ocean, clothes whipped by helicopter blades.

He got to one knee, and then the other, pushed up on his good leg and gripped the lowest rung of the ladder, held onto it and pulled himself to his feet. The agony was too intense to allow him to scream and he made a low, animal sound.

Ash drove his body upward using his arms and his right leg, until he was looking over the edge of the tank at Scooter, floating, hair fanned in the water, shirt billowing out.

Ash pulled himself forward, belly on the lip of the tank, and he stretched out and feared Scooter was too far from him, but his fingers found fabric and he closed his hand like a vise and pulled the boy to him. He flipped him over and yanked the cloth from his mouth.

Scooter wasn't breathing.

Ash slipped and they fell ten feet to the ground, his son landing on top of him.

The impact had Scooter gagging and filthy water spilled from his lungs and he coughed.

Ash got on top of him and pumped his chest and more water spewed out. Scooter's eyelids flickered and he looked at his father.

"Scooter," Ash said.

"Pop," Scooter said, his voice a torn whisper. "Is it over, Pop?"

"Yes. Yes, it's over," Ash said as he passed out.

ONE HUNDRED NINE

Victor Fabian sat in the lounger like a codger. He seemed to have lost the desire to move, and even if he did rouse himself, where would he go?

So he sat and the clock ticked and the generator hummed, and then the wind grew too loud and insistent to hear anything else but its moan.

His body shook and his palsied fingers tugged at the plastic seat cover and disobeyed his order to be still.

Tears of self-pity trickled unchecked down his cheeks and dampened his collar.

His sobs and moans were drowned by the howl of the wind.

The room darkened as the wind roared across the desert plain, throwing a curtain of dust over the house, sand pelleting the windows, leaving Fabian lost in a dim brown world. A drainpipe clanked and then was torn loose, clattering away.

It grew darker still, and the ghost city disappeared into the tide of dust. And the house, and Victor Fabian inside, disappeared with it.

ONE HUNDRED TEN

John Dapp slept all the way to Shanghai. Nicola looked out the helicopter window at nothing. This craft wasn't like her father's flying boudoir, it was stripped down and noisy. That seemed to have no effect on Dapp. And neither did the bouncing when they hit pockets of turbulence. His chin bumped against his chest, but his sleep went undisturbed.

The blade slap on landing woke him, and she found herself wondering if he were accustomed to this. If he'd been a man who'd been choppered out on dark missions, sleeping and then waking and doing the unspeakable things that men like him did.

Better not to know.

Nicola left the helicopter and stood on the remote airfield and moved a tendril of hair from her face and felt lost.

"Do you have anywhere to go?" Dapp said, appearing from behind her.

"No."

"Then ride with me."

They got into a taxi driven by a man who looked embalmed.

"Do you want to go to the British Embassy?" Dapp said.

"Not really. All those bloody questions. God."

"True."

"And then the media. Inevitably."

The car passed a dozen eel-like bullet trains waiting in a train yard. The sky was yellow with smog.

Dapp nibbled at a hangnail. "Just a thought ..."

"Yes?"

"How attached are you to being you?"

"Why? Are you thinking of killing me?"

"Just your identity."

"Meaning?"

"A reboot. As somebody else. No Fabian history."

"No karma?"

"That's outside my purview."

"You're serious? About the identity thing?"

"I don't joke."

"No, you don't, do you?" She looked at his blunt profile. "I think I'd quite like that."

"You're sure?"

"Yes."

"Okay," Dapp said, "I'll facilitate it."

"What do you want in return?"

He shook his head. "Nothing."

"Oh good, because that's about all I can offer you."

Dapp scratched at stubble on his cheek. "I don't mean to pry ..."

"Pry away."

"I'm imagining that you were dependent on your father's largesse?"

"Gosh, that's delicately put, John Dapp. Jane Austen couldn't've said it better."

Not even a smile. "Well?"

"Yes. I am. Was."

"Okay."

"Okay what?"

"We'll take care of that."

"You'll give me *money*?"

"Enough to get you started. I figure I owe you that much."

"You're being very kind."

"No, I'm not."

They passed rows of faceless gray apartment blocks reflected in a murky paddy field.

"Are you going back to America?" she asked.

"No, Jesus," he said, yawning. "I think I'll stick around here for a while. The food agrees with me."

"Maybe I will too." She watched a wooden boat churning up a narrow brown canal. "Perhaps you can show me the sights?"

Nicola turned toward Dapp, smiling. But he was asleep again.

ONE HUNDRED ELEVEN

When Danny Ash woke, he no longer reached for his dead wife, but he lay, eyes closed, as he did each morning, feeling her presence, inhaling her scent, feeling the texture of her skin on his fingertips, in the way an amputee feels a phantom limb.

Ash was not an afterlife kind of guy, so he knew this manifestation of Jane was just an engram, a memory trace stored in the soup of his brain. And as he aged, as the neural pathways shriveled and atrophied, so she would fade like a Polaroid left in the sun.

He sat up, trying to cast adrift these morbid thoughts. He was helped by the searing pain in his thigh where Orlando Peach had shot him.

He had learned the man's name but very little else about him.

The secret of whoever he'd been had died with the woman who had stolen and raised him.

Ash sat on the edge of the bed in his boxers and massaged his left leg. There had been surgeries and skin grafts and plates and screws. Arteries and sinew and veins and a switchboard of nerves had been rewired and repaired and tamped off and cauterized.

His leg was withered and raw and scarred.

He would never be a swimwear model.

Ash pulled on sweatpants and reached for the antique ebony

cane that stood beside the bed. It had a silver eagle's head for a handle. Something a riverboat gambler may have swaggered around with. He'd picked it up in a junk shop in Seattle after one of his weekly sessions of physical therapy.

He lifted himself, grunting, and used the cane to walk to the door and open it. He stood a while, leaning on the cane, listening to voices coming from the kitchen.

His son's and Mrs. Dempsey's.

Mrs. Dempsey was a local woman whose logger husband had been laid off. She came in each morning to help with breakfast and clean the house and run a few errands.

"C'mon, Greg, eat," she said. "Bus'll be here in no time."

His son went by Greg now. Scooter had been left behind in that furnace in Pennsylvania.

Ash limped down the corridor and stood in the kitchen doorway, looking into the sunny room. The wall that he'd run through like a wannabe Buster Keaton had been restored by an old hippie with a beard and a ponytail who'd whistled Creedence while he'd worked.

His son sat at the table eating cereal. Mrs. Dempsey leaned against the counter drinking coffee. A jovial redhead in her fifties with a face so plain it was almost beautiful and the squat body of a power lifter, she couldn't have been more different than the person Grace Zima had pretended to be.

The boy had grown in the last four months. Filled out. He would soon be taller than his father.

He looked up when Ash tapped his way into the room.

"Hey, Dad."

Pop, too, was a relic of the past.

"Hey, son. Morning, Mrs. D."

"Morning, Mr. A."

Ash enjoyed the Beckett-like absurdity of these abbreviated names. A reassuring daily ritual.

He folded himself into a chair at the table and listened in on his son's conversation with Mrs. Dempsey.

Small talk.

Which summed Greg up. He spoke again. But he said nothing.

Greg's communication was as bland as an infomercial. Ash and his son had exchanges that were remarkable only for what was left unsaid.

Greg would barely speak of his mother.

He did not speak of Grace Zima.

And he would not speak at all of those blood-filled days he had spent with Orlando Peach.

He spoke about food. About TV and computer games. About school in the most general terms.

He smiled. He was unfailingly polite. But his eyes were blank and shuttered. The eyes of someone who'd seen hell.

Ash had taken Greg back to the therapist in Seattle. The man, again, had counseled patience.

"He's young. He has time," the therapist said.

"Does he?"

"Yes, he does. He's busy reconstructing his narrative."

"You say that like it's a good thing."

"It is. He's deciding on what terms he wants to deal with the world."

"Really?"

"Yes. It's a mark of intelligence. Of maturity."

Ash had tried to embrace the man's optimism, but he feared there was a tab that would be paid in a year or two when the hormones of manhood started to surge through his son's body.

The school bus rolled up and Greg grabbed his pack, still chewing, and said, "Bye, Mrs. D. See ya, Dad," and he was out the door.

Ash went outside and stood in the sun, leaning on his cane.

The Anderson kids from across the street were on their way to the bus, and Greg walked with them. They let him board first, an unspoken acknowledgment of the celebrity he still enjoyed after the events of earlier in the year.

Events that had rocked an administration. That had sent a domino-tumble of apparatchiks falling on their swords to protect an increasingly isolated and embattled president.

Ash had been left free of taint.

He and his son dubbed the innocent victims of a terrible conspiracy.

Ash had turned down endless invitations to do network talk shows. He'd ignored emails from New York publishers eager to foist ghostwriters upon him. He'd even taken a call from Oliver Stone himself, listened to his hyperbolic pitch for a Hollywood paean to paranoia, and had politely said, "No. Thank you, but no."

For nearly a month after he was discharged from the hospital in Pittsburgh and he and Greg had come home, the house had been surrounded by the media, and it had seemed like they would lay siege forever. But then other horrors had leached them away, and life had returned to some kind of normality.

Mrs. Dempsey passed Ash on her way to her battered little yellow Hyundai.

"I'm off to Costco, Mr. A. Any requests?"

"No thanks, Mrs. D. I'm good."

The small car protested when she lowered herself into her seat, and it coughed and prevaricated before it fired and she took off at breakneck speed. If Orlando Peach had been the malevolent manifestation of a dark and dystopian video game, Mrs. Dempsey was a cartoon. A throwback to an earlier, more naive and hopeful era. To *The Flintstones* or *The Jetsons*.

Ash returned to the kitchen. Mrs. Dempsey had left him a mug of coffee on the table. He leaned the cane against the counter and sat, using the remote to rouse CNN.

He was looking at a courtroom sketch of Ahmed Ashraf. Bearded, glowering, standing manacled in the dock as he listened to a judge sentence him to forty years in prison.

His accusations against Ash had been dismissed as opportunistic fabrications. As the lies of a desperate man.

Ash clicked off the TV and stirred sugar into his coffee. He sat and stared at the swirling surface of the drink, but saw bodies and debris floating in the ocean.

He remembered the last time he'd seen Ahmed, sitting beside him in the departure lounge at Sanaa airport, the minutes ticking away to when the doomed plane would leave. Ash had closed his eyes against the horror of it all. Closed his eyes and fallen asleep.

When he'd woken Ahmed was gone and so was the plane.

Ash had wandered through the chaotic airport and found a taxi to take him to a hotel. He'd called Jane and Scooter and then he'd sat and watched the same footage of the crash site repeating on all the news channels, sound muted. Watched the images over and over until he could anticipate when one of the bodies, a woman in an orange dress, would be flipped onto her back by waves from the blades of the hovering helicopter, her face digitally blurred.

After Jane died, in his nightmares it had been his wife's face he had seen through the pixelation.

Sitting in his kitchen, holding his coffee mug, Ash closed his eyes.

He had to believe that the only truth is the story we tell ourselves. That time would be his ally, that it would rewrite his memories, fashioning a version of those events in Yemen that would be easier for him to live with. That a point would be reached, eventually, when he would be unable to tell where true memory ended and false memory began.

He had to believe that.

Ash stood and limped to the kitchen window. He heard voices and looked across at the house that had once been Holly the Imposter's.

A truck was parked in the driveway and movers were carrying furniture through the front door. A youngish man and woman and a boy around Greg's age stood in the yard. They turned and smiled at Ash, and the woman waved.

Ash waved back.